The Golden Promise of Cripple Creek

Also by Mary Ellen Johnson

Travels Across Time

Before I Wake

Eternal Beloved

The Golden Promise of Cripple Creek

The Knights of England

The Lion and the Leopard

A Knight There Was

Within A Forest Dark

A Child Upon the Throne

Lords Among the Ruins

Flames of Rebellion

The Golden Promise of Cripple Creek

LOVE DURING THE BOOM TIMES

TRAVELS ACROSS TIME
BOOK THREE

MARY ELLEN JOHNSON

ePublishing Works!

December 2025
ISBN: 978-1-664457-712-7

ePublishing Works!
644 Shrewsbury Commons Ave, Ste 249
Shrewsbury, PA 17361, USA
www.epublishingworks.com
Phone: 866-846-5123

To my dad, my uncles, and all those who lived it.

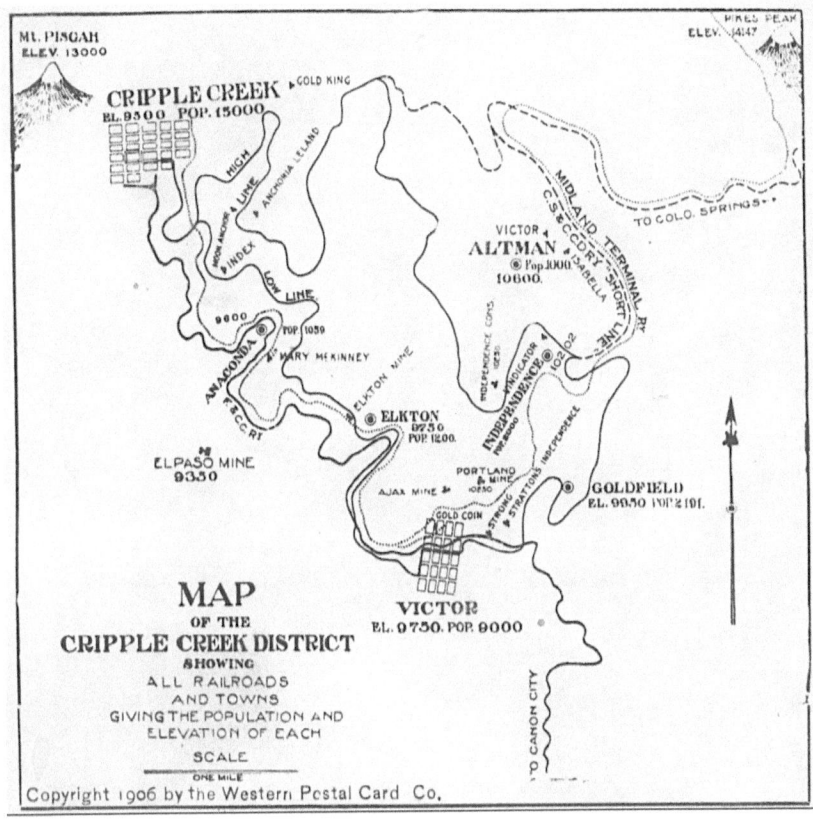

MT. PISGAH
ELEV. 13000

PIKES PEAK
ELEV. 14147

CRIPPLE CREEK
EL. 9500 POP. 15000

GOLD KING

HIGH LINE
IRON ANCHOR & LINE
INDEX
ANCHORIA-LELAND

LOW LINE

9600

TOP 1039

MARY McKINNEY

ANACONDA

F & C C RY

ELKTON MINE

ELKTON
9750
POP. 1200

TO COLO. SPRINGS

MIDLAND TERMINAL RY
C.S. & C.C.DRY. "SHORT LINE"

VICTOR
ALTMAN
Pop.3000
10600

INDEPENDENCE CO'S

INDEPENDENCE
EL. 9000

VINDICATOR
10102

EL PASO MINE
9350

AJAX MINE

PORTLAND & MINE
10250

GOLD COIN

STRONG

STRATTON'S INDEPENDENCE

GOLDFIELD
EL. 9950 POP. 2191.

MAP
OF THE
CRIPPLE CREEK DISTRICT
SHOWING
ALL RAILROADS
AND TOWNS
GIVING THE POPULATION AND
ELEVATION OF EACH
SCALE
ONE MILE

VICTOR
EL. 9750. POP. 9000

TO CAÑON CITY

PART ONE

Today

❧❧❧

When all else fails there's always delusion.

— CONAN O'BRIEN

One

"And remember," Sabrina Darling reminded her "besties" before signing off, "You are on your way to better best!" While patting her sweating face with a towel sporting the "Better Best" logo ($11.99 on Sabrina's Better Best online store), Sabrina grinned into the camera.

Ignoring her older brother Padrick's phantom comment, which never failed to put in an appearance: "What the hell does 'better best' even mean?"

"It's called branding, moron," Sabrina—real name Maeve Mooney but Maeve Mooney was a ridiculous name for a fitness influencer—muttered to an invisible Padrick. She, Sabrina/Maeve, turned off the camera and stumbled from her makeshift studio into her living room where she collapsed atop the white boucle surface of the sofa her interior designer had assured her was "tres chic."

It was still uncomfortable.

"Gawd!" Maeve groaned. "Just kill me now." She knew her breathing remained way too fast, though she no longer wore her fitness smartwatch (available with pink or purple bands, a steal at

$49.95), which would have reminded her of how out of shape she'd gotten these past months.

The main reason she'd begun editing her videos to include more close-ups of her face and various body parts rather than the entire package. Thank God for skinny apps. Besties were getting so mean, even questioning her credentials, as if her still-perfect guns weren't credentials enough.

Regardless, she was no longer following the advice Sabrina Darling chirped out to her besties. *"Eat healthy shit. Exercise until you have to fall asleep or crash into bed without taking your clothes off because you're more than exhausted. You're comatose."*

It had worked, hadn't it? One million subscribers spread across various platforms, along with accompanying products and merch. By any measure Sabrina Darling, aka Maeve Mooney, was a success.

So why do I feel like Wile E. Coyote with an anvil about to be dropped atop my head?

"Beau," Maeve breathed, as if the name of her soon-to-be-fiancé would motivate her to do more than pant and sprawl on her sofa with all the grace of a pregnant warthog.

Warthog? Where did that come from? Do I even know what a warthog looks like? I think they have tusks. Or is that a rhinoceros?

"Beau Strank looks like Humpty Dumpty," she imagined Padrick, who lived rent-free far too often in her head, commenting. Yeah, because *Alice in Wonderland/Through the Looking Glass,* with its many illustrations, was Padrick and Celia's five-year-old Lily's favorite book. Which meant it was pretty much the entire Mooney clan's current frame of reference.

Except Beau *did* look like Humpty Dumpty—if Beau had been an egg who wore quaint clothing and perched on walls. Well, Beau Strank did kind of wear quaint clothing. Maeve had first glimpsed the scion of one of Colorado Springs' oldest families in the lobby of the Broadmoor Hotel, where he'd been dressed in a purple golf shirt and hideous yellow plaid Bermudas and leaning on a 9-iron. So maybe more like a character from *Clue,* which Padrick and

Maeve used to play before her brother had turned into such a butthead.

"I suspect Professor Plum in the lobby with a golf club."

"Get it together, girlfriend," she said to the empty room.

Maybe I should buy a cat or a hamster, so I don't look like a crazy person talking to myself.

"Alexa, what time is it?" Maeve called out to her substitute human.

"Good morning, Sabrina Darling," replied Alexa from its perch on a nearby coffee table. "The time is 9:55."

Suppressing the urge to thank the computer, which possessed quite a pleasant female voice, Maeve muttered, "Shower." She envisioned rising from her couch, staggering into the kitchen for a granola bar and maybe a Skinny Cow Ice Cream Sandwich. But then she would be reminded that she'd dropped sixty grand on a Tuscan kitchen remodel when everybody was suddenly painting their old cabinets and putting in hideous mirror upper cabinets or tearing them out and replacing them with open shelves while designers pontificated, "No more Tuscan kitchens. No! No! NO!"

Why were interior decorators so fickle?

Another thing Maeve didn't like to think about: when she'd videoed her sister-in-law Celia making her famous sweet kale salad. **(Note to self at the time**: *Focus on Nana Grace's antique china and Celia's hands rather than outdated surroundings. Pretend I'm the creator, which I pretty much am, masterfully aided by my* pitch-perfect *voiceover.)* She had quickly deleted the subsequent "bestie" comments asking rude questions like, "When did you start wearing a wedding ring?"

"Credit Celia!" Padrick had texted, followed by a middle finger emoji. Padrick Mooney had the crazy-making habit of perusing Maeve's channels in order to leave nasty comments like "Way to go, Moonface," which might not sound so horrible, but she'd outgrown that nickname twenty years ago.

Anyway, Maeve would not waste her Beautiful Mind on Padrick or the rest of her family who she dearly loved because they really,

really were wonderful people, but the Mooney clan was also, let's face it, embarrassingly "redneck." When she'd hurled that particular epithet at her brother, he'd responded, "Since striking coal miners who wore red bandanas around their necks were called rednecks, I'll take that as a compliment." Followed by a shrug of broad shoulders. "Just my opinion."

Unfortunately, thanks to all his reading and podcast listening, Padrick was full of opinions. He knew way too much about subjects nobody cared about.

Padrick Mooney—named for Padrick Sean Mooney, who'd purchased the family's Shamrock Ranch about a thousand years ago —had no conception of important things like branding or advertising or Instagram or anything other than climbing utility poles where he risked being incinerated by a billion volts of electricity. Who fancied himself some 21st-century homesteader because he and Celia had constructed their own cabin on part of the ranch where they raised an Old McDonald's assortment of farm animals and grew a massive garden and pickled or canned anything that vaguely resembled a fruit or vegetable. They even slaughtered, prepared, and packaged their own meat.

Makes total sense when Safeway is forty minutes away and Cripple Creek is right down the mountain.

Sad, really: Padrick Mooney didn't even realize he was an anachronism.

Maeve reminded herself she really must get up, even though every muscle in her body screamed, "Don't ever move again!" But today was going to be very, VERY special. Today she and Beau Strank would attend Cripple Creek's Donkey Derby days, though that wasn't the special part. Today she would introduce Beau Strank to her family. While she'd known Beau from working at the Broadmoor's Golden Bee and he'd helped her purchase her gorgeous though undeniably compact home in the ritzy part of Cheyenne Canyon, they'd only been dating four months.

And as down-home folksy as Donkey Days was, at least it

provided a break from Beau Strank's routine. When it came to dating, her pending fiancé really didn't have much of an imagination. Being June, he would "suggest" dining on the Golden Bee's terrace, not because of the atmosphere, but because the food was cheap for the Broadmoor and Maeve had worked there three years as the English-style pub's piano player, which might not make it her preferred dining destination if you thought about it, which Beau obviously hadn't because Beau Strank wasn't much given to deep thinking, though he did have a shark's instinct for making money and talking in platitudes which had served him well as a real estate investor, state senator, and potentially, next governor of the great state of Colorado. Beau fancied himself the Republican version of Will Rogers—whose Shrine of the Sun was nearly within spitting distance of the Golden Bee—and who'd said he'd never met a man he didn't like. So, after finishing his fish and chips and yard of ale, Beau would lean across the table, pat her hand and say, "Excuse me, sug, gotta go press some flesh," and make the rounds, backslapping golfing buddies and introducing himself to total strangers because he was always on the hunt for possible real estate commissions or future votes. Left alone, Maeve would pick at her spinach and pear salad while dreaming of Domino's Chicken Taco Pizza plus a side order of Cheddar Bacon Loaded Tots.

Yep, Donkey Derby Days would be a definite improvement.

After Maeve stiff-walked her way into her also recently renovated bathroom, which she'd be paying off until the year 3000, she showered, washing herself with Chanel Coco Mademoiselle Foaming Shower Gel. It didn't smell any better than her niece's Softsoap Body Wash, but it cost a lot more. Meaning her unsophisticated nose must be missing something. Meaning she needed to *pretend* she could tell the difference.

"Eyes on the prize," Maeve reminded herself. Thirtieth birthday in two months. Marriage proposal any day now.

Visualization: *I will act so surprised when you propose. "Of course I'll marry you," I'll say. "And I'll be the better bestest wife forever."* Which

15

was kinda ironic because as soon as Maeve became Mrs. Beau Strank, she had no intention of ever working again.

Except as Colorado's First Lady. The governor's residence, aka Cheesman-Boettcher Mansion, was quite lovely. Maeve had Googled it. Built in 1908. Late Georgian Revival style. Massive columns and curliqued-thingies. She particularly loved the semi-circular sunroom looking out onto a lovely park.

Every morning I'll drink my coffee and read my newspaper there. Okay, well, more a smoothie, and nobody actually subscribed to newspapers anymore. Her smartphone then, where she would read all the local news, no matter how boring. *Promise.*

And so, Maeve Mooney dried her still incredibly toned body with the plush, organic bath towel she'd retrieved from a nearby towel warmer and readied to embrace her future.

When Maeve was small, her Nana Grace had been fond of saying, "You're dreaming with the fairies half the time, Maeve Mooney. That's the Irish in you." As if the Mooney family had just gotten off the boat rather than having emigrated during the Great Hunger. Maeve's grandmother could have been described in a variety of ways, but "sweet little old lady" didn't number among them. Nana Grace was tall and gaunt with white hair plaited in two severe braids she wrapped around her skull. While she sometimes referenced her fashion modeling days, Nana's uniform of choice was a shapeless sack that skimmed the tops of her lace-up boots. A don't-even-think-about-messing-with-me-attitude completed her ensemble. Nursing a nest of grievances she could express subtly, with so much charm you forgot the toxicity of whatever underlying message she peddled, or with a wrath that caused the most fearless to back off, hands up, crying "Sorry!" When contemplating Maeve's penchant for singing and playing piano, reading anything she could get her hands on and scribbling bad poetry, Nana Grace had alternated between being pleased and irritated. Maeve never dared ask her grandmother to clarify her opinions lest she risk a thump on the head, which was Nana Grace's favorite way of communicating.

Now that Maeve Mooney was nearing two milestones in her life —her thirtieth birthday and her engagement—she regarded her ten-year-old self with embarrassment. In the summer you'd likely find young Maeve sprawled upon the grass near the mine shaft Nana Grace referred to as the "holy well" and Maeve insisted on calling the "White Rabbit," since Lewis Carroll's books were perennial favorites. Maeve was prone to cloud gazing and reading aloud to the occasional cow grazing in the middle distance while the family dog snored at her feet. That long ago Maeve likened words to gemstones. She'd been enchanted by their rhythm, texture, shape, their very arrangement on a page, the sounds they made when she repeated them using various voices and inflections. Once she'd polished and refined her gemstones to perfection, she'd carefully enter them in the leatherbound journal Padrick gifted her each Christmas.

"It's all fine and dandy to have your head in the clouds," Nana Grace would scold. "But you can't eat clouds. Practical is the proper trait to be cultivating."

In fairness, Maeve *was* practical. She had plans. She just had no idea how to implement them.

She blamed her parents.

"Dream your dreams, my baby," Mama would say. Never adding a "but" such as... "Learn a trade like your brother," or "Pull up those grades and apply to Harvard." "You're okay just as you are" turned out to be an extremely destructive message, leading Maeve to assume success's stars would miraculously align themselves in her favor without any effort on her part.

Reality had smacked her in the face like a wet fish after Padrick had taken her to Ireland as a high school graduation present. Padrick had just completed his lineman apprenticeship and insisted the trip was a reward for them both. (This was when Padrick had still been her fun, sweet brother.) It was only during their excruciatingly long and uncomfortable flight home that Maeve had begun dissecting her conflicting emotions regarding their experience. Three weeks of breathtaking scenery, tours of everything from Blarney Castle to the Jameson Distillery, pub crawling and late-into-the-night conversations with new friends still left Maeve wondering why she wasn't disappointed exactly, but discontented maybe? Confused? Uneasy?

When Maeve and Padrick had introduced themselves to some of the Mooney clan who'd settled in County Offaly, they'd been welcomed as long-lost relatives. The Mooneys were warm and generous, laughed easily and often and certainly lived up to the Irish's fabled reputation as storytellers. "Blessed with the gift of gab," as Nana Grace would have said.

Eventually though Maeve noticed that beneath the bucketloads of charm, their relatives seemed obsessed with grievances, suffering, tragedies, and death. While they could elevate the wounds of the past to poetry, a decidedly dark cast tainted most conversations. If Maeve complained of a headache, someone mentioned the ancestor whose head had been chopped off at the Battle of the Boyne. If she remarked on a particularly delicious dish, her hostess reminded her that during the Great Famine, all of Ireland had been reduced to eating nettles, seaweed, turnips, and cabbage leaves.

The Irish, it seemed, nursed their grievances as diligently as they nursed their pints.

The Troubles were a favorite subject, though Maeve never knew whether they referred to the 17th-century Wars of the Three Kingdoms or PBS documentaries like "Once Upon a Time in Northern Ireland." The Emerald Isle was ever awash in Troubles. Its heroes were invariably some version of Michael Collins; the women Grace O'Malley, the pirate queen who refused to bow before Elizabeth I. Grand and glorious and doomed. If you could throw in a bit of treason and treachery, all the better.

When William Faulkner said, "The past is never dead; it's not even past," he could have been referring to the Irish.

America is about today, Maeve had decided during her and Padrick's flight home. While her brother buried himself in a tome about the Easter Rebellion and its aftermath, her thoughts revolved around her future. *America is where we can invent ourselves however we please; where we always look to the future and where we may build castles in the air, but that's better than stumbling around in the rubble of the past.*

Somewhere over the Atlantic, Maeve had put aside childish things. She'd vowed to pursue success as ardently as her Irish relatives pursued their psychic injuries. They might lament they were helplessly buffeted by fate, but they had marinated in their victimhood so long they wouldn't have chosen another outcome even if it had been offered.

Maeve Mooney would craft her own destiny.

And she pretty much had, or at least she was as far along as any twenty-nine-year-old could be. Though sometimes Maeve wondered whether she was missing...something. When she felt restless and confused, she bought something or created another Better Best video and hawked some new vitamin or makeup wonder. That usually kept the doubts at bay. Still, Maeve wished she had someone, her own personal "bestie," with whom she could share her darker moments. She didn't actually have friends. As a prominent influencer, Maeve had learned that too many people just wanted to bask in her reflected glory, produce hurtful and totally untrue vlogs criticizing her, or post Better Best comments she immediately deleted. She could probably dump on Padrick's wife, who was level-headed and non-judgmental, but inevitably Celia'd blab to Padrick and he'd be on her like a tick on a hound. Mama and Daddy and Granda were always willing to listen, but their advice had nothing to do with real life, at least real life in the 21st century.

"Move back to the ranch," Mama would say. "Relax. Take long walks. Reconnect."

"Don't marry any man with soft hands," Daddy would say.

"Let me tell you about the time I nearly made a fortune panning for gold over near Fairplay," Granda would say.

I'm on my own, Maeve thought, as the minutes ticked by until one, when Beau Strank would arrive.

Then they would drive up Ute Pass to Cripple Creek.

And she would inch several steps closer to the destiny she so deserved.

Two

Donkey Derby Days was a tradition commemorating Teddy Roosevelt's 1901 visit to Cripple Creek. Teddy had been vice president then, whistle-stopping on behalf of President McKinley. When he'd learned Cripple's donkeys spent their lives carrying sacks of ore through pitch-black tunnels, often resulting in their blindness, legend went that Teddy demanded miners release the animals from their servitude.

Festivities consisted of three days of parades, dancing, music, arcade games, gold panning, booths displaying food and homemade crafts, and kitted-out donkeys racing up Bennett Avenue to cheering spectators. The entire Mooney clan generally attended. Last year Padrick had participated with their very own donkey, purchased because Lily insisted her parents must add to their collection of animals rivaling Noah's Ark. Since Lily was also a big fan of *Winnie-the-Pooh*, the donkey, to no one's surprise, had been named Eeyore. But for today, at least, all the family—including Eeyore—remained tucked away at Shamrock Ranch, awaiting Maeve and Beau Strank's arrival.

When she reminded Beau they really must be going, her

intended life partner demurred. "Gotta press the flesh, sug. It's politics."

Because of his political aspirations, Maeve understood that networking was a full-time job. Still, how annoying! Not only did Beau need to make a good impression on her family, but wasn't his comment patronizing? Dismissive? Yeah, well, Maeve knew a bit about politics her own damn self. The Stranks might have been political in the sense that they had lots of relatives elected to public office, but the Mooneys were political in the sense that if this were the 1930s, they would have been communists.

While Beau worked his magic, Maeve wandered in the opposite direction, taking lots of selfies and videos of the brick, western-style buildings. *When I'm First Lady, I'll create an Instagram account:* "Maeve Strank Visits Quaint Colorado Towns." *That's why Colorado needs a young First Lady. New Ideas. Bring everyone together.*

Maeve tried to remember who the current governor's wife was, but she really, really didn't follow politics... except, oh, yeah, the current governor was gay, so she'd be restoring tradition. Perfect!

By the time Maeve neared the old courthouse on the corner of First and Bennett, the crowd had dwindled to a handful. Hard to believe Cripple Creek had once been dubbed the "Paris of the West." Today's gambling "industry" was a puny substitute for the riches provided by turn-of-the-century gold mines. Maybe that was why Maeve always thought of Cripple Creek as an afterthought struggling for relevancy. Still, when little, she'd enjoyed all the tales of its history. She'd particularly enjoyed Nana Grace's visits to Rocky Mountain Canary General Store, where she'd buy Maeve a chocolate chip ice cream cone and homemade fudge and toffee for the rest of the clan.

"There are ghosts here, Cailin."

Maeve could almost hear Nana Grace's voice. Despite the fact that Nana's side of the family, the O'Connors, had fled Ireland following the 1880s' Fenian dynamite campaign rather than risk arrest for blowing up British buildings, Maeve's grandmother had peppered her speech with Irish words delivered via a definite brogue. While licking her ice cream, Maeve and Nana Grace would stroll Bennett Avenue, Nana filling her head with outlandish tales involving leprechauns, banshees, changelings, spells, holy wells and the like. Here in Cripple Creek, ghosts took pride of place. The owner of the Imperial Hotel, on the corner of Bennett and Third, had been cracked over the head with an iron skillet by his mentally ill daughter, leaving his ghost to walk the corridors wearing an old-fashioned top hat. Colorado Grande Casino was haunted by the beautiful Maggie, dressed in a white blouse and blue skirt and with her long hair piled atop her head, who sang Irish tunes and danced in its old ballroom.

Then there was the young girl who'd been spotted inside Bronco Billy's Casino.

"She likes to play with visiting children," Nana Grace explained. "She also likes to sit at the top of the stairwell where she draws on the walls. No matter how employees scrub off the drawings and other graffiti, they always come back."

While Maeve always expected Nana Grace to launch into a lecture about defacing public property, instead she continued, "Sometimes you can see her gazing out the window, looking for a *cara*." Her grandmother would gesture to the huge arched windows beneath the "Turf Club" sign carved into the original brick. Once, Maeve fancied she spotted a figure wearing a white dress and with a big bow in her long hair, elbows on the windowsill, gazing down at her.

Maeve had loved those stories until she grew old enough to wonder whether her grandmother might not be crazy superstitious but simply crazy. In Maeve's opinion, her entire family had way too many fanciful or deluded ideas, not the least of which was their embrace of their peasant roots, as if there was something noble about living in bogs and starving from potato blight and railing against the fates. Maeve preferred focusing on the part of the Mooney heritage tracing their lineage back to the Gaelic kings.

Certainly not the Mooney heritage as it pertained to Cripple Creek.

Maeve hadn't always felt this way. As a child she'd been enchanted by its history—Bennett Avenue with its trolleys and elegant National Hotel; Myers Avenue, one block south, teeming with brothels, opium dens, dance halls and cribs for miners too poor to afford the high class whores at the Old Homestead House on the opposite end of the avenue. She too had been familiar with ghosts, though not the kind Nana Grace peddled. They peeked out from fading photographs in the Mooney library and local museums; flitted about Mt. Pisgah cemetery; watched and waited like shy children until Cripple was quiet, save for the occasional ding-ding-ding of slot machines, signaling it was safe to come out and play. What had it been like when ragtime music wafted from saloons, when miners trooped in and out of assay offices, hardware, and department stores, when workers and their wives dressed in their best to enjoy Enrico Caruso and Sarah Bernhardt at the Cripple Creek Opera House? When mine explosions shook the earth and whistles shrieked shift changes or warned of danger in the tunnels, when miners burrowed like voles thousands of feet down, extracting tons of ore in order to produce one ounce of gold? When newsboys shouted the day's headlines and swaggering mine owners displayed gold pocket watches adorned with jewels? When her great-great-grandfather, Saint Paddy, as her family referred to him, had been responsible for turning the Western Federation of Miners into Colorado's most powerful union?

Even now, their presence lingered like steam rising from a winter pond, which was one of the reasons Maeve disliked visiting Cripple Creek. Just as she'd jettisoned her Irish heritage over the Atlantic, she'd laid her romantic notions of Cripple Creek to rest as neatly as the graves in Mt. Pisgah Cemetery.

Contemporary Cripple Creek was nothing more than T-shirt-clad tourists and dead-eyed seniors with portable oxygen tanks mechanically yanking the arms of their slot machines.

I'm destined for a much wider world, Maeve thought, glancing at her cellphone for the time. *And nothing will stop me.*

Beau Strank emitted a low whistle. "Quite the spread," he said, after his Mercedes had eased over the cattleguard beneath the wrought iron "Shamrock Ranch" sign. Maeve found herself viewing her family "spread" with new eyes, or more precisely her soon-to-be fiancé's eyes. Rolling pastureland dotted with livestock and round hay bales from the season's first cutting, sprawling farmhouse on a rise surrounded by outbuildings and a corral. Maeve was familiar with every rock formation, every hiking trail on their two hundred-acre property.

"Prime piece of real estate, sug," Beau commented approvingly.

"Yes."

Maeve suppressed the urge to knead her stomach where a knot had formed. When she'd worked at the Golden Bee, she'd enjoyed driving around the Broadmoor gawking at the mansions, custom homes, multi-million-dollar condos, and estates glimpsed behind iron gates. She'd dreamed of living in one, of transforming herself into the perfect Broadmoor resident—refined and well-bred (because she'd invent her pedigree) without being smug, like the Broadmoor resort itself—impeccably tended private and public lawns and golf courses; immaculately kept buildings that while grand, would never be so gauche as to attempt to compete with the surrounding Rockies. An oasis of good taste where even the animals at Cheyenne Mountain Zoo lolled contentedly in their cages and the ducks trolling the Broadmoor Hotel's lake begged politely while maintaining their honks at acceptable decibels.

The American Dream for people with manners.

Was this all a mistake? Did I miscalculate somewhere along the way? Forget to factor in a few critical details when storyboarding my life?

She side-eyed Beau, who was obviously calculating the

numbers on the asset side of Shamrock Ranch's balance sheet and coming up with an impressive bunch of zeroes. Here he was, the fifty-five-year-old man who held her future in his pudgy, well-manicured hands. Definitely not a looker, not with his egg-shaped body and hinky hairline that screamed "transplants."

Don't care, she reminded herself. During her wilder years, Maeve's body count had included plenty of boy toys and Alpha males. Sex had never been that great with any of them.

Strank craned his neck in the direction of a weathered head-frame, set apart behind a wrought iron fence like a cenotaph to some grand historical figure. Beneath the headframe was the White Rabbit/holy well Nana Grace had insisted was an opening into another world—"Like Alice in Wonderland, *ceann milis.*" The truth was less magical: it was an abandoned mine shaft with a fence erected to prevent animals and the Mooney children from falling to their deaths.

"It was always a dry hole," she explained to Beau, who was still rubbernecking. Nearby was the rock foundation of some mansion that had burned down in the aftermath of the labor wars, but by the time Padrick had explained its history, she'd no longer been interested, and the details had slipped away like butterflies at twilight.

Beau pulled his SUV behind a trio of well-worn pickups and a Jeep Cherokee (all American-made). Free-range chickens clucked and scattered across the manicured lawn in the direction of the Mooney residence. Maeve might have grander aspirations, but she was proud of their rambling white farmhouse with its gingerbread trimmed dormers marching across the upper story (complete with wooden shutters that could be closed during hailstorms); its copper metal roof and wraparound porch decorated by elaborate hand carved posts and railing; window boxes popping with herbs and flowers.

Maeve's feeling of well-being disappeared when she realized

who was watching them from the interior of said wraparound porch.

"My family can't wait to meet you," she lied. While her parents and Granda valiantly supported her various "life choices," Padrick was forever crying, "What the hell's happened to you, Moonface? You know better than..." whatever decision he disagreed with.

"Let's get on with it," she muttered, exiting the vehicle.

The sacrifices one had to make to achieve one's goals!

Padrick Mooney watched the Mercedes G 63 AMG wind up the dirt driveway. *What a pretentious fuck.* A foreign-made SUV costing a couple of hundred thou when you could buy a used Ford Expedition for ten grand. For the millionth time, Padrick wondered what had happened to his little sister. Sabrina Darling, yeah, Maeve had pretty much created an alter ego that proved she'd lost her ever-loving mind. Fake blonde hair, fake hair extensions, fake tan, fake nose, because apparently the Mooney nose was too big for Pop Diva Princess, and dressing in designer duds that screamed, "Look at me. Marvel at the size of my wallet."

From his position with arms crossed and leaning against a porch pillar, Padrick called out, "Hey, Moonface!"

Ignoring him, Maeve bent down to pet their border collie, Mutt, who'd scrabbled off the porch steps to greet her with excited whines and tail wagging.

"Hey, Moonface!" Padrick repeated.

"Daddy!" Maeve yelled. "Tell Moron Brain not to call me that!"

A mild "Behave yourselves" from the front porch where Daddy and Granda were ensconced in their rockers.

A grinning Padrick descended the steps and nudged Maeve's shoulder before welcoming Beau with an outstretched hand. While the Mooneys were generally a hair below average in size, Padrick was the lineman version of the Incredible Hulk. His garb of choice was Carhartt overalls, with flannel shirts underneath in the winter and nothing in the summer.

Padrick ignored the look of alarm on Maeve's face at his bare torso. He might pretty himself up for Sunday Mass or a night out with Celia and Lily, but not for this slimeball.

Beau Strank flashed his salesman smile and shook Padrick's hand firmly, but not too firmly because there was a trick to the proper way of shaking hands if you were a politician and you thought people were too stupid to know you were as phony as your concern for their pedestrian problems.

Soon after, Mama, Celia, and Lily exited the interior to join them. After an awkward round of introductions, Mama asked Beau whether he would enjoy a tour of their house. Playing docent was one of Mama's favorite pastimes.

"What the hell, Maeve?" Padrick whispered after Beau and Mama moved out of earshot. "D'you know who that dickhead is?"

"Of course," Maeve said, lifting her chin. "He belongs to an important local family like the Tutts and the Penroses."

Padrick snorted, but before he could make some further nasty comment, Maeve scooted after the disappearing pair.

The first floor of the Mooney home, which consisted of the usual kitchen, dining room, parlor, living room, library, music room, and an entire wing where Granda resided, was chock full of antiques, many dating back to the time of Saint Paddy. Even viewing each room from her current ruthlessly critical viewpoint, Maeve found it all beautiful in a shabby chic sort of way, like the manor houses she and Padrick had toured in Ireland—a bit down at the heels perhaps, which only added to their charm.

Beau possessed a familiarity with antiques Maeve wouldn't have guessed from the mid-century vibe of his Broadmoor condo. "Is that a Tiffany table lamp?" he gushed after Mama led him into the living room. "I've never seen a fainting couch like this. Such exquisite material!"

He sounded like an estate appraiser readying for an auction.

Erase your cynicism, Maeve Mooney.

When they reached the parlor with its clear pine floor, worn rugs, and mishmash of periods furniture, they paused in front of one of the house's eight fireplaces. Above its carved mantel was a large oval portrait, executed in badly faded shades of grey and black. To Maeve, it looked more like a paint by numbers than a work of art.

Saint Paddy.

"Not only did Paddy Mooney purchase the acreage, but he also built the original house," Mama explained. "Though it's been added on over the years."

"Ah, yes," said Beau, hands behind his back, pretending to study the sun-bleached painting of a long-dead ancestor he'd probably never heard of.

Maeve wouldn't describe Saint Paddy, in his high collar shirt, tie and vest with watch chain peeking out of a side pocket, as handsome, particularly with that unfortunate Mooney proboscis. He'd always reminded her more of Darby O'Gill from *Darby O'Gill and the Little People*. This painting had been commissioned near the end of his life when he'd been bald and quite rotund and the Mooney nose appeared to have been smashed several times. She'd never express her real opinion of her quite plain (but merry-looking!) ancestor, not when Paddy Mooney had achieved the status of Saint Michael the Archangel in Mooney mythology.

While Beau and Mama chatted about her boring ancestor, Maeve's gaze drifted to the adjacent tintype—six officers of the Western Federation of Miners, which had once ruled the District. Her great-great-grandfather was seated, legs crossed and bowler tilted low so you couldn't really see his face other than a huge grin, which further cemented Maeve's (unspoken) belief that Paddy Mooney was a man who harbored secrets—such as being your typical hard-drinking, story-telling, full-of-blarney Irishman.

But it was the man standing directly behind Paddy, with his

hands resting upon her great-great-grandfather's shoulders, who held her attention.

Ronan Doyle. President of Cripple Creek's Western Federation of Miners (WFM), Local Union 40. Seeing him again caused her heart to feel a little strange, as if reigniting a yearning long after she'd forgotten it existed. Yet, she hadn't been wrong. Ronan Doyle remained the handsomest man she'd ever seen. Taller than the rest and looking, at least to Maeve's mind—harkening back to the time travel books she'd once devoured—like a transport from the 21st century. While the others were dressed in suit coats and vests, Ronan wore a collarless white shirt, open at the throat revealing what appeared to be several necklaces, but which she'd decided were religious medals and chains because no turn-of-the-century miner would wear something that looked at home on a model gracing the cover of *Esquire.* Hatless with a neatly clipped beard and hair far longer than the others and looking off to the side, as though seeing something or not wanting his face on camera. During her first crush phase, Maeve had endlessly studied the tintype, even taking out a magnifying glass to determine whether those necklaces were merely peculiar shadows.

Who is Ronan Doyle? she'd wondered, as if the photo might reveal his secrets. A broody sort, naturally, aloof and fighting his attraction to the heroine—in this case Maeve herself, at least during the stage she'd discovered and devoured Mama's historical romances.

Intense. Passionate as a union leader had to be at that time. But not just passionate toward a cause. Quite the ladies' man until tamed by the charms of one Maeve Mooney...

Ronan Doyle had sparked her interest in turn-of-the-century Cripple Creek, but even after scouring yellowing newspapers and local histories in the Mooney library, Maeve had only come across a few mentions of him—reminders of weekly meetings at the WFM union hall, congratulations when Ronan won some bareknuckle fight, speechifying at a Fourth of July extravaganza.

A memory intruded, ancient, when she'd been in the throes of her silliness.

Lounging on the Victorian settee with its poky springs—before Mama had reupholstered it—she'd been writing in her journal. A poem that included Aengus, the Celtic God of Love, but she couldn't think of something to rhyme with his name. Maybe the "gus" part, something like rust or dust or trust or...

"Head in the clouds again?" Nana Grace had swept into the room without her realizing it. Dressed in yet another version of those shapeless sack dresses she wore and those combat-style boots, she stood beside Maeve, who'd angled the settee to face the tintype head-on.

"The problem with Ronan Doyle was that he needed a decent piano player. And his uncle needed to leave the Demon rum alone."

With that, she'd swept from the room. Huh? Since Nana Grace spent a lot of time in the family library, Maeve had assumed she'd found some reference in a local history book.

And forgotten the whole business.

Besides, since Maeve had replaced fantasy with flesh and blood, she'd learned that romance existed only between the pages of novels. She'd sampled enough of the male menu to conclude men were like brushing your teeth—necessary for your health, but beyond that just another chore.

"I don't know when I've eaten a more delicious meal," Beau Strank said, helping himself to the last piece of Celia's cheesecake, which was made from goat cheese, courtesy of her Alpines. "And all home-grown." Leaning back in his chair, he patted his impressive stomach. "If y'all opened a restaurant, you'd make a fortune!"

Everybody appeared pleased by Beau's praise and charmed overall. Except for Padrick. Throughout dinner, Maeve's brother had remained uncharacteristically silent, his gaze repeatedly drifting from Beau to her and back again.

Really, what is your problem?

She kicked Padrick beneath the table. He responded by discreetly flipping her off before ordering Lily to finish her corn on the cob.

After dinner, Celia and Mama cleaned up, Daddy excused himself to feed the animals, and Padrick, Granda, Beau and Maeve retreated to the front porch. While Alexa played Dead South in the background and Lily sprawled on Mutt's stomach with an open book, Beau and Maeve sat on the porch swing.

This is going well, she thought smugly. *Beau is already like a member of the family.*

Gazing across the landscape, Maeve's heart swelled with affection. She'd forgotten how beautiful Shamrock Ranch could be on a summer evening. A hint of violet appeared in the west, heralding sunset. Shadows crawled across meadows riotous with lupine, wild asters and Indian paintbrush. Old Red, their ancient Percheron, and Eeyore the Donkey grazed near a rock formation she and Padrick had once pretended to be Fort Laramie, Old Ironsides or the Alamo, depending on what book had most recently captured their imagination.

"Auntie Moonface, would you take me to the White Rabbit?" Lily had abandoned Mutt to gaze up at Maeve with those adorably huge blue eyes. She didn't have the heart to remind her niece that "Auntie Moonbeam" was her proper title.

Maeve glanced at a frowning Padrick. "I told you, butterfly, there's nothing to see there."

Since that day no one *ever* mentioned, Padrick had been skittish about the entire White Rabbit business, even arguing the area should be bulldozed and the shaft completely filled.

"I promise we'll be careful." Maeve slipped her hand into Lily's. "And we'll take Mutt." As if Mutt could protect them from...what? Anyway, Beau might enjoy getting better acquainted with his future in-laws without her hovering.

They strolled toward the headframe, Lily clutching an ancient copy of *Alice's Adventures in Wonderland/Through the Looking Glass,* just as Maeve once had and chattering happily about the Cheshire Cat, Humpty Dumpty and queens who cut off people's heads.

Maeve's mind drifted back to her own childhood visits with Nana Grace. How many different tales had her grandmother spun about what she insisted on calling the holy well? The well could tumble you down into the past, to the time when it had been excavated. Its waters could cure illnesses and divine the future. Which was kind of impossible since there was no actual water in the so-called well, but when Maeve pointed that out, Nana Grace had thumped her on top of the head and said, "I'll be showing you water when I wash that smart mouth out with soap."

After Maeve had unlocked the wrought iron gate and they'd entered the enclosure, she tightened her grip on Lily's hand. It seemed like yesterday when *she'd* been clasping that same battered copy of *Alice in Wonderland* and pressing her small body against the iron bars, peering at a very unprepossessing circle of dirt, hoping she might see something magical.

A breeze sprang up, carrying with it the cooling breath of evening. Maeve shivered.

I did see something, didn't I?

Only it hadn't been magical.

She looked down at her feet. Had it been here, at this very spot, where she'd found a delirious Nana Grace?

Lily continued chattering and tugging her forward, closer to the shaft. Immersed in memories of that dreadful time, Maeve answered by rote. That summer, that horrible summer, the summer following her senior year. The summer Nana Grace disappeared.

Nothing unusual had distinguished that day, nothing had warned the Mooneys this would be a monumental "before and after" in their lives. Nana Grace sometimes went off on what she called "walkabouts," visiting relatives or friends (Nana Grace had friends?) for weeks at a time. Glad of the reprieve, nobody questioned her much. This particular time, there'd been no warning or declaration of "I'm going to visit Mother Cabrini's shrine. I'll be gone as long as it takes." As usual, the family had enjoyed a hearty breakfast. The usual conversation—work, weather, neighborhood news. Nana Grace had glowered at her husband because he'd spent the previous evening drinking and gambling at Johnny Nolon's Casino. But that wasn't unusual. Nana Grace loathed the wickedness that was alcohol, asserting it was the greatest curse of the Irish. Afterward, she'd helped Mama and Maeve clean up before retreating to the library, or so they'd assumed. No one noticed Nana's absence until dinner time when Granda sounded the alarm.

Thinking she'd gone on another of her walkabouts without bothering to tell them (Nana loved spiteful gestures), they'd waited several days before alerting the authorities. Afterward, a search party had scoured the ranch and the surrounding countryside. Local media speculated that Nana Grace's disappearance might be connected to recent cattle mutilations.

Weeks later, when mourning doves cooed and rain from the previous night's storm still lingered in the air, Maeve had spotted her grandmother sprawled inside the iron fence, mere feet from the White Rabbit. Nana Grace's faded blue eyes, intent upon Maeve's face, clawed hands reaching up imploringly, palms black with soot or something, still haunted her dreams.

After Maeve knelt down beside her, Nana Grace whispered, "Wonderland...Not what you think..."

Those were her last words. No one ever uncovered why Nana Grace had disappeared, where she'd gone or how she'd returned. Nana's secrets had been scattered along with her ashes across the highest point of Shamrock Ranch, overlooking a valley of lodgepole pines, red granite formations and, far in the distance, the jagged, white-capped spine of the Sangre de Cristos.

Maeve shivered. To the west the sky had caught fire, looking as it must have more than a century past when an overturned gas stove had caused all of Cripple Creek to burn.

"I want to get closer," Lily complained, jerking Maeve's arm. "I can't see anything."

As ever, the world went about its business, the living and dying unseen and unremarked. Maeve thought about that sometimes, how they'd all continued their lives, as ignorant of Nana Grace's pending fate as they were of their own.

But maybe that was the way it should be. *If we could tap into our fates, would we lie in bed, pull our covers over our heads and refuse to leave?*

"Time to go, sweetheart," Maeve said. "There's nothing to see here in the dark."

~

Maeve should have known. When she and Lily returned, songs from *the Little Red Song Book* were blasting away, courtesy of Alexa. All the way up the path, Maeve heard,

Workers of the world, awaken!
Break your chains, demand your rights.
All the wealth you make is taken
By exploiting parasites.

She didn't need the entrails of a chicken to interpret what that IWW music meant. Padrick was pissed. Yet when she and Lily reached the porch, the scene looked normal enough. Beau was still seated on the swing, cradling a bottle of Budweiser (union made!) and looking as if he owned the place. Granda and Daddy, returned from their chores, had settled into their rockers. Padrick leaned against one of the porch columns, legs crossed in front of him. "Come here, butterfly," he called, holding his arms out to Lily. Maeve knew her brother well enough to hear the tension in those three words, note the narrowed blue eyes, pugnacious jut to his jaw.

"You realize you've got a primo piece of property here," Beau was saying. He'd used the same voice when convincing Maeve to purchase her Cheyenne Canyon home from his Broadmoor Premium Real Estate firm.

You couldn't possibly be so stupid as to be talking business, not when I've repeatedly warned you not to.

"With the proper investment guidance, you're sitting on a gold mine." Absently, Beau picked at the label on his beer bottle.

All righty then. You could be that stupid.

Porch windchimes tinkled; Celia and Mama's voices drifted from the kitchen. Granda hummed along to *Workers of the World, Awaken!,* using his beer bottle as a metronome.

"Only real gold mine around here is the Cripple Creek & Victor," Padrick countered, his tone growly the way it got when irritation was sliding toward rage. "Richest gold mine in state history." He adjusted Lily, who cuddled against his shoulder. "So you'd think its owners would be open to a union in order to share their profits."

Beau didn't even blink at the word "union." "Actually, I was referring to your magnificent property. They're not making any more land, you know. And our beautiful state continues to be a treasured destination." Maeve listened in horror as he continued, "If you sold Shamrock Ranch, your beautiful baby daughter down to your great-great-grandchildren would never have to work a day in their lives."

*Join the union, fellow workers
Men and women, side by side;
We will crush the greedy shirkers
Like a sweeping; surging tide;*

"Okay, that's enough," Maeve muttered. She stalked inside the house to face the source of her distress, that little black ball so innocently placed on the hallway table. Bending close to the troublemaker that continued warbling revolutionary verses, Maeve hissed, "Alexa, shut the fuck up!" She returned to stand inside the screendoor, which was the perfect position from which to view the derailment of her future. If only fate allowed do-overs. Maybe she'd rewind way, way back before she'd storyboarded Beau Strank to be her husband and her passport to achieving the American Dream.

"It'd be my pleasure to work up some figures, a back-of-the-hand appraisal," Beau droned on. "I guarantee you'll be pleasantly surprised." For someone who prided himself on reading the room, Beau Strank was oblivious to the hostility sparking off Padrick like a downed power line. "Just imagine what you could do with more money than most people dream of—"

Daddy interrupted. "Two things count in this world, your family and your land." He gestured into the dark. "Here is the Mooney legacy. Been in our family for more than a hundred years. No price you can put on a man's birthright."

For her easy-going father, that was the equivalent of punching Beau in the face.

Padrick spoke up. "Gotta question about your ancestor, one Horace Strank." His neutral tone was belied by the "look," which meant he was about to start spouting his socialist nonsense. Or rip Beau's throat out.

"Ask away," Beau said amiably. Unaware that he had just stepped into a mantrap.

"During the labor wars, Horace Strank was one of the founders of the Citizens' Alliance, which helped destroy the Western Federation of Miners."

"Padrick!" Maeve called out. "Remember what they say about mixing politics and religion."

"Was it Horace Strank's idea, as a leader of the Alliance, to persuade Governor Peabody to bring in Gatling guns and declare martial law and to murder strikers? How many deaths was your relative responsible for?"

"I wouldn't know anything about that," Beau responded blandly. "I'm not really a fan of history."

Maeve pushed open the screen door and let it slam behind her. "Daddy, Beau said he can get us season tickets for the Broncos."

The entire Mooney clan, save Maeve, loved football, though she pretended to because she enjoyed ogling the players' butts.

Everyone except Padrick seemed relieved by the change in subject. Celia came outside to retrieve Lily, who'd fallen asleep on his shoulder, which left Padrick free to glare more menacingly at Beau. The Mooney men were still upset over the outcome of the 1904 strike, though Saint Paddy had tried his mighty best to fight Colorado's governor, the state militia, the National Guard, the various mine owners' alliances... and Horace Strank.

Soon after, Maeve ended the day's disaster with, "We really must be going. Traffic down Ute Pass can be bumper to bumper."

Beau shook hands all around and handed out business cards. "If you change your mind, give me a ring. I promise you won't be disappointed."

Though they were not a huggy family, Padrick pulled Maeve to him. *"Bloody hell,"* he whispered against her ear. "You can do a million times better than that fucking bastard. Just say the word and I'll kick his ass."

Oddly touched, Maeve clung to her brother for a long moment before pushing away. "I'm fine," she whispered back. "Promise. Everything's great."

Only it wasn't.

As Maeve Mooney would soon find out.

Three

Maeve didn't believe in karma. At least the bad kind. At least the bad kind when it came to her.

But something was going on.

In the space of eight weeks, she'd lost *everything*!

I don't understand.

What had happened? What is happening?

One thing was clear. If karma didn't have it out for her, somebody did.

But who?

Beau Strank topped Maeve's list. Following the Donkey Days disaster, he'd ghosted her, blocking all her calls and texts. She hadn't found him at his office, his condo, the Broadmoor Golf Club or any of his other usual haunts.

He was obviously *somewhere*, though, since two weeks past an eviction notice had been posted on her front door.

"How can this be?" Maeve cried. "I'm not a common renter."

Turns out, she was.

Maeve hadn't actually purchased 212 Canyon Street. She'd signed a lease with an option to buy. Before they'd ever been an item, Beau had arranged financing, no easy feat, he'd said, since banks were reluctant to lend money to the self-employed. Maeve had been so grateful after he'd put together the deal, particularly the way he'd patiently explained the contract while she'd scribbled her initials in dozens of places. When her parents had suggested she hire a real estate attorney just to be sure, she'd answered a bit snarkily, "Mr. Strank is a real estate broker. He knows what he's doing!"

"You broke the terms of the lease," Padrick said, after she'd called him in hysterics and he'd driven down Ute Pass, implementing a big brother rescue. (Padrick might be a pain, but he was the smartest guy Maeve knew and she couldn't afford a legal consultation.)

"The lease is null and void if you miss any payments, which you did—"

"But I made them up, and I never got any notices." (That she knew of. Maeve wasn't always on top of opening her mail.)

As it turned out, Beau Strank was the actual owner of 212 Canyon Street. "Right there, legal as you please." Padrick tapped the first page of the contract. Maeve was grateful her brother didn't castigate her for being so stupid and when he said, "I'm gonna kill the fucking bastard," she spent several pleasant moments imagining Padrick squishing Beau Strank like an overripe tomato before he intruded on her fantasy with, "Didn't you put two and two together?"

Maeve blinked herself back to the present. "What do you mean?"

"Don't you know your own history?" Padrick had forced her to shower, after which he'd dragged her into the kitchen where he'd wrestled up a meal from the few unspoiled ingredients remaining in her refrigerator. Maeve certainly no longer looked like Pop Diva Princess, which was okay, but he wished she'd lose that hangdog expression.

Between bites of a cheese-and-something omelet, Maeve

assured Padrick she was familiar with the origins of the Mooney clan, as well as bits and pieces of the Orange Rebellion and she at least recognized the Battle of the Boyne involved the Irish...

"Not that history. The foundation beside the White Rabbit. Horace Strank built the original mansion in 1900. Bloody hell, Maeve, didn't you ever listen?"

Maeve placed her head in her hands. Once she had, but she'd prided herself on erasing all that blue-collar propaganda from her mind. "Gawd, I'm trapped in a nightmare."

"You know what I think?" Padrick removed her plate and continued tidying up her sadly neglected kitchen. "Beau Strank finagled a visit to Shamrock Ranch thinking he could talk us into selling and then buy it himself. That's the piece of shit he is."

Maeve felt like pulling out her hair, though that was already happening because her tape-in extensions were shedding like Mutt in the summer.

"We'll move you back home this weekend," Padrick said before leaving. "Store your furniture in the tack room and ready your old bedroom. You know Mama and Daddy will be thrilled."

After Padrick left, Maeve tottered back to bed where she examined the titanic-sized disaster that had become her life. Night after night, her mind endlessly racing until she fell into an exhausted sleep.

Determined to count her blessings, Maeve reminded herself that at least she wouldn't be homeless. Which would otherwise be a real possibility. Because losing her home wasn't the end of her problems. Sabrina Darling, a fabulously successful social media influencer, was pretty much out of business.

From earning hundreds of thousands a year to subscribers demanding their money back because her fitness program was a rip-off and she was a scam artist who hadn't provided the promised personal consultations regarding their fitness "journey." Oh yeah, and subscribers were upset because Sabrina Darling's response to their whiny texts with their whiny questions had been pretty much a generic version of, "You're doing great, girlfriend!" Not to mention the diet pills and other products she—*and dozens of other influencers, so don't blame me*—had promoted on behalf of a company now being investigated by the FTC.

Maeve felt particularly betrayed by Tommy, her Domino's Pizza deliverer, who'd posted several detailed accounts of her penchant for late-night food orders.

Maybe I should have tipped him better.

After deleting her platform—which meant starting the process, but it was too complicated right now so she just disabled her comments—Maeve burned up countless mental calories trying to uncover who, other than Beau Strank, was hell bent on destroying her.

Grade school classmates who'd been mean to her for no reason?

Some heartbroken guy she'd slept with during her "body count" phase?

Jax Ajax, her long-ago personal trainer who'd taught her every-thing she'd needed to know about physical fitness in order to bypass all that silliness about certification? But she and Jax quit fooling around after he got engaged, and why would he pop back up after all these years?

Kaitlyn, the waitress from the Golden Bee who'd smashed her car windshield after accusing Maeve of stealing her boyfriend? Which she kind of had, but Roy had been a computer nerd who'd helped her set up Better Best, and he hadn't seemed upset when she'd dumped him. He'd seemed almost relieved, in fact, if she could remember that far back.

Her college interns? They should be grateful for learning how to launch their own businesses, rather than, well, some of them had been downright bitchy.

The workers who'd remodeled her kitchen and bathroom? *When you're paying out that much money, you have a right to expect perfection.*

What more could go wrong? Maeve wondered. She tried not to

think about it because that might be poking the karmic gods and they'd already caused enough havoc.

Still, she wasn't at all surprised when she turned on the local news to hear its anchor report: "Beau Strank announced his run for Colorado's governor. With his new fiancée at his side."

Before pulling her blankets over her face, Maeve whispered, "I'm definitely going to vote Democrat."

"In the gardens of memory, in the palace of dreams, That is where you and I shall meet."

Maeve and her niece had snuggled against the pillows propped against Maeve's headboard reading *Through the Looking Glass*, when she'd come across the phrase that had once so captivated her, a phrase she'd long forgotten. *"In the gardens of memory..."* Maeve read slowly, savoring each word along with the images they evoked. She found herself catapulted back to her ten-year-old self, when she'd marveled how someone as eccentric as the Mad Hatter could utter such an exquisite sentiment in such exquisite fashion, though she hadn't been sure what any of it meant.

After copying it into my journal, I underlined it so many times I tore the paper.

The realization awakened a yearning inside her, too ephemeral to articulate, though she couldn't dismiss it as sentimentality or self-pity because her life had become a catastrophe.

What exactly would a memory garden smell like? Maeve had wondered. *Would a palace of dreams be made of cobwebs or ice? What would "you and I" do after they met?* She'd imagined herself, when she was grown and possessed of a garden full of memories rather than a handful of potted plants, as a wraith-like form draped upon a shadowy window seat, gazing out at a smudged grey landscape in a musing sort of way. While tracking the raindrops slipping like tears down the windowpane, she would contemplate the identity of that "you."

How had "you" morphed into Beau Strank? How had all those shining possibilities degenerated into peddling fitness subscriptions when, let's get real, Maeve's actual credentials consisted of sleeping with Jax Ajax and adapting his training sessions? Selling questionable vitamin supplements and made-in-China merchandise? Purchasing a hand-carved five-thousand-dollar Christopher Guy bathroom mirror so she could brag about it to her "besties"? Believing money—the getting and spending of it—was the most important measure of success?

In the three months Maeve had been home, she'd roamed her psyche the way she'd roamed Shamrock Ranch, the way she'd played Chopin's "Funeral March" for hours on end, the way she'd hidden herself away in her old bedroom with its faded flowered duvet and matching sheets edged with pretty little ruffles grown limp with time. She was vaguely aware that the entire Mooney clan kept the outside world at bay. If there were lawsuits being filed, news reports aired, Sabrina Darling TikTok haters by the thousands, her family never let on.

Still, Maeve wasn't entirely disconnected. She didn't need her parents or Padrick to tell her she'd lost her home, her business, her reputation, her intended fiance—okay, that was definitely a plus. All of which had brought her to the following painful, but undeniable conclusion.

I'm to blame. My bad choices. My pursuit of wealth and status, my manipulation of others for my benefit. My upside-down priorities.

All of that's on me, no one else.

Well, maybe one other person, Maeve had concluded: Nana Grace.

Since Mama worked full-time at the county courthouse, Nana had been Maeve's primary babysitter. And as Maeve disassembled her past, she realized how toxic her grandmother had been. Selfish and self-deluded and ready to punch the world in the face at the slightest provocation. Had it begun with her disillusionment over her marriage?

"Never marry a handsome face," she'd lectured Maeve, "for they'll mistakenly believe a seductive grin, a twinkling set of eyes and a silver tongue will make all of society bend its knee."

And:

"If it hadn't been for your daddy working from the time he was knee high to a grasshopper, Brady Mooney would've drunk and gambled away Shamrock Ranch or sold it to finance some get-rich-quick scheme, you mark my words."

Marriage had also kept Nana Grace from fulfilling her own potential. At various times, she could have been a doctor, a lawyer, a real estate mogul, a fashion designer or model, if she hadn't been tied down young to a whiskey-guzzling dreamer and a child.

Nana Grace's opinions found fertile ground in Maeve's young mind. She'd diligently soaked up the superstitions; the fabulisms used as much to frighten as to entertain; the caustic view of humankind in general and men in particular; the endless lectures on all matters right and wrong, according to Grace O'Connor-Mooney's moral code.

Maeve Mooney, Nana Grace in the making.

Not blaming her. Simply trying to understand.

Which is what had brought Maeve here to the White Rabbit on this moonless, starless night. Around her, God's wild creatures had taken possession of Shamrock Ranch. Foxes and raccoons crept near the chicken coops, hoping to find them unlocked; coyotes yipped upon the ridge, claiming the moon; mountain lions stalked the deer and elk that had drifted down to graze the meadows.

Maeve couldn't remember an evening so black or so still, like stepping into a painting: *Black on Black on Black*. Was this what hell would be like, not only the absence of God, but the absence of light?

Maeve remained Catholic enough to believe in hell, but best not to think of it out here when she was quite alone and who knew what might be observing her? She thought of the Great Horned Owl, all glowing eyes and razor talons, that had nested seemingly forever in the lone pine near the mansion ruins.

Owls, harbingers of death. Liaisons to the Otherworld.

Maeve shivered. She buttoned the pink and blue plaid shacket she'd shrugged over her wool sweater in order to blunt the November cold. Retrieving her smartphone (no longer connected to WiFi) from her Levi's, she clicked the flashlight app to maneuver the complicated latch.

Maeve stepped into the enclosure, her booted feet releasing the petrichor from a recent rain. She paused at the approximate spot where she'd discovered her grandmother that terrible day.

"From the moment we're born, we walk toward death," Nana Grace was fond of saying, and this was where her walk had ended. (Not literally. She'd died two days later in Woodland Park's UC Health Hospital.)

Which was why Maeve was out here, in the wee hours, when her parents and Granda were long to bed, as she would normally be.

Maeve had been contemplating Nana Grace's last disappearance, or more precisely, obsessing over it. What if, like Maeve's own life, Nana's disappearance wasn't at all what it had seemed at the time? Or all the times she went off chasing whatever caught her fancy, with no one caring enough to really question. Simply relieved to enjoy time away from her judgments.

What if what had seemed a tragedy had been a reprieve? What if Nana Grace had embarked on some grand exploration—though how a grand exploration could end near a dirt hole Maeve had no clue—and her last words, *"Wonderland... it's not what you think..."* hadn't been deluded ravings, but the solution to a puzzle whose pieces Maeve was supposed to assemble?

Such peculiar thoughts one has, when one has thoughts to think. It sounded like something Lewis Carroll would have written, which pleased her.

A flash of gray. With a whisper of its outstretched wings, the

Great Horned Owl skimmed the foundation of the burned-out mansion, seeking mice cowering in the tall grass.

Padrick had chastised Maeve for being ignorant of the history behind the ruin, but Nana Grace had filled Maeve's head with so many crazy fables—largely knockoffs from the "auld sod"—that the commingling of the two was enough to confuse any child. Nana had tied the mythical mansion to ghost tales from an Irish castle called Leap, when an eleven-year-old named Emily had fallen from its battlements—or had an identical thing happened *here?*—and her poor sister Charlotte was left to drag her deformed leg behind her. (Maeve had imagined carting an amputated limb around like a piece of luggage.)

"They live on as ghosts because that's what happens when you think you know better than your elders," Nana had finished ominously.

No wonder Maeve had nightmares. No wonder she had an aversion to the ruin.

Yet, Maeve remembered another conversation right on the ruins of the mansion, one she hadn't thought about for how many years? After Nana Grace had returned from one of her earlier "walkabouts."

Tapping her temple. "You can bend time to your will," she'd said. *"We in the O'Connor clan. The magic's been passed down."*

"I don't understand." So Maeve had been young enough to yet be intrigued by her grandmother's nonsense.

"If we were not here, but in Leap Castle, that very place. I might say, 'Take me to the Bloody Chapel,' and there I'd be. With the murdered priest lurking in the stairwell, before he became a ghost. Or a later or earlier incident, if I chose." She'd paused dramatically. *"Once I located the portal."*

Maeve had looked around at the White Rabbit, its shadow nearly reaching the ruins as the sun inched behind them. "What's a portal?" she'd asked, a reminder of her youth.

That's when Nana Grace had reverted to the nasty piece of work with whom Maeve was most familiar. *"You've obviously got not a drop of the O'Connor mystic in your veins. I'll not be wasting my breath on the likes of you. Forget we've had this talk."*

And she had.

Maeve shivered. Even now, more than a decade after her grandmother's death, she couldn't puzzle her out. Why had Nana Grace possessed such a malicious heart? She always said she loved Maeve, loved them all. (Except for her husband.) Wasn't that the sadness of it? How we rationalize our cruelties and call them love?

I don't want that. I want to be different.

While it was easy to make promises when one was sheltered from the consequences of one's bad decisions, Maeve whispered, "Right here, right now I *will* change my ways." She imagined her words rippling out into the darkness, stirring awake magic she no longer believed in.

Maeve closed her eyes. She realized, for the first time in how long, her stomach didn't hurt; her heart no longer felt perpetually squeezed. A sense of peace enveloped her, a determination that she was on the precipice of a new beginning. She would embrace it, and she would triumph over all the challenges awaiting her after she ventured beyond her current haven back into the real world.

A gentle brushing of her cheek. Fingers? A feather? The breath of a breeze? A rustling in the undergrowth beyond the enclosure, the plaintive hooting of her owl. Followed by something so indistinct, it didn't immediately register. Music? More of an impression than an actual sound. She held her breath, listening. A distant radio? But the farmhouse remained dark. No restless residents on the prowl. Then she heard the faintest tinkling of a piano, like distant windchimes. Louder. A plaintive melody, familiar, yet its identity eluded her.

Maeve cocked her ear to better hear. The music seemed to increase in volume. Her gaze swung in the direction of the White Rabbit. Was it her imagination, or was the darkness less intense? Could the music be emanating from there? From a dry hole? But what if it wasn't a dry hole? Maeve wasn't sure anyone had ever actually inspected the shaft, at least in her lifetime. Could there be a kernel of truth among all the folk tales and superstitions she'd been fed?

Oddly, Maeve felt not fear, rather a sense of anticipation.

Am I being offered a new adventure?

She suddenly thought of the fairy rings that sometimes grew right beyond the enclosure. Fairies danced inside the rings and used the mushrooms as dining tables, though Nana Grace warned her never to step inside lest she be kidnapped and whisked away, never to be heard from again. Padrick explained that fairy rings were caused by a fungus, but what if the truth of fairy rings, of all those tales, lay somewhere in between?

One step closer to the light, to the shaft. Maeve imagined the night leaning forward along with her, curious to see what unfolded.

It was fascination
I know
And it might have ended
Right then, at the start.

A female, singing a song she indeed recognized. "Fascination." Granda always requested it when the family gathered round on a Sunday for a sing-along. "Though," Granda would say, "Nobody can sing it as smooth and mellow as the late great Nat King Cole!"

Just a brief romance
And I might have gone
On my way
Empty hearted.

Huh. Goosebumps rose on Maeve's arms. She recognized the wistfulness, the longing behind the woman's singing. *She's in love and he doesn't love her back...*

She wanted to weep at the thought.

Maeve dared another step closer; still not close enough to see the origin of the glow. A waltz tempo. *One, two, three, one two three.* If she gazed down into the hole or the shaft or whatever it was called, would she see, far below, men in black tie and women in long dresses, strong arms around corseted waists, couples gracefully swirling around a candlelit ballroom?

Had Nana Grace heard something similar the day she'd disappeared? Had she been passing the White Rabbit, decided to explore the origin of the sound, and then... what? Might there actually be some sort of portal to another world as Nana claimed? Could you fall down the hole the same way Alice had on her own adventure? Is that what Nana had meant by "wonderland"?

> *It was fascination*
> *I know*
> *Seeing you alone*
> *With the moonlight above*

Maeve fancied she could see the words drifting up from the shaft, swaying gently, as if buoyed by a draft.

"Enchanting," Maeve breathed, captivated rather than frightened. That was the kind of night it was.

"Photos," Maeve breathed, removing her smartphone from her back jeans pocket. Is that what this was all about? Some benevolent being had led her here to present her with a new and exciting business opportunity, a platform that explored paranormal phenomena? A social media *Ghostbusters*? Maeve snapped several photos, anticipating how this would work. Later, upon close examination, she would see faces or dancing lights or maybe even a string of musical notes emerging from the hole. And, voila, a new career!

> *Then I touch your hand*
> *And next moment*
> *I kissed you*

Fascination turned to love.

Maeve tiptoed closer. Wouldn't it be lovely to spend time in a world so different from her own? Where orchestras played "Fascination," dance partners bowed and curtsied and were oh, so polite, and nobody knew Maeve's identity, where her mistakes were decades in the future, where the karmic gods granted her a do-over?

Another step and the toe of Maeve's hiking boots edged the lip of the hole. *I'm going to look!* Heart racing in anticipation, she leaned over the hole, hoping she might view...

The ground beneath Maeve's feet crumbled. Too quickly for her to jump back to safety. She lost her balance, grabbed onto...nothing for there was nothing to hold onto and before she could even shout, Maeve Mooney was falling, falling down, down, down...

PART TWO

November–December 1901

❦

The past is a foreign country; they do things differently there.

— L.P. HARTLEY

Four

Easy as shooting clay pigeons, ten in all. Thump, swish, gasp from onlookers, from the hanged men. From them all?

"Look, lad, and don't forget," Da had said, his huge hands on Ronan's tiny shoulders, his mam's hand squeezing his own.

The Day of the Rope, when three of Ronan's uncles had their necks snapped, their jerking limbs silhouetted against a woolen nothingness from which mist seeped onto the faces of the dignitaries in Schuylkill County's jail yard; onto onlookers like Ronan who'd lined the curbstone of the street fronting the jail, watched from nearby fields, and squatted on the stoops of surrounding houses.

"As if heaven itself is weeping for the injustice of it," Mam had sniffed through the handkerchief she'd brought to her eyes.

Had she really said that? Had the hangings taken place in a mist-ridden fog or beneath a glowering June sun with air so thick it caused the gallows to shimmer? Ronan mentally replayed the scene from that angle and countless others. He remembered a trio of gallows, lined up like soldiers, with the Molly Maguires hanged in pairs. Each had been trussed in leather straps and carried a red rose. But how reliable was Ronan's memory and what had blended together only to be served up in some macabre witch's brew? He'd only been seven years old, after all. His family had kept the newspaper accounts, which remained tucked inside a wooden box on one of Ronan's bookshelves, but what did it matter whether his uncles had each clutched a rose, or the priest had kissed them and the sheriff shaken their hands or that Hugh McGehan had taken sixteen minutes to die? The lone irrefutable fact was this: three of Ronan's uncles had died after the Molly Maguires had been convicted and the organization crushed and twenty hanged because of that fink Pinkerton bastard, James McParland.

Sighing, Ronan locked the main door to Cripple Creek's WFM union hall, pulled up the collar of his sheep-lined jacket, jammed his worsted gloves inside his pockets and struck out along Bennett Avenue.

Why am I poking the devil by dwelling on the past? That's just borrowing trouble, and we've enough of that in the present.

Tonight's meeting had been less contentious than usual, maybe because Leprechaun hadn't been there to stir things up. Small men and small dogs had a lot in common—always yipping and snapping at your heels and behaving as if they were the giant Finn McCool rather than an ankle-biter. Leprechaun would have been yelling the usual, "Better to die on your feet than live on your knees," and "An injury to one is an injury to all." Paddy Mooney was like a pull-string toy. Pull the string and out would come some cliché that sounded like Pope Leo's own truth when Paddy spoke it. Paddy Mooney had a voice and manner smooth as Irish whiskey, which is what made him such a crackerjack organizer.

Ronan's breath puffed in the razor-sharp air. The smells of wood and coal smoke, along with the effluvium belching from various smokestacks, lay particularly heavy in his lungs as he walked. A mercy, since that precluded snow.

Why was he feeling so uneasy this cold November night? It couldn't be work, not really. Compared to the coal mines of Pennsylvania, Colorado's gold mines bordered on paradise. Most of the District was organized. Eight-hour day; three-dollar-a-day wage. Non-union products were forbidden to be sold in saloons, grocery and other related stores; retail clerks were mandated to close their shops at six o'clock in the evening. Laundries were prohibited from shipping clothes out of the District to non-union shops; boarding houses and restaurants hired union help, including cooks and waiters who'd negotiated a six-day work week.

And we, the WFM, are at the heart of it all.

So Ronan told himself. Assured himself. Argued with himself when the black dog snarled at him from the shadows, threatening to take him down.

Remember how they executed your uncles and crushed the Mollies? From the coal company to the politicians to the judge, all of them working together to frame your kin and their like. Ah, boyo. Do you really believe your fate will be different?

Always that immutable truth lurking in the background of everything Ronan said and did. Was that some sort of sixth sense, or simply the whispered voices of all those who'd been sacrificed on the altar of capitalism?

"The arc of the moral universe is long, but it bends toward justice—except for America's working class."

It had always been a mystery to Ronan—whether as a breaker boy inside the Glen Carbon or here as a powder monkey—how mine owners could be so ignorant of one basic fact. *Without our hands, our backs, our brawn, and aye, our desperation, you all would be up shite creek.*

Ronan passed under one of the newly installed electric streetlights. Electricity had recently arrived, thanks to the remarkable Woods family, who'd virtually built the town of Victor and the Skaguay dam and power plant that lit up nearly every residence in the District. Not that Cripple Creek, with nearly a hundred saloons and gambling emporiums—most open round the clock—was ever really dark. Closed mercantile stores; a meat market. More saloons. To the west, beyond Cripple, only an occasional pinprick, like embers escaping a fire, emanated from the tents, shacks and houses crawling up Mount Pisgah.

He loved the aggressive endlessness of Colorado's night sky, though it could never be wide or open enough, not with the claustrophobia that had plagued him since... But Ronan hadn't gone below in years, so he'd laid that particular demon to rest. At least during daylight hours.

Ronan was so used to the noise of a city numbering thirteen thousand residents, it was only now that he tuned into the piano and fiddle music, the singing, the laughter and voices. Before night put itself to bed there would be brawls, maybe a couple of knife fights and a shooting, not to mention the regulars who passed out on sidewalks or wherever they fell. But what could one expect when the moment a man crawled into the belly of one of five hundred area mines, he risked being burned or crushed to death from a misplaced charge, asphyxiated from poor ventilation, or expiring from heat stroke? Aye, the very thought of burrowing into the earth like some mutant worm was enough to make Ronan want to drown himself in a barrel of beer.

Ronan neared his destination, the Pick-Axe, located next to Johnny Nolon Saloon & Gambling Emporium. Tonight he'd slip up the back stairs to his room without alerting Leprechaun, who was tending bar. Which his Uncle Liam should have been doing, but Uncle Liam was on the sauce again and not good for much of anything.

Pausing near the bottom step of the stairs to his room, he groped inside his jacket for his room key.

"Where am I? Am I dead?"

Ronan jumped. He looked around. The alley wasn't completely

dark, not with the lights from Johnny Nolon's. He didn't spot any crumpled lumps, and the voice appeared to be feminine.

"Help! You, who are you? What am I doing here?"

Didn't sound drunk; disoriented maybe?

On the opposite side of his position near the stairs, swathed in shadows, he glimpsed a half-reclining figure. A patch of light revealed a pink and blue plaid arm.

Skirting the stairway, Ronan moved closer to the figure. The clicking of roulette wheels from Johnny Nolon's and from the Pick-Axe, Uncle Liam, leading a rousing rendition of "Little Brown Jug."

Pushing back his cap, Ronan bent toward the figure, careful not to get too close. Illnesses were ever making the rounds. If the creature wasn't drunk, she might be sick.

The figure shifted; a face joined the sleeve in the light. Yep, female.

"Are you ill? Do you need help?"

Huge green eyes gazed into his brown ones. "Have I died and gone to heaven? Aren't I supposed to be met by relatives? Though I'm not sure I want Nana Grace to be the first—"

"You're not dead, lass, though some might say Cripple Creek is hell."

Ronan allowed himself a closer step. The woman's gaze didn't appear feverish, though she wasn't making sense.

"Oh, I know you, I'm sure I do. It can't be you, can it?"

"Where do you live?" Ronan interrupted again. "Who might I fetch to help you? Are you in need of a doctor?"

"No!" The woman vigorously shook her head with hair that barely reached her shoulders. Probably shorn at one time to combat lice. Ronan skimmed her body as best as he could. She appeared to be wearing Levi's, but women didn't wear Levi's or any other pants, and those boots, he'd never seen such strange soles—

"I just need...You say I'm in Cripple Creek? Then a ride home? Would you call me an Uber?"

"A trolley, you mean? It's past ten so they'll not be running again until six on the morrow."

From inside the Pick-Axe, *"The rose is red, my nose is too, The violets blue and so are you;"*

"It's just...it's really cold out here and I need, oh, oh..." The woman raised her hand and touched his bearded jaw, her gaze suddenly intense as fire. "Ronan Doyle? It can't be, but is that really you?" Before Ronan could respond, she collapsed against the brick wall.

~

Maeve had no idea how long she'd slept or where she was when she cracked open her eyes to sunlight pouring in through a pair of windows. Full-size bed, cast iron frame, a horsehair mattress from the feel of it, feather pillows.

Maeve's eyes drifted closed again. She wasn't sure whether her head hurt or if it had been stuffed with socks. She had to figure this —whatever *this* was—out.

What do I remember?

The White Rabbit. Falling? She must have blacked out and awakened here. Or maybe staggered here from somewhere else.

Noise drifted from the street—not the roar of cars, but a cacophonous hum she was sure she could distinguish individual noises one from the other if she could concentrate. But her mind wandered like a toddler chasing soap bubbles.

All Maeve knew for certain was that *something* had happened after she'd heard that peculiar music and followed it until she'd tripped on a lip of dirt and tumbled down...down...

I fell... But it wasn't really falling. By all rights, she should have broken her neck, or dropped like a stone since shafts could pierce the earth for hundreds, even thousands of feet. But she'd been more like a dandelion puff, drifting sometimes up, sometimes down, through a place that didn't seem to have walls or boundaries, but consisted of a vague dusky light.

I asked for an adventure. Could this be it? A peculiar night it had been, with magic in the air. "You, Maeve Mooney, are going to embrace this...glitch," she whispered, giving herself a pep talk. "Whatever, this can't be worse than what you left behind."

After groping for one of the two pillows behind her head, she pulled it over her face. The scent was pleasant—orange with a hint of cloves. Familiar, too, though she couldn't quite grasp...Then she remembered. Florida Water. Granda sometimes used it. Though this particular version was infinitely more appealing.

"So that's what you smell like, if you're real," she said to her invisible savior.

Ronan Doyle? But it couldn't be. Maeve felt thirteen again and drooling over a tintype. Impossible. She was mixing up what she knew—a fragrance—with delusion. Besides, if Ronan Doyle wasn't a figment of her imagination or whatever, where was he?

I didn't carry myself into this room.

Had Maeve's mind simply conjured everything? But why would it? Unless she was dead. But if that were so, the afterlife wouldn't be so pedestrian.

Maeve looked around what was most likely Ronan Doyle's room. Next to her bed, a dresser with a lamp atop it, a coiled rosary and three books, their spines toward her. *The Communist Manifesto*, *Progress and Poverty*, and *Looking Backward*. The only author she recognized was Karl Marx.

The rest of the area consisted of a small wardrobe and a marble-topped washstand with a plain matching jug and bowl. Beside it was a soap dish, a broken handled cup with a toothbrush, a glass jar labeled Colgate Dental Powder, the narrow-necked Florida Water glass bottle, and other items she didn't recognize. Above the stand, an oval mirror so speckled and discolored you'd be lucky to see your face. The usual things one finds in a studio-style apartment—even in the 21st century

—save for the huge, cluttered desk and rows of shelving covering one wall. Books, wooden crates that appeared to double as filing cabinets, various memorabilia such as a violin case and miner's hat and in front of a desk chair, the framed logo of the WFM—a pick-axe crossed with a shovel. Beyond that, a door, hopefully leading to at least a water closet.

Footsteps on the stairs. One sharp knock. The door opened.

Him.

Wow. Just wow.

No words could accurately describe her childhood crush. Thick dark hair, shoulder length and kind of mussy, but it suited him; the darkest eyes; longest lashes. Neatly trimmed beard; perfectly proportioned face. Taller than she'd imagined, but perhaps that was due as much to that mysterious quality called charisma, which Ronan Doyle oozed by the bucketload. He was wearing black pants, a white collarless shirt, and suspenders that somehow looked sexy on those very broad shoulders. Maeve glimpsed the necklaces she'd once examined with a magnifying glass. A celtic cross, a crucifix and saints' medallions. Because Ronan Doyle, a mere miner, *would* be a Catholic.

"You're awake then?"

Maeve reached out to grasp Ronan's wrist, in case she was dreaming a very extended dream and her fingers would clutch empty air.

Ronan stared down at her hand, then up to her face, a frown only enhancing those flawless features.

So this must be real. She'd go with real. "Are you really Ronan Doyle? Is this your room? How long did I sleep?"

"Aye, that I am and this is my room, above my uncle's establishment. I'd venture you've been out about a day and a half."

Pleasant voice, conventionally deep with the barest hint of a brogue. Probably a decent baritone.

"Did I snore?" What sort of stupid question was that?

Ronan frowned. "I wouldn't know. I slept on a cot in the backroom downstairs. I had Bridget Kehoe—housekeeper at the National Hotel—checking on you."

Maeve shifted to directly face him. "What's the date today?"

"Did you not hear the church bells?" When she didn't answer, he continued, "Sunday, November 24... 1901."

Maeve flopped back on her pillows and closed her eyes, considering. This couldn't be real, but if it was, she was back in the past, during Cripple Creek's boom times. *Wait till I tell Padrick.* But how could she tell him anything? Would her family fear her dead? Is this what had happened to Nana Grace? Had she too fallen down the White Rabbit? If so, Maeve should be able to return the same way her grandmother had.

Interesting! Why not stay right here then, at least for a while?

"Your name?" By Ronan's tone, he'd asked her more than once.

"Maeve Mooney."

"If you don't mind my asking, Maeve Mooney, what were you doing outside my establishment dressed so peculiar and kind of babbling, if truth be told?"

How was she supposed to respond? She certainly couldn't tell Ronan Doyle the truth.

Maeve heard him shift, heard him repeat her name, as if prodding her.

That's when Maeve decided to use a literary trope so worn that anyone possessed of a lackluster imagination would be ashamed to utter the following words: "I don't actually know what I'm doing here. I can't remember anything other than my name. I...I must have amnesia." Was that a word in 1901?

Ronan frowned. "You recall your name, but nothing beyond?"

She nodded.

"Well, Maeve Mooney, that's a bit of a problem, isn't it?"

"I'm sure with a few days' rest, I'll remember. That's the way it is with amnesia. One moment you can't recall a thing, and the next it all comes flooding back."

Ronan frowned. "We've a doctor I'll send to talk with you, maybe run tests for such things."

"No," Maeve cried in alarm. "I mean...I don't have the money to pay for that."

Ronan shook his handsome head. "'Tis paid for by the union. I'll send him 'round tomorrow. We can even get you a nurse, if need be."

At that moment, an explosion strong enough to rattle the casement windows and shake the bed caused Maeve to gasp and grab Ronan's forearm. "What is that? Are we being bombed?" She looked around for a place to hide.

Ronan raised an eyebrow. "Just some dynamiting down below."

Releasing his arm, Maeve collapsed back upon the bed.

"I think we can safely say one thing, Maeve Mooney. You've not lived in a mining camp before."

Despite growing up in Nana Grace's to-put-it-kindly credulous world, despite herself having been magically transported back in time, Maeve experienced no flash of precognition upon first meeting her great-great-grandparents.

Had she known, Maeve would have petitioned the universe for do-overs.

First, great-great-grandmother Bridget Kehoe: the housekeeper Ronan promised would "check in" on her. A petite, curvaceous woman with a stack of fiery red hair barely tamed by a maid's cap and a face that might once have been beautiful. Unfortunately, in the way it sometimes is with the very fair, her skin had prematurely settled into a map of wrinkles and sun spots. Or perhaps her rotten interior had disfigured her exterior, because Bridget Kehoe was one of the most hateful creatures Maeve had ever met.

Upon their first official meeting, Bridget had barged into her room, tossed several bundles on her bed and snarled, "Mr. Doyle told me to purchase you some decent clothes. 'Miller's Fashion Emporium,' he tells me, when I could've rounded up some hand-me-downs, which is what you merit, and saved him some coin."

Maeve's entire new ensemble, down to her fleece-lined cotton stockings, was a dreary shade of grey. When she'd politely thanked her great-great-grandmother, Bridget had growled something and stomped out the door.

The second, her great-great-grandfather: Saint Paddy himself! Initially, Maeve thought Leprechaun—as everyone called him—a charming bundle of nonsense who delivered ridiculous Irish jokes along with her nightly dinner. A shade over five feet, sporting a mischievous grin and genial manner that charmed most everyone, Leprechaun was one of those who, Nana Grace would have said, owned a tongue that would pick a lock. It took Maeve weeks to learn his real name and months to question the myth of "Saint Paddy."

Far longer to realize the part both Bridget Kehoe and Paddy Mooney would play in destroying Ronan Doyle, and in the process, the strike itself.

Maeve's favorite new "friend" was a newsboy named Timmy Fein, who each morning delivered a stack of newspapers and magazines along with her breakfast.

"Yes, I do go to school, but I also work because Ma needs money," Timmy explained in his shy, earnest manner. "Mr. Doyle lets me sweep out the saloon sometimes and Uncle Liam has me fetch phosphate sodas when his head is right, and Leprechaun has me running messages. Mr. Doyle says I'm very responsible."

At nine years old, Timmy Fein was a beautiful child with huge dark eyes and unruly brown hair that stuck out beneath a flat cap. Dressed in a patched wool jacket, knickers, and black stockings encased in worn but carefully polished boots, Timmy was the picture of every newsboy in every film and tintype Maeve had seen. But in real life, it was impossible to ignore the dark circles under his eyes and his stick-thin body. Following their first meeting, she always saved Timmy an apple, bread and cheese or desserts from her previous meals.

"When I grow up, I'm going to be a bricklayer," Timmy volunteered one day. "My da told me they earn $6 for a day and it's easy work and I would enjoy that very much."

Curious about Timmy's circumstances, she'd questioned Leprechaun, who was an inveterate gossip.

"Declan Fein was a mucker—meaning he shoveled broken rock into tramming cars and also sorted the ore that goes from the mill to that which goes to the tailings dump. Backbreaking work and dangerous. Which is why it pays better than most."

Eight hours a day, year after year. How could a man's body survive?

"What happened with poor Declan is that a powder monkey was called in to blast a larger rock into smaller pieces so our Declan can lift them easier." Dramatic pause.

Maeve's stomach sank. "Don't tell me," she whispered, as if that might alter the fate of Timmy's father.

"Misplaced charge," Leprechaun continued. "Not enough left from both of them to even be buried in Mount Pisgah Cemetery."

I must do something, Maeve decided, her long dormant social justice instincts stirring back to life. *I must help Timmy and his family.*

First, she needed to find a job. No, first she needed to leave this room, which alternated between prison cell and sanctuary.

Every day Maeve scoured the help wanteds in various newspapers. Should be easy enough to find *something*—store clerk, maid like that horrid Bridget Kehoe or maybe even a teacher. Instead, employers were seeking sewing girls and wasted dressmakers, shorthand writers and typewriters (?), and grocery travelers.

What do those words even mean?

Several palmists, trance mediums and healers were available, but they were selling their services for a "full and happy life," which Maeve would be totally unqualified to promise. Piano lessons? She'd need a piano. When she came across a classified advertisement for a "good delivery horse, young and sound," she gave up. Far less stressful to linger over advertisements for elegant dresses with sweeping hems and tightly corseted waists ($2); Levi's ($1.25); and Sudsy Soap "that won't shrink your flannels."

Plus, local news was fascinating. While 21st-century media made a big fuss about being "fair and balanced," District papers were the opposite. *The Daily Press* and *Victor Daily Record* proudly served as "an advocate and defender" of labor by challenging publications representing the "all-powerful combination of capital." Didn't matter whether you were Republican or Democrat—though don't even think of voting third-party cuz that's "rainbow chasing"—but you'd damn sure better be carrying a union card in your back pocket.

The Colorado Springs Gazette hadn't changed in the past hundred years—a cheerleader for capitalists and disdainful of unions. After coming across an article accusing the Molly Maguires of exercising a reign of terror like the French Revolution, Maeve ordered Timmy to exclude it from her daily stack.

Maeve particularly enjoyed *The Miner's Magazine* and *The Crusher* because they sometimes mentioned "WFM No. 40 President Ronan Doyle," who apparently "enjoyed bare-knuckle fighting Fridays at the Topic Theater."

Since bare-knuckle fighting most likely included naked chests, skimpy trunks and oily muscles, Maeve decided she'd pop in on one of his matches.

Once she dared leave her room.

Both magazines were chock-full of information about forth-coming Christmas balls, myriad smokers, socials, and family-related events. All hosted by various unions and lodges.

Life might be tough in 1901, but her ancestors certainly shared a strong sense of community.

As the holidays neared, she noticed Christmas 1901 was way less commercial. Sure, Santa was his future fat, jolly, white-bearded self with a penchant, it seemed, for wearing long johns, but he promised children simple presents like marbles, baseball cards and various pull toys. No advertisements screaming "Buy! Buy! BUY!"

She was surprised by the seemingly friendly relationships between mine owners and their workers. According to *The Crusher*, Jimmy Burns, former plumber and current owner of the Portland Mine, gifted each of his seven hundred employees a five-dollar gold piece. Conversely, miners at the El Paso presented their superintendent a diamond stud in appreciation for his fairness.

What would Padrick make of all these seeming contradictions? she wondered for the thousandth time.

But thoughts of Maeve's family inevitably led to memories of all the Christmases she'd taken for granted or regarded as an embarrassment—primarily because of what social media referred to as the "Mooney Tradition."

Right after Thanksgiving, the Mooney men would begin decorating the lower meadow and the drive leading to the farmhouse with enough lights that you could view the display from outer space. Frosty the Snowman, Nativity scenes, caroling scenes, a miner leading a donkey or a lineman climbing a pole scenes, dancing candy canes, animatronic elves, ornaments the size of boulders, flashing green leprechauns that popped out of the most unexpected places. Because of all the resultant publicity, people from as far away as Denver drove the hundred miles to gawk and marvel or complain that the Mooneys were wasting too much energy.

What will it be like this year? Maeve wondered. *Maybe they'll skip it altogether.*

No doubt her family was still searching for her. They'd have long ago contacted the police, alerted the media, and even after search and rescue teams had given up, still be scouring the area. Had her disappearance made the front page of *The Gazette?* If so,

Beau Strank and whoever else hated her would snark, "She got what she deserved."

So much pain. But not once her family knew the truth.

Which was when Maeve decided to journal her experience.

After which I'll toss the journal down the White Rabbit where Padrick or somebody will be sure to find it and then it'll be like Indiana Jones, where you have tons of sequels, each more exciting than the last. Finally, after she (and all her misdeeds) had totally faded from the public eye (Maeve might have been delusional about the level of her fame and/or related public interest), she'd reappear, captivating the entire planet with her tale.

I'll be rich, rich, rich.

Which didn't hold the appeal it once might have.

Nor did it help her pocket so much as a silver dollar here in 1901 Cripple Creek.

~

Bored! So BORED!

What to do? Observe the outside world from a window, venture out in her drab new duds, snoop through Ronan Doyle's things? She was repeatedly drawn to Ronan's work area, but what sort of work was getting done since Ronan hadn't bothered to show his own fine face even once since their initial meeting?

Subtle questioning of Leprechaun had revealed some interesting information, including the fact that Ronan wasn't dead, so one had to question Mr. Union President's work ethic. Yet, as curious as Maeve was, she couldn't bring herself to snoop through his nightstand drawers or wardrobe or the papers on his desk or the wooden boxes stuffed with union files. Rather she confined herself to studying his mini-library, which contained lots of biographies and polemics railing about independence, equality, working class dignity, class warfare and the solution to it all: socialism. His "light" reading consisted of authors like Shakespeare, Byron, Wilde, Voltaire,

Darwin, and Dickens. Maeve wasn't in the mood for that sort of reading either. She did retrieve a copy of W.B. Yeats, *The Countess Cathleen,* because it looked short enough to be manageable. But when the play opened naturally to a page with the heavily underlined phrase, *"They say that now the land is famine struck/The graves are walking,"* Maeve snapped it shut. Too personal. Too private. Too much a betrayal of Ronan Doyle's kindness toward her, no matter how indifferent.

Maeve did peruse one of the three books, *Progress and Poverty,* he'd left atop his nightstand, which was not snooping but simply passing time. She chose *Progress and Poverty* because it had a makeshift bookmark—a receipt from "The Miner's Emporium" for dynamite—indicating Ronan had been reading it.

"Take now ... some hard-headed businessman, who has no theories, but knows how to make money. Say to him: 'Here is a little village; in ten years it will be a great city—in ten years the railroad will have taken the place of the stagecoach, the electric light of the candle; it will abound with all the machinery and improvements that so enormously multiply the effective power of labor. Will in ten years... the wages of common labor be any higher; will it be easier for a man who has nothing but his labor to make an independent living?'"

Okay, enough of that. Obviously, the author, Henry George, was a communist. Which made Ronan a radical, as if she needed *Progress and Poverty* to confirm it.

Padrick, at least, would approve.

Each day Maeve gave herself one of the Sabrina Darling-style pep talks she'd once laid on her "Besties." "Get out there and explore your new world. Engage! Embrace! Adventure!"

Gawd, was I ever that ridiculous?

Still, it had been nearly three weeks and Maeve hadn't yet gotten beyond opening the front door to stand on the landing. The air smelled horrible, like rotten eggs; Bennett Avenue, with its phaetons, stagecoaches, barking dogs and yammering humans, was so noisy it hurt her ears, and the mere thought of descending the apartment stairs and setting foot on solid Cripple Creek ground caused her to hurry back inside and slam the door.

Have I become agoraphobic?

Watching the world go by via her casement window was plenty exciting, in a safe, silent movie sort of way. Maeve could gauge the time by the trolleys which ran every ten to fifteen minutes during peak times—much more entertaining than simply glancing at Ronan's alarm clock—and by the different kinds of people who swarmed the part of Bennett she could see each day at specific times. An everchanging parade of humanity—plainly dressed women with shawls rather than bonnets on their heads; elegant ladies in fur trimmed coats with matching ermine muffs and hats; men in fancy day suits and black silk top hats; sportsmen flanked by English bulldogs or mastiffs; dandies walking their dachsunds all decked out in Christmas plaids; miners tramping in and out of the assay office on the corner of 3rd and Bennett where a Salvation Army band passed around their tambourines after playing Christmas music.

Never once did Maeve spot Ronan. Not that she was looking.

At night, her sleep was marred by the noise drifting up from the Pick-Axe, which was tolerable except when its invisible pianist played songs with his trademark enthusiasm and lack of talent.

Increasingly, she found herself drawn to a tintype tacked to the wall between the shelves flanking Ronan's desk. A pale, delicate woman, a tall, broodingly handsome man and between them, a dark-haired boy. Obviously, Ronan and his parents. Maeve spent way too much time staring from Little Ronan to his father and back again, placing Little Ronan's face over Big Ronan's for they were like enough to be twins. From the eyes, the forthrightness of Big Ronan's stare to his widow's peak, to the identically shaped lips with the lower plumper than the upper cupid's bow. Little Ronan in knee pants with his hair carefully parted and his father's hand taking up most of one narrow shoulder. Big Ronan's expression was bold, as if daring the photographer, any man, to cross him, while Ronan's mother looked more suited to lounging in a drawing room than scrubbing dirty clothes on a washboard outside a company house. Surely, both dreamed of a better life for their son. No doubt Big Ronan, with his movie star looks and determined expression, had taken his fragile wife in his arms and promised to flee the Pennsylvania coalfields, the company towns, the company schools, the company scrip, and the company noose.

"We will go west," Maeve imagined Ronan's father murmuring against his wife's ear. "Where there are blue skies and you'll breathe pure mountain air, Mama, that will cure your tuberculosis, and we'll homestead with a log cabin kind of like *Grizzly Adams*, only with a family and..."

So, I'm reduced to this. Concocting imaginary lives for the Doyle clan.

She could hear Nana Grace scold, *"There you go again, Maeve Mooney, wasting your life building castles in the air."*

Regressing back to her childhood when she'd spent lazy afternoons alternately cloud gazing and scribbling foolishness in her journals.

Maeve found the newspapers beneath a violin case inside a wooden box with "Red Diamond Explosives" stamped on one side. The box had been tucked away on a bottom shelf next to a pile of WFM's *The Miner's Magazine*.

She'd sworn she'd not snoop, but here she was. With no excuse other than she was bored out of her skull.

Maeve carefully lifted out the top newspaper, yellow and brittle with age, from the box.

The Philadelphia Enquirer, June 21, 1877 edition. **Headline: "Hour of Doom!"**

The rest of the front page was a reporter's very long eyewitness account of the hangings of ten Molly Maguires within the walls of the Schuylkill County jail.

One name Maeve recognized...Doyle

Cold fingers traveled her spine. Ronan's father? Her gaze traveled to the beautiful man in the tintype. "Is that how you died?"

Knowing she'd intruded upon a painful event in Ronan's past, Maeve quickly returned the box and violin case to their rightful place. While the discovery might help explain the man she absolutely was not obsessed with, she'd had no right.

"I'm sorry," Maeve whispered to the empty room.

Five

I t was adorable Timmy Fein who unwittingly shattered Maeve's ennui and pushed her into the next phase of her adventure.

"Mr. Doyle told me you're coming to live with us," Timmy said after devouring the gingerbread cookies she'd saved for him. "Would you like that, Miss Mooney?" He flashed a beatific smile.

Maeve was so stunned she barely choked out a response. What was Timmy talking about? Was Ronan kicking her out? While he had every right to, how could he be so cruel as to pawn her off on a widow with four children? Besides, Maeve might like to think she'd overcome her elitist attitudes, but she wasn't about to squander her adventure in some one-room shack slapped on the side of a hill. Nor to be smacked in the face by the reality of poverty in 1901 Cripple Creek. As much as she was trying to be a better person, bunking at the Widow Fein's was NOT a viable solution.

After Timmy departed, Maeve yanked Ronan's fur-lined winter cap from the pegs in back of his apartment door, tucked her hair underneath it and tossed Ronan's Carhartt coat over the shacket and jeans she wore, rather than the drab garments Bridget Kehoe had dumped on her bed.

Agoraphobia miraculously cured, Maeve thundered down the apartment stairs and into the Pick-Axe, seeking her benefactor. The saloon looked marginally like those depicted in the movies with a parade of whiskey bottles in front of a mirrored backdrop; barrels of beer behind a long wooden bar; hand printed chalk board advertising free lunch with five cent beer; broad unpainted floor planks, scattered tables, Wellington upright piano near a tin sign that read: "If you expect to rate as a gentleman, do not expectorate on the floor."

The room was empty save for a large figure slumped against the bar.

Maeve approached the lump. "Hello! Excuse me. Is Ronan Doyle here?" A closed door tucked in a corner most likely led to the kitchen, storage area and Doyle's sleeping quarters.

The lump stirred, slowly turned in her direction. The man's face was a map of deep lines, his nose appeared to have been broken more than once and his complexion, the entire cast of his face, screamed "alcoholic." Despite that, he was attractive in a well-lived way with a full head of gunmetal grey hair and familiar dark eyes which landed somewhere in Maeve's vicinity.

This must be Uncle Liam.

"Ronan's at the hall, laddy," Uncle Liam slurred. "Which you should well know." He blinked before pouring himself another shot from a nearby bottle of Jim Beam. Downed it. Paused. Rubbed a hand over his face. "Did I tell you about what happened that day with Ronan a wee lad of seven, when they killed me brother?"

Remembering the "Hour of Doom" newspaper, Maeve was torn between correcting Uncle Liam's "laddy" nonsense, circumventing any rambling reminisces, and learning more about wee lad Ronan.

"No, but I'd like to hear."

"One of my three brothers," Uncle Liam amended. "They took them out to the Mauch Chunk gallows in pairs and before my Mikey was dragged from his jail cell—number 17—it was, Mikey slaps his hand upon the wall and cries out, 'This is the hand of an innocent man!'" He downed his shot of whiskey in one gulp. "And do you know, laddy, his handprint has been whitewashed and scrubbed and painted over, but it always comes back. As it will until Jesus's Second Coming to mark the crime done to all the Mollies, curse the bloody buggers."

Maeve shivered. Uncle Liam's bleary eyes swiveled to the mirror behind the bar, as if observing the haunted handprint.

"I'm so sorry," she managed. Trite words, but what could anyone say that would ease such pain? Here she'd been stewing over Ronan and her petty problems when this man, both the Doyles, had suffered unspeakable misfortune.

"I was blessed to flee the mines. Only one who did. Owned a boarding house next town over before Ronan and me..." He paused and looked off into the distance, as if about to add something more, "pulled up stakes and came out west."

"Wha...what happened to Ronan's dad?" That beautiful man in the tintype? "Was he also hanged?"

Uncle Liam's eyes swiveled in her direction. Eyes that mirrored Ronan's own, with the addition of decades more tragedy.

A lone tear slipped down the crevices of his ruined face. *"There was a star that lit my life,"* he said softly. *"It hath set to rise no more."*

After which Liam Doyle poured himself another drink.

As was his habit, Da carried me home from the Glen Carbon. As was my habit, I fell asleep in his arms.

"You're not to the mines tomorrow, mo bhuachaill óg, *my baby boy,"* *he'd said against my ear. I may have nodded, though I was so exhausted. Twelve-hour shifts as a breaker boy? How could I not be dead in his arms?*

Pow. Pow. Rhythmically hitting the makeshift canvas sack filled with sand. Jab left, jab right. Mind the footwork.

Da talking to Mam, soft and low, his face golden in the lamp light. In my cot near the stove, I could both see and hear him, though his words drifted to me as in a dream.

"I heard the Tommyknockers meself," Da'd said.

Even at age eight, I knew about Tommyknockers, that their presence could be an ominous sign. Struggling through the fog of sleep, I shifted to better view my parents' interplay.

Jab left, the impact against the bag so intense it reverberated through Ronan's arm and body all the way to his teeth.

Mam's usual soothing voice tinged with alarm. "But that could mean good fortune, couldn't it?"

"Not believing so. Dylan swore he saw one, wearing a helmet and carrying a pickax, no bigger'n a red squirrel, he said."

Mam made the sign of the cross. "Dylan's always speaking daft."

Jab, cross, hook, uppercut. Repeat.

"Nevertheless, keep the boy home. An early Christmas present, we'll say."

Here's where Ronan always tossed aside footwork, technique and proper form to stand with feet planted square upon the wooden floor, pummeling the bag so hard he sometimes split his gloves.

Da buried so deep they'd not even tried to dig him, any of them out. So much for a gentle way and a head full of dreams for a better future when it all came down to the worst explosion in a decade and the superintendent shaking his head. "Not even worth the time to give them a proper burial."

An arm around Ronan's shoulders abruptly returned him to the WFM gym with its boxing ring, speed and punching bags, wrestling and calisthenics areas designed to let off steam, keep the body strong, and for a few like Ronan, provide them a decent shot at winning bareknuckle fights.

"Enough, lad. Save your anger for tomorrow night and the Topic." Stepping away from the bag, Ronan took the proffered towel and wiped it across his sweating face and chest. *It's this time of year. Tonight I'll bury myself in my room with a bottle of Jack Daniel's.* But he couldn't even do that, not with Maeve Mooney having taken up residence. Ronan missed the familiarity of his mattress, his books, his violin, his makeshift office, his recently installed clawfoot tub and flush toilet in the adjoining room. His uninvited visitor had brought chaos into his life, but that was about to change...

After Ronan tossed aside the towel and gulped down a tin cup of water, he became aware of a shift in atmosphere. He glanced toward the opened side door where an average-sized figure stood backlit against the afternoon sun, a figure wearing a coat like his and a hat like his. The figure approached.

"Fecking hell," he muttered. Somewhere during his workout, Ronan had divested himself of his undershirt, so he'd be conversing bare-chested with a woman, which was beyond inappropriate, scandalous really, even though he doubted onlookers realized they had a woman in their midst. Until Maeve Mooney opened her mouth. Quickly he strode to her and pulled her away from curious eyes. "What are you doing here?" he asked, deliberately keeping his voice low. "Where are your proper clothes?"

Did this woman's amnesia extend to forgetting how to dress like one?

Maeve blinked several times before her gaze roamed his body. There it was, that look he hated because he had absolutely nothing to do with his face or his form or anything related to his physical appearance. *"Don't look at me that way,"* he wanted to snap.

For her part, Maeve had already formulated a plan during her trek to the union hall. In the space of five minutes, she'd devised a far superior plan to Ronan Doyle's harebrained idea of moving her into a hovel where she'd be a burden to an already over-burdened family. First, she'd rely on her physical appeal to soften him up. (Despite the fact that she was makeup free and wearing clothes no 1900s man would find attractive, Maeve was confident she remained at least an eight out of ten on the attractiveness scale. Particularly with her surgically pert nose.) She would flatter Ronan, appeal to his gentlemanly instincts as a damsel in distress and he'd fold like a lousy hand of cards.

"Surely, an important union official such as yourself knows all manner of folks," she'd say. "Surely, you'll be able to find me a job with someone willing to advance me enough money to rent a room in a nice boarding house." She might even clap her hands and coo, "Problem solved!", though Maeve had pretty much given up cooing in the weeks following her public disgrace.

"I couldn't think to intrude on Timmy Fein and his family," was how she actually began. Ignoring Ronan's glistening chest, the remarkable contours of his body, Maeve kept her gaze locked to his while presenting her case, punctuated occasionally by a coy glance and licking of the lips. She was both surprised and irritated when Ronan focused, not on solving her plight, but on the current state of her amnesia, which she'd (ironically) forgotten long ago.

"Have you finally remembered where you're from?" Ronan gestured for his trainer to hand him his undershirt. Now that the sweat on his skin had dried, he was cold, in need of washing up, getting back to union business and swiftly concluding this unwelcome conversation.

While Maeve watched, she reminded herself not to be distracted by all those rippling muscles. Particularly because she suspected he was deliberately trying to distract her. "Well—"

"Do you have a family we can wire, or who you can write to in order to request funds? Just enough to tide you over until you're properly employed? Or, if not that"—Ronan glanced down at Maeve's left hand, as if seeking her invisible wedding ring—"did you recall the identity of your husband?"

While she sputtered an answer, he studied her. An attractive woman, he supposed, and he rather liked her attitude, like a wild horse pretending it had been tamed. Until it bit you or stomped on you. Ronan knew all about that sort of female...

"What sort of employment might you be suited for?" he prodded. Certainly, she had no chance of making it in the "sporting" profession. Too high class for a crib girl and too long in the tooth to be a draw at the Old Homestead House, even if she were so inclined. And, truth to tell, a woman wearing men's britches would be lucky to find work mucking out stables.

Maeve's face had flushed crimson. "I'm sure you can come up with something appropriate." She lifted her chin, leaving it a tempting target if she'd been a male and this was a sparring match. "Isn't that what men are supposed to do, help the fairer sex?"

Grabbing one of her hands, Ronan turned it over and traced her palm with his thumb. "Think you'll find work as a housemaid or laundress? Not with that soft skin."

Maeve jerked free of his grip. "You don't need to be rude about it."

Time to try another tack. Aware of his effect on the weaker sex, Ronan forced his expression to soften, disregarding the feeling that this was not a time for cheap tricks that only worked because he'd inherited the Doyle males' beauty.

"Miss Mooney, I will speak frankly. If you are still afflicted with your amnesia, then I am duty-bound to help. And, if per chance, you are hiding from something or someone or seeking a new start, you are no different from ninety percent of the District's residents. I suggest you accept my offer of assistance and let us be done with all of this back and forth. I've already spoken to the Widow Fein. She'd be thankful for an extra pair of hands to help with the house-work and wee ones."

Maeve balled her hands into fists, as if readying to attack. She'd obviously not been impressed by his half-assed attempt at seduction. The same way he'd not been impressed with her fluttering eyelashes and flirtatious manner.

"Timmy Fein chatters about you all the time," he quickly added. "You'd not want to disappoint the lad, would you?"

Maeve's shoulders slumped; she let out a defeated sigh. "Have you ever heard the expression, 'Stranger in a strange land?' No, of course you haven't, but that's how I feel. I'd just like everything to stop. Or rush ahead a hundred years or so."

Not understanding any part of what she'd said, Ronan still felt a twinge of sympathy. "Don't you worry. The Widow Fein knows everyone. Soon enough, you'll have full employ and be renting a nice room and your circumstances much improved." He hesitated, considering his next words. "Or if you recall you're single, the District has plenty of fine men looking for a wife."

That certainly snapped Maeve Mooney out of her discomposure. If looks could kill, Ronan would be dead on the spot, which he secretly found amusing. Before she could further protest, he ordered her to return to his room and pack her things. "I'll be along as soon as I make myself presentable." When she hesitated, he made a pushing gesture to hurry her along. "Oh, and be sure to change into proper clothing. You'd not want the Widow Fein mistaking you for a lad. "

Aye, if looks could kill, Ronan's heart would have already stopped a dozen times over.

Six

C hristmas Eve. Maeve had been settled at the Fein household for more than a week. The house wasn't as dilapidated as she'd feared, though it only consisted of three rooms—two bedrooms and a combination living room/kitchen. (An outhouse was in the back yard.) Cheap but well-maintained furniture and children's drawings, nature scenes from magazines and framed photographs decorated the walls, all contributing to a homey atmosphere. From the front door you could see Cripple Creek going about its business below; in the middle distance, headframes, smokestacks, shafthouses and men crawling like crippled flies across the denuded earth. On the far horizon the Sangre de Cristos, looking exactly the same as they would one hundred, or one hundred thousand, years from now.

Maeve's sleeping quarters was an uncomfortable cot near the pot-bellied stove, which she periodically fed with coal and which at least kept her warm. She did her best to contribute to the family— checking Timmy and Danny's homework, helping with the cooking, cleaning and child tending. She'd even tried her hand at laundry, though the lye soap had eaten her hands so thoroughly she had blisters.

"Think you'll find work as a housemaid or laundress? Not with that soft skin."

Annie Fein was a kind soul with the patience of all heaven's saints. Her main source of income was her seamstress work, though she received death benefits from the WFM and five dollars a week from Ronan, who explained that would be the cost for renting a room in an actual boarding house.

Seated on a wooden bench in front of the Fein residence, Maeve gazed out at the scattered city lights. Smoke from chimneys hung listlessly above nearby houses—many of them more shacks, really. Quiet, cold and peaceful here. Earlier, Annie and her two boys had left for Midnight Mass at St. Peter's Catholic Church. Maeve had stayed behind to mind three-year-old Dilly and Baby Katie, currently asleep in their shared bed.

Singing from St. Peter's and St. Andrew's Episcopal drifted across Golden Avenue. Odd, to see both churches brand spanking new, though they'd survive largely untouched into the future. As would the hospital currently run by the Sisters of Mercy, though it would be transformed into Hotel St. Nicholas, a Bed and Breakfast reportedly haunted by nuns, mental patients, children, a miner missing his torso and a ghost called "Stinky," who announced his presence smelling like a sewer.

Tonight, Maeve's ghosts tormented her in the form of memories. Cripple Creek Christmases had once been magical. Giant headframes, lonely outposts of a discarded past, strung with rope lights and light bulbs in the shape of bells and candy canes and "Oh, look!"—a giant Santa face, a Christmas stocking and a starburst snowflake upon the Hoosier Mine overlooking the town. There'd been parades, ice sculptures, and a Christmas-themed performance at the Butte Opera.

"It's all pretty enough," Nana Grace would concede, as the Mooney clan strolled Bennett Avenue admiring the businesses outlined in colored lights and topped by cascades of icicles. "But do not be forgetting Baby Jesus was born so He could suffer and die on the cross to save the souls of all us miserable sinners."

As a child, Maeve had found it all enchanting, pretended not to as a teen, and dismissed it as an adult.

And now?

Nana Grace: one ghost who needed to stay buried.

Maeve's thoughts turned to Ronan Doyle. Had he attended Midnight Mass? She'd not seen him since he'd dumped her off with a warning to dress like a woman and mind her cursing lest Annie wash her mouth out with soap. Had he been serious? A few days later, a sober Uncle Liam had arrived carrying a four-foot Christmas tree and stayed, much to the Fein children's delight, to help decorate with strings of popcorn, cranberries and chains of colored paper. Afterward, they'd all gathered round to sing carols and drink spiced cider. Picturesque as a Hallmark movie, only sincere.

Was Uncle Liam courting Annie? If so, he needed to stay off the sauce.

Note to myself: Quit sounding like Nana Grace, judging matters you've no right to.

While no one spoke much about Annie's deceased husband, judging from the wedding photo atop her dresser, Declan Fein had been a glowering simian of a man, bowler tipped back in cocky fashion, sausage fingers splayed possessively across his bride's shoulder. A seated Annie, wearing a plain white dress, enormous hat and clutching a bouquet of roses, looked extremely young and vaguely terrified. Had Declan beaten her? Forced himself upon her, resulting in a shotgun wedding? Upon receiving the news he'd been blown to smithereens, had Annie shed tears of relief?

There you go again.

Maybe you could earn a living as a novelist.

A whistle blast shattered Maeve's reverie. Not even Baby Jesus's birthday could shut down the District's mines. Annie had explained the different meanings; tonight's shriek simply announced a shift change. Any unexpected sequence and the wife hanging her laundry outdoors or tending her wee ones; the independent miner working his small claim; the union secretaries checking union cards as miners began their shifts; even the crib girls on Myers Avenue would cock an ear, subconsciously waiting for the specific code announcing a shaft had been blown to hell or collapsed in upon itself. What the whistle couldn't tell you—you would have to wait for that—was how many men would die that day. And if your loved one is numbered among them.

Had a whistle blown for Annie's husband?

Shivering, Maeve wrapped her shawl closer. As soon as she found a job, she'd purchase a wool coat, just like the ones in the Sears catalog that doubled as the Feins' wish book.

But therein lay Maeve's biggest problem.

Money. More precisely, the lack of it.

Who controlled the wealth in 1901 Cripple Creek? Certainly not the miners. If Maeve were to do more than survive, she must be on the side of the winners—the Horace Stranks, Spencer Penroses, Charles Tutts, Jimmy Burns, W.S. Strattons, and the Woods family, who would have an entire avenue named after them in future Colorado Springs. How she would accomplish that, she had no idea. But the prudent, practical thing would be to distance herself from the losers in this game. People like Ronan Doyle and Annie Fein and even Timmy with his sweet, shy smile.

That's what her head told her. The practical side of Maeve Mooney.

But already her heart was at war with her head.

Ronan Doyle played a mean fiddle, Maeve would give him that. And Uncle Liam was a surprisingly accomplished banjo picker. The fifer and guitarist were strangers, though she certainly recognized the pianist as the epically untalented twenty-something who'd tortured the ivories at the Pick-Axe. With each misplaced chord, Maeve wanted to leap upon the makeshift stage and shout, "Stop! Let a professional show you how it's done!"

Ronan and Uncle Liam took turns singing. While Ronan possessed a mellow baritone, Uncle Liam sounded like Leonard Cohen with a cold. Which Maeve found surprisingly appealing.

"May I have this dance, Miss Mooney?"

Maeve's parade of partners had begun early this New Year's Eve when Timmy Fein had asked her to navigate a polka, which in 1901's iteration appeared to be a bouncy waltz.

"Of course."

"Mam said she's gonna have to put Baby Katie to bed, so we'll be leaving." Timmy addressed his feet even while holding out his skinny arm for her to grasp. He was obviously in the throes of his first crush, which was pretty darned cute. Not only because he reminded Maeve of her much-missed niece, but he was so earnest that if he were twenty years older or she were twenty years younger, she would promise to be his girl simply to tease out a smile.

Timmy was also very patient and encouraging, which he needed to be because Maeve had no idea how to execute the steps to this polka business. "You're not so very bad, Miss Mooney," he gallantly —and erroneously—assured her.

Their pairing was interrupted after one turn around the hall, decorated with pine boughs, leftover Christmas decorations and kerosene lanterns hanging from overhead beams, when Annie Fein beckoned her son to the sidelines.

"Come along, my pet. You should've been in bed an hour past."

"I'm not a baby like Katie. I can stay up late," Timmy mumbled, his cheeks turning strawberry red at being caught out.

After thanking Timmy (over-effusively) for being such a *fabulous* partner, Maeve said, "I'll come with."

Annie waved her away. "You deserve a few hours to yourself so's to enjoy grown company."

Which was how Maeve found herself dragged around the floor

by a parade of partners attempting to teach her two-steps, polkas, quadrilles, and other dances that were impossibly complicated and more strenuous than her "Better Best" routines. How did people who performed brutal physical labor eight hours a day, six days a week have the strength to call such a taxing cardiovascular workout "fun"?

"I can't remember ever dancing so much!" Maeve finally gasped after staggering off the floor following something that might be called a set dance. Whatever it was, a ballet master would have trouble navigating it. She bent over to ease a stitch in her side.

"Not sure I'd call whatever you've been doing dancing," Ronan Doyle commented. Throughout the evening, he'd alternated playing and singing with supervising the night's celebration and mingling with fellow union members. Now he stood near the stage, sipping a cup of sweet cider.

"Did you just make a joke, Mr. Doyle?" Maeve straightened to face him. Up close, hair rumpled, sleeves rolled up, religious necklaces peeking from a shirt sticking to him in various places—it *had* gotten hot in here—Ronan was undeniably a visual feast.

No way to hide all that beauty. Annie said some woman had broken your heart. How could that be so? Stop it. Remember, men are like brushing your teeth... And even more, remember soon enough you'll be returning to the White Rabbit and all these people, including Ronan Doyle, are names on a headstone or nameless in a pauper's grave.

Around them, the laughter and buzz of conversation, the stomp and shuffle of feet. The odor of cigarette smoke blended with that of coal from the hall's lone stove, kerosene, pine from the Christmas decorations and leftover food.

Ronan's gaze swung from their surroundings to her. "Wonder how many of your partners will be able to walk tomorrow."

Maeve laughed. "Should I be flattered you were watching me?"

Ronan snorted. "How could I miss? I'm assuming your misplaced memory also includes forgetting any dance lessons."

Okay, past time to put that old chestnut to bed. Instead of

replying, she removed Ryan's cup from his hand and finished it, pleased by his shocked expression.

"You are a bold one, Maeve Mooney," he said, though the side of his mouth twitched up in amusement. The way he addressed her as "Maeve Mooney" reminded her of Padrick's 'Moonface,' which was both irritating and oddly comforting.

"And you are quite the talented musician," she replied, placing the cup on the edge of the stage. "You and Uncle Liam both. When you played 'Cripple Creek,' you had the entire hall stomping and clapping." She hoped he missed the wistfulness that had crept into her voice. She should be the one playing piano, accompanying Ronan and his makeshift band, or performing solo. When the pianist stumbled through the opening chords of Scott Joplin's "The Entertainer," she felt like shouting, "Arrest this guy. He just murdered ragtime."

Oblivious to the crime being committed a handful of feet away, Ronan continued surveying his domain. He reminded her of the watchers who'd once kept guard over the dead to make certain they were truly dead, or if foul play was suspected, for signs of bleeding when the killer came into the corpse's presence.

Maeve shivered. *Morbid thought. Where did that come from?*

In a few hours, 1902 would push aside 1901. One more year when the WFM kept the wolves at bay, when the District blindly shuffled about its business, ignorant of impending doom.

But aren't we all? At the beginning of 2024, I had no idea my dreams would collapse, that I'd wind up in an alternate universe.

A different song, this time a waltz Maeve recognized from her Golden Bee days.

Ronan held out his hand. "Dance, Maeve Mooney?"

"What? You're going to risk your feet with me?"

"New boots," he said, leading her onto the floor. "Reinforced toes."

Ronan placed a hand above her waist while she put one tentative arm around his shoulder and her other in his free hand. His fingers and palm were calloused; she fancied she could feel the warmth of his other fingers splayed against her dress. He was so tall and broad, nearly as tall and broad as Padrick, though Padrick looked like a grumpy moose whereas Ronan... She wondered why he chose to dress so plainly, to wear his hair long and sport a beard. Annie had said he didn't like to call attention to himself. If so, he'd need about a billion dollars worth of plastic surgery.

In his low, gruff voice, Uncle Liam began:

It was fascination, I know
And it might have ended
Right then, at the start
Just a passing glance

The song Maeve had heard the night she'd tumbled down the White Rabbit. Goosebumps sprang along her arms.

"One, two, three, One, two, three," Ronan said, near enough to be heard above the din. He pulled her closer to more easily guide her movements. Maeve closed her eyes in concentration, melting into the rhythm of his count. Was that Florida water she smelled, certainly a hint of clean sweat...

"One, two, three. One, two, three."

Maeve imagined the picture they made—she so petite and slender contrasted to his bulk; her skirts swirling gracefully as they glided among the other dancers because she certainly was responding perfectly to his instructions and every movement of his body. Like the couples she'd imagined the night she'd fallen down the White Rabbit. "What a handsome pair are Ronan and this Maeve Mooney," everybody would be saying. "I wonder when he'll be proposing!"

Don't even go there. You know he's not for you.

Uncle Liam growled,

Seeing you alone

with the moonlight above
Then I touch your hand...

"Keep counting, keep moving," a clueless Ronan murmured. "You're doing fine."

...And next moment I kiss you
Fascination turned to love.

～

According to the huge clock over the WFM officers' dais, 1902 was fifteen minutes away. The crowd had dwindled and the musicians had begun putting away their instruments. The tradition of welcoming in Baby New Year with funny hats, party favors and belting "Auld Lang Syne" was obviously in the future.

"Bossman," called out Leprechaun. He'd been drinking all night and was now slumped against a glowering Bridget Kehoe. "Before we're off, play 'Londonderry Air.'"

Others echoed the request. Maeve had never heard of "Londonderry Air," but within the first dozen notes of Ronan's violin, she recognized it as "Danny Boy." How many times had she performed it at the Golden Bee, at Mooney gatherings? How many times had she watched listeners brush away tears when singing along to the lyrics? How many times had she herself been nearly overcome with the melancholy of it all?

Ronan played beautifully, eyes closed, his execution evoking images as poignant as if lamenting a lost love. But without Danny Boy's lyrics, "Londonderry Air" was the night sky without stars. No summer's gone and dying roses, no praying Aves in front of a grave. Certainly, no parent lamenting the loss of a son off to war or to foreign lands.

Spontaneously, Maeve added her voice.

O Danny boy, the pipes, the pipes are calling
From glen to glen and down the mountainside

Ronan's eyes jerked open; his pace momentarily faltered. After joining him on stage, Maeve crossed over to the piano and eased herself onto the stool, her fingers automatically finding the proper keys.

But come ye back when summer's in the meadow
Or when the valley's hushed and white with snow...

While Maeve's voice was rusty, it soon soared in concert with their combined instruments. God, it felt wonderful to perform again, as if she'd finally surfaced after nearly drowning.

And when you come and all the flowers are dying
If I am dead, as dead I well may be...

She experienced the power of lyrics that weren't hers and a melody that wasn't hers, but which she could present as a gift to this community—something that didn't need to be purchased at the Emporium or earned at the cost of broken bodies or hoarded for fear of barren cupboards.

You'll come and find the place where I am lying
And kneel and say an Ave there for me.

With the fading music, Maeve felt as if she were in the presence of something sacred, the way she sometimes did when standing at the topmost ridge of Shamrock Ranch, gazing across a valley of red rock and Ponderosa pine, or singing "O Holy Night" at Midnight Mass, or standing on the Cliffs of Moher at sunset.

A sense of the sacred that was all too fleeting before you realized you had to walk a hella distance back to the farmhouse; that St. Peter's was uncomfortably warm and you needed to go to the bathroom; that the tour guide was scolding you all for lingering on the cliffs when you were behind schedule and needed to get back on the tour bus.

Maeve realized that the hall had gone completely silent and Ronan was staring at her. Something flicked across his face, gone before she could put a name to it and she suddenly remembered those crumbling newspapers and the hangman's noose that had claimed his uncles. Was that what Ronan was thinking of? All the graves he'd knelt and prayed before?

The sudden, sharp blast of whistles caused Maeve to jump. A cacophony, all in discordant harmony. The mines! An accident! Expecting gasps of alarm from the crowd and a rush toward the exits, she bolted off the piano stool. "What's happened?" she cried, clutching Ronan's arm.

He blinked, as if emerging from far away. "Midnight," he said, after church bells joined the whistles. "'Tis a new year you've welcomed in."

Around them people laughed, clapped and hugged each other, the melancholy mood broken.

"Here's to 1902!" Ronan declared, raising his violin and bow above his head like a trophy.

Maeve wished she could share in the jubilation. But how could a song about a boy returning to loved ones cold in the ground portend anything but tragedy?

PART THREE
Summer–Fall 1902

❦

We must not allow the clock and the calendar to blind us to the fact that each moment of life is a miracle and mystery.

— H.G. WELLS

Seven

You wouldn't believe it! I'm firmly ensconced in the National Hotel. The hotel is breathtaking—four stories, 117 rooms and a lobby that rivals anything we saw in Ireland. Why such magnificence was ever torn down is beyond me, but maybe it's a metaphor for America, which you can articulate way better than I can. Anyway, I have my own room and private bath and there's even an outlet for a telephone. I'm writing from a sitting area overlooking Bennett Avenue, which is always a mess of stagecoaches, horses, wagons, the occasional runaway team and even a steam-powered Locomobile! Cripple Creek is like some enormous beehive. Though here money is the honey...

Maeve put down her fountain pen. She'd begun keeping a journal as soon as Ronan had agreed to a tryout as the Pick-Axe's entertainer, after which the money rolled in. At first, she'd addressed her missives to her entire family, but over the months, she found herself writing directly to Padrick. And while she probably mentioned Ronan Doyle way too often, here she went again.

I'm really grateful he took a chance on me since saloons are no place for a real lady, as I've been repeatedly told. But nobody can sing and play songs like 'Rocky Mountain High' and 'This Land is Your Land,' cuz they haven't been written yet! Even the founding fathers you've read about—Spec Penrose, Charles Tutt, the Woods brothers—stop by. And they do tip well, unlike so many of the big shots who used to patronize the Golden Bee!

Maeve stretched and leaned back in her chair. Horace Strank had invited her to perform at his Strank's Manse on the Fourth of July—*Now that will be an experience!*—which was when she planned to toss what had become a bundle of journals down the White Rabbit. She imagined her family's excited reaction upon finding them and realizing Maeve Mooney was on an extended adventure, like those 18th-century Grand Tours of Italy!

Maeve dipped her pen in a nearby ink well, wiped off the nib and hesitated over the page. The following would be the most difficult part, though she'd written about Saint Paddy before. She watched him sometimes, this great-great-grandfather of theirs, this champion of labor rights. Even knowing that without him, there would be no Shamrock Ranch...

His personality isn't what I'd imagined. He talks a lot and he's charming, but he's not charismatic and serious enough to be a union leader—though that must be an act since Ronan chose him as an organizer. Leprechaun is certainly NOT a saint, though I'm sure he wouldn't call himself one either.

Maeve put aside her journal. She was particularly pleased by her luxurious suite, since it provided confirmation that this stranger in a strange land was making her way. Her rooms weren't anywhere near as fancy as Winfield Scott Stratton's fourth-floor apartment which had a bedroom covered with mirrors, or so she'd been told; then again, he was the richest man in the District, maybe the state. Stratton also had a fifty-year lease, which the help breathlessly chattered on about, to which Maeve made no comment because W.S. Stratton's life measured in weeks rather than years. Only occasionally had she even glimpsed the millionaire miner—a thin, white-haired man shuffling through the lobby, always with an air of sadness, the pall of death already upon him.

After Maeve dressed for her evening performance, she surveyed herself approvingly in the room's full-length mirror. Once Ronan had hired her, she'd purchased a sewing machine (Sears catalog $15) for Annie Fein, who'd sewn the outfits they'd sketched together. Bypassing the uncomfortable corsets Maeve so hated, they'd fast-forwarded to the Roaring Twenties and flapper dresses that skimmed the floor in a nod to current fashion, but sparkled with beads and tassels.

After leaving her suite, Maeve approached the National's elevator, which was the first in the District and so slow and jerky it would have been faster to take the back stairs to the lobby. But VIPs frequented the National. Who knew what distinguished businessman she might meet, which would lead to yet more bookings so she could support herself, continue helping the Feins and maybe indulge in a little turn-of-the-century travel?

"Miss Mooney!"

Horace Strank, her former non-fiance's great-great-grandfather and semi-regular at the Pick-Axe, approached her.

"Mr. Strank, how lovely to see you again."

Strank bowed. It was a curious thing. Horace Strank was a younger version of his great-great-grandson, a good two decades younger than the Beau of Professor Plum clothing and used car salesman demeanor. And yet, somehow his progeny's pig eyes, round, florid face, Humpty Dumpty physique—and who could forget the hair transplants—had been tweaked and rearranged and improved upon in the person of Horace Strank. He cut a compelling figure, no doubt helped by his bespoke suit with its fancy grey waistcoat sporting a pocket watch the size of a dinner plate and tailoring that transformed a "rotund" physique to "solid."

Responding to his greeting, Maeve ducked her head as if shy, which seemed the preferable behavior for "ladies," though she did it to avoid looking at the gold ore stick pin Strank always wore to secure his silk ties because Ronan had once observed it would take at least two tons of rock to retrieve such a nugget.

"I am so looking forward to your performance on the Fourth of July. You've never visited Strank's Manse, have you?"

Not in its current iteration. "I've heard it's magnificent." Actually, she'd heard it was hideous, overblown and tasteless.

"I believe James Peabody, our next governor, will also bless us with his presence. He's campaigning, you know." As if Maeve were too stupid to read Cripple Creek's five daily newspapers. "And you do know I entertained Teddy Roosevelt there last summer, right before he became president?"

Before Maeve could respond, he rushed on. "I purchased a Steinway Grand Piano, which was shipped all the way from New York City. Perhaps you would honor Mr. Peabody and the rest of my guests with your rendition of 'America the Beautiful?'"

Maeve suppressed a snort. Just like his great-great-grandson, the execrable Beau, who grew teary-eyed because "its purple mountain majesties" referred to Pikes Peak and had always requested it when he patronized the Golden Bee.

Refraining from fluttering her eyelashes, Maeve demurely replied, "I promise."

Ronan Doyle sometimes imagined dressing like a woman, the way the Mollies had back in Ireland before embarking on their raids—donning some enormous bonnet stuck with flowers to hide his face and a gunny sack of a dress so he could better blend in and not be gawked at. (If there were women over six feet who were built like an ox.) From childhood on, Ronan had known the Doyle men's looks commanded attention. All of them, his Da, his uncles, and so the stories went, his grandfather and before. Ronan sometimes wondered whether a long-ago ancestor had made a deal with the devil. "Bestow upon me and mine pulchritude," that fool had said. "In exchange, we'll give you shortened lives and violent deaths."

"We Doyles are wildflowers, plucked before our time," observed Uncle Liam, who was himself pushing against the outer ranges of longevity.

Until Ronan had been elected to the presidency of Local 40, he'd been a powder monkey. Since public speaking was part of his job description, he'd studied the speeches of Eugene Debs, Albert Parsons and Clarence Darrow. During solitary hikes across meadows of Indian paintbrush, columbines and seas of blue flag, Ronan had honed his voice until he might not be St. Francis, capable of charming all God's creatures, but he could hold an audience. His mission. His duty. So that there would be no more six-year-old breaker boys, no more old-before-their-time men coughing out their lungs or unable to straighten backs crooked from decades in the tunnels; no more wives who feared being widows every time a whistle blew; so no more workers would have to bow their heads or beg for their jobs before the fat-arsed, fancy-suited, pomaded worms who held a proper man's hopes and dreams and paychecks in their manicured hands.

On this Fourth of July morning, Ronan entered Pinnacle Park, preoccupied with the execution of his forthcoming speech. Feeling good. Optimistic. Yeah, James Peabody was an anti-union banker and a Freemason to boot, but the election was four months away. During the strike of 1894, a previous governor had sided with the workers, refusing to call out the National Guard, which helped strikers beat back employers' demand for ten hours' work for eight hours' pay. Precedent, it was called. Since then, business and labor got on well enough. In fact, mine owners and investors, who mostly lived on Millionaire's Row down in Colorado Springs, still helped fund and organize celebrations such as these.

It can remain that way, Ronan thought, waving to familiar faces while striding in the direction of the Zoological Gardens where he was to meet his uncle. The Woods family was proof that capital and labor could work together. A symbiotic relationship, like the Nile crocodile and its plover bird: the bird cleaned the crocodile's teeth and gums in return for the crocodile's protection. A win for both. Ronan even banked at the First National Bank of Victor, where youngest son Frank Woods was president, as did most local miners.

Strange though, if you thought about it. Directly beneath the depositors' feet, beneath the bank's foundation, First National customers just like himself were shoveling muck, loading extracted ore into carts and transporting it to the surface. An entire underground city largely forgotten until a blast rattled windows and caused the structure to groan and crack before everyone returned to normal business.

Upon reaching the gardens, Ronan bent to kiss Annie Fein's girls, ruffle Timmy's hair and shake grown-up Danny's hand. He was pleased for Uncle Liam, who seemed content courting the Widow Fein and spending time with her children. After his—their—past disaster, Annie was a gift from the saints.

However, Ronan immediately felt uneasy, more than that, as if insects were crawling over his skin. At its heart, Pinnacle Park's Zoological Gardens was a prison masquerading as a zoo. Hundreds of cages—deer in their paddock, bears in their pit, wolves, foxes, and coyotes peeking out from manmade caves built into the side of a hill. While cages came in many shapes and sizes, they were still cages. Day after day, year after year, Ronan had been packed in a cage that plunged him and fellow miners a thousand feet down. As trapped as these innocent creatures here today. Only in fetid air and in near-impenetrable darkness, crushed with the weight of despair. *Is that all there is to a man's life?* he'd wondered, as he positioned his dynamite, inserted the cap and lit the long fuse, all the while praying he'd not bring an entire mountain down around his head. *Is that all there is to me?*

Ronan caught his uncle's eye. "I'm going to stretch my legs a bit more before my speech."

A look passed between them, a look acknowledging all their past, all their shared pain.

"Aye," said Uncle Liam, the lone keeper of the entire Doyle family history. "But don't be forgetting this, *nia*, nephew."

"What's that?"

"All the world's a stage, and most of us are desperately unrehearsed."

Ronan laughed. "Truer words, Uncle, have never been spoken."

~

"The mine owners do not find the gold! They do not mine the gold, they do not mill the gold, but by some weird alchemy all the gold belongs to them!"

Cheers erupted for words that weren't Ronan's own, but belonged to Big Bill Haywood, who'd recently become second in command of the WFM on a national level. Haywood believed in "One Big Union" and Ronan admired him more than any man he'd ever met. Except maybe his Da. And his uncles.

"Capitalism threatens our democracy," Ronan continued. A fine crowd today, four hundred or so eager for something more than the usual patriotic pablum. "Only organized labor can save democracy. We are the lone barrier between the people and absolute serfdom. Today, more than ever, money makes this nation's laws. The press and the pulpit have joined in an unholy alliance to hide truth from you and to maintain the status quo, which suits all of them and none of us."

He spotted familiar figures among the spectators, faces upturned, expressions enthralled, because truth didn't need to be dressed up, but was most powerful spoken plain.

Ronan had given similar speeches countless times—courts declaring laws that favored workers unconstitutional; counseling patience rather than addressing injustices; refusing to agree to arbitration since "there's nothing to arbitrate." Make changes through the ballot box? Not if the wrong side wins.

"And when we're pushed past the point of desperation," Ronan thundered, "we're labeled traitors and thrown in prison. After which we face the rope."

During this part of Ronan's speeches, memories threatened to overwhelm him. While he was surrounded by Colorado's natural beauty, it was the slag heaps of his Pennsylvania childhood he saw.

Ronan blinked, his attention once more anchored by the breeze feathering his hair, the sun warming his back, the trickles of sweat stinging his eyes. *This is not Schuylkill County but Teller,* he reminded himself.

"They tell us our demands will scare away capital. 'Then you'll have no jobs,' they bluster. To which we reply, 'Go ahead then: mine your own coal and your own gold and launder your own sheets and tailor your own clothes and muck out your own stables and build your mansions using your own lily-white hands.'"

There was always a point during Ronan's speeches when something inside him shifted, when words poured forth like a stream tumbling over river rocks, racing to the ocean and beyond until they rippled across the Universe where they were embraced by the Creator who Ronan instinctively knew was immensely *more* even than his own Catholic Father, Son and Holy Ghost. Who acknowledged the words and the anger and pain and the longing behind them as part of Himself, for He and His creations were the same.

Children's laughter and the faint strains from a carousel's calliope drifted to him; from yet another open-air pavilion, the Gold Coin Club's band belted out "The Stars and Stripes Forever," once more anchoring Ronan to this red, white and blue bunting-draped pavilion, this sea of faces. He ended his speech with: "For it was Jesus who said, 'Blessed are those who are persecuted because of righteousness, for theirs is the Kingdom of Heaven.'"

The crowd erupted. Uncle Liam, with Dilly Fein perched on his shoulders, blinked back tears. How proud would his brother Colm, Ronan's Da, be to see his son so eloquently going shoulder to shoulder against those who'd oppressed the Irish forever and a day. Beside him, Annie Fein, clutching Baby Katie's hand, thought how nice it was to be courted by such a big-hearted man as Liam Doyle. Leprechaun, already halfway to belligerence via several bottles of Cripple Creek Lager, cursed his boss for relying on his good looks rather than actual oratorical skills to, oh, I don't know, convince everybody who already believed in the WFM, that the union was mankind's savior. Nearby, Bridget Kehoe stared at Ronan Doyle, with the sun at his back causing his unbound hair to shine like something holy, and cursed how bad luck had left her at thirty with faded looks and limited marriage prospects. By picking the wrong Doyle, she'd lost them both, hadn't she, though through no fault of her own. And then there was Maeve Mooney, who despite having lived most of her life at near nine thousand feet, feared she was suffering from altitude sickness. Witnessing Ronan, she was reminded of Pentecost Sunday when the Holy Spirit descended upon the apostles and a divine fire flickered above each of their heads. She felt excited, humbled and awe-struck, all at the same time.

I wish I had a smartphone. I wish I could send Ronan's speech to Padrick. And after that create some sort of social media account with a caption like "Wow! Just Wow!"

Ronan Doyle, who would have thought?

Eight

Another surreal experience, seeing Shamrock Ranch before it became Shamrock Ranch. Familiar meadows dappled with wildflowers; red rock formations she'd climbed countless times; hillocks scarred with walking and cattle trails—at least in her time if not in this. Like a palimpsest, one scene atop the other—the white Mooney farmhouse with its copper roof and surrounding outbuildings scraped away to be replaced by a far less weathered White Rabbit, and *Jesus, Mary and Joseph*, was that Strank's Manse?

As the coachman maneuvered the surrey with its several guests behind a line of carriages, Maeve gaped at the monstrosity. A monument to too much money and too little taste. Four stories of sapphire blue trimmed in red; turrets on opposite ends of the residence; an observatory rising like an enormous pimple out of its mansard roof.

Once inside the already crowded foyer, Maeve was greeted by Horace Strank, dapper in dinner suit and tails.

"How lovely you look, Miss Mooney," he said, gaze assessing the cream-colored damask gown with its rhinestone and lace bodice that Annie Fein had so lovingly created. "We are all looking forward to your performance later this afternoon. That will be following our soon-to-be governor's speech."

Maeve wouldn't say the interior of Strank's Manse was as grotesque as the outside, though who would have thought of building a giant pond stocked with native trout? Or hiring a harpist dressed as a Greek goddess? Or installing more stained glass than in a cathedral? *Or,* Maeve thought while inspecting the wall murals, *commissioning an artist to paint the District as Ancient Rome, with a toga-dressed man resembling Horace Strank standing in front of a building resembling the White House?*

Wait till I write Padrick.

As soon as politely possible, Maeve slipped away to the White Rabbit. Sheltered inside the headframe, she opened her dance bag to retrieve journals that were tightly wrapped in canvas and thoroughly trussed with string. Not daring to peer down the hole for fear of what she might or might not see, Maeve tossed her package into the dark. The moment felt simultaneously anticlimactic and surreal. Like those hypnogogic states when only after your dead relative appears, or the floor opens beneath your feet, or you're soundlessly screaming *do you realize you're dreaming?*

Or when you look uphill to an untouched mountain meadow where the Mooney farmhouse should be.

"We must resist militant unionism," bellowed James Peabody, soon-to-be elected 13th governor of the great state of Colorado. "We must resist the leadership of the Western Federation of Miners. Its leaders are thugs and night assassins."

Maeve, seated near the Steinway grand piano upon which she'd soon perform, had jumped when Peabody had launched into his harangue. How could such a thunderous voice emerge from such an innocuous-looking individual? James Peabody was the Everyman of bank presidents—portly, handlebar mustache, pomaded hair neatly parted in the middle, oleaginous manner.

Except when it came to organized labor.

"The WFM is the most powerful, unprincipled, and unforgiving organization on the face of the Earth," Peabody continued to the audience of forty or so seated in the reception room. All powerful businessmen, many of who Maeve recognized, though she was the only woman. Apparently, today's broadside would be confined to the masculine sex. "These labor leaders are greater oppressors of the laboring man than employers have ever been. Wherever the WFM rules, violence erupts. Threats, intimidation, assaults, dynamite outrages, murders—the catalogue of its crimes affronts humanity."

Hadn't Peabody just met with Ronan and other labor leaders to pledge his neutrality?

Maeve forced her gloved hands to remain demurely in her lap. Reminding herself she was just a breeze passing through. Anything she said or did or thought wouldn't change outcomes one whit.

After Peabody finished his speech and Maeve was introduced to polite applause, she sat down in front of the Steinway. If she pleased Strank's audience, some would hire her. For an hour's performance in a private mansion, she'd earn more than an entire week at the Pick-Axe.

Focus on that, not anyone's political beliefs.

After a spirited rendition of "Maple Leaf Rag," Maeve ran through her usual repertoire—a mix of contemporary ballads and ragtime pieces, along with songs composed by artists not yet a twinkle in God's eye.

When she played the opening bars of John Denver's "Rocky Mountain High," the atmosphere shifted. A crowd favorite, whose reputation had preceded it. Maeve sang of Colorado's cathedral mountains, its clear mountain lakes, its starlight "softer than a lullabye." And here in this overwrought parlor, with its imported Italian fireplace mantel and ceiling beams wrested from a Tudor manor house, the robber barons who were tearing down the mountains and scarring the land sipped their expensive whiskey, smoked their Cuban cigars and blinked away sentimental tears.

Don't judge. But in the future, some of Colorado's high mountain streams still ran orange, so contaminated that not even an insect could survive. And the District's only remaining mine was an open pit ecological disaster plunging some three thousand feet into the earth.

What is the balance? Maeve wondered as she curtsied to enthusiastic clapping. She wanted to be neutral, had to be neutral but...

If only she could flee this grotesque monstrosity, race up the hill to her family, find them standing on the front porch of the Mooney farmhouse, waiting for her with welcoming smiles and outstretched arms.

"Miss Mooney, may I congratulate you? You sing like an angel."

Maeve looked into friendly blue eyes peering from behind frameless glasses. Receding hairline, bushy mustache, standard height and build. Suit not bespoke, but not a working man's either.

The stranger took her hand. "The main reason I attended Horace's *soiree* was to enjoy your performance." Trace of an Irish accent, which explained the obvious blarney, "May I introduce myself? James McParland at your service." Accompanied by a small bow.

Maeve's blood chilled. Instinctively, she pulled her hand free. "James McParland? THE James McParland?"

A surprised lift of the eyebrows. He cocked his head to the side, studying her. "Have you heard of me?"

Maeve could barely think over the buzzing in her head. James McParland. The man who might as well have personally placed the noose around the neck of each of the Molly Maguires?

"The name's familiar," she managed, hoping her manner appeared relaxed. "Are you a friend of Mr. Strank's?"

"We do run in some of the same circles." He smiled his charming smile. "Though my office is in Denver."

James McParland. Pinkerton spy. Kind eyes, a benevolent expression, and an engaging manner. All a mask. Before her stood the equivalent of Satan, Master of Disguise, Father of Lies, one of the greatest actors of his time, and he'd never set foot on the stage. What was he doing in Cripple Creek? Had he already infiltrated the WFM and the other unions? Would he and the Pinkertons play the same part here as they had in Pennsylvania?

I must warn Ronan.

~

"James McParland is here in the District," Maeve said without preamble.

Boom! Fireworks exploded upon the night sky in the baseball field surrounding Cripple Creek. Oohs and aahs from thousands of spectators.

Ronan's eyes widened before his expression settled on neutral. His gaze swept her body, taking note of her costume. "And how might you know that, Maeve Mooney?"

"I met him at Strank's Manse."

"Did you now?" Ronan gazed down at her, his face changing color with the kaleidoscope of fireworks.

"Not four hours ago. He said he has an office in Denver and he runs in the same circles as Horace Strank. I know what he did to your...the Molly Maguires, so what's he doing here? Does he have spies stirring up trouble?"

Ronan studied her, her face painted orange and blue and red, her expression so very...un-Maeve like. Suddenly, he grasped her chin and lifted her face to meet his.

"Which side are you on, Maeve Mooney?" His fingertips burned her skin, and he gazed at her with the same passion as when he'd been speechifying at Pinnacle Park. But it wasn't directed at her, of course it wasn't. Besides, Ronan was probably already aware of McParland's presence. The Pinkertons weren't the only ones with spies. What was wrong with her, attempting to impress him while making a fool of herself?

"You didn't answer," Ronan said roughly. "Which side are you on?"

A question that had been asked for centuries. Which would be asked so long as the underclass struggled beneath the upper class.

Maeve swallowed. Who did she think she was, championing a losing cause and a man who'd never been more than distantly pleasant to her, who'd certainly never asked for her interference?

"My side," she finally said.

Ronan dropped his hand from her chin. "Of course you are," he said and turned back to the fireworks.

Nine

Ronan had a list of men he hated—with a blind hatred that went back to a time he could scarcely remember.

He still hated the pit bosses at the Glen Carbon, who were British or Welsh, and who'd cuffed him and the other breaker boys for no reason other than they were Irish, while insulting those like his Da and his uncles for being drunken, lazy and superstitious.

He hated Franklin Gowen, president of the Reading Railroad, who'd hired the Pinkerton Detective Agency at a cost of $100,000 to infiltrate the coal fields. One hundred thousand dollars which would have paid for installing emergency exits, proper pumping systems and ventilation that the miners so desperately needed.

He hated the newspapers that, after the Mollies' arrest, likened all the Irish, not just the Mollies, to the KKK, called them violent and depraved, "scum" and "lawless wretches."

He hated all the prosecutors in all the trials, with Franklin Gowen once again the lead attorney, who did the bidding of the railroad and coal magnates—and most of them English—with their witnesses on the payroll of the railroad and mining companies. In other cases, defendants were persuaded to turn state's evidence to help convict their alleged collaborators. Some of the juries were populated by Germans who didn't even understand English, and the crooked judges presiding overall.

He hated the state of Pennsylvania, which provided the court-room and the gallows and said not a word about a private corpora-tion initiating the investigation through a private detective agency, the Pinkertons, or the private police force that arrested the Mollies, and the private attorneys for the coal companies who prosecuted them. Not a word from the politicians who passed a law—written by Frank Gowen—authorizing the formation of private police forces to patrol the coal fields, and suspending constitutional guarantees.

But most of all, he hated James McParland, who'd headed Denver's Pinkerton office for nearly a decade. An ill wind that blows no good. Not that Maeve Mooney had told him anything he didn't already know. The District was awash with spies, including his own.

Maybe I'll mention McParland to W.S.

He opened the wrought iron gate to Winfield Scott Stratton's property. Hidden behind shrubbery and forty-foot oaks and with awnings covering even the second-story windows, it emitted a secretive, even forbidding air, rather like its owner, who'd built it himself. Comfortable enough, but nothing that could compare to the mansions on Millionaire's Row a few streets over. When Ronan had first met Stratton, he'd lived in a shack mere steps away from his Independence Mine. It had been small enough to fit into Stratton's current front room, which doubled as a mini art gallery filled with paintings from famous or soon-to-be-famous artists. Unfortunately, a world-class art collection would remain another of W.S.'s unrealized dreams. Death could be a ruthless bastard, though a fifty-four-year-old man who drank two quarts of whiskey a day was taunting the Reaper. It would be Stratton's own weaknesses, as it is with most of us, that would take him out.

"How is Mr. Stratton this afternoon?" Ronan asked his long-suffering housekeeper, who escorted him to Stratton's study.

"'Bout the same," Eliza said with a shrug.

"Welcome, President Doyle!"

Stratton's customary greeting was more a breath than an utterance, adding to Ronan's disquiet. W.S. half-reclined on a red velvet day bed, shot glass in hand. On the floor beside him was a stack of newspapers topped by a book, probably one concerning geology or smelting. Stratton had studied geology at Colorado College and metallurgy at the Colorado School of Mines and was always contemplating the possible geological origins of the next big strike. Or maybe, since his tastes were eclectic, it was simply a dime novel.

Ronan held up his violin case. Each visit he played for his friend, whose study, with its grand piano and wax cylinder phonograph, could double as a music room.

"'Greensleeves' first today?" asked Stratton.

"If you'd like." While Ronan removed his violin and readied it for use, he surreptitiously studied his old friend. Always wiry, Stratton was so thin his limbs barely stirred the fabric of his suit. Even his white mustache, usually upturned at the ends, had lost its jaunty air.

Closing his eyes, Ronan tucked the violin beneath his chin and touched bow to string. "Greensleeves" always had him imagining Tudor ladies in velvet and ruff-wearing lords. If Henry VIII had actually composed "Greensleeves" for Anne Boleyn, it accurately tracked the arc of most love affairs. Somewhere along the way, someone was bound to lose their head.

As Stratton could relate. He'd been sued by girls of the half world and unhappy mistresses and his one short-lived marriage had ended when his wife announced she'd become pregnant before their wedding. And not, according to Stratton, by him.

It was safe to say that neither he nor W.S. was lucky in love. Which was why, save for his unfortunate youthful delusion, Ronan had left love very much alone.

"You have the touch," Stratton said, after he finished his mini-performance.

From a nearby sideboard, Ronan poured himself a shot of whiskey and settled in a nearby wing-backed chair. During their visits, he would nurse one drink—two at the most. One of Ronan's secret fears was that if he ever succumbed to the habit, he'd be the most hopeless drunk of all. Before him reclined the living embodiment of the horrors of alcohol, as if he didn't already know from Uncle Liam and half the men and women he interacted with daily. Work like an animal. Drink yourself blind and stupid. Rinse and repeat. Until cirrhosis and diabetes get you, the way it had Stratton. Or the mines. Or life itself, in the endless variety of ways it could feck with you and yours before tossing you onto the scrap heap.

"One hundred thousand dollars is as much money as any person of ordinary intelligence can take," Stratton said, voicing a familiar lament from the man who'd sold the Independence for eleven million dollars. To be fair, before gold had been discovered, a gambler named Pearlman had offered him a five-thousand-dollar, thirty-day option. Had Pearlman not passed on the option and ridden a first-class coach to San Francisco accompanied by a painted lady, Stratton would have been paid one hundred fifty thousand dollars for his stake. Rich enough. But not criminally so...

That is the land of lost content,
I see it shining plain,

quoted Ronan softly, knowing Stratton would understand A.E. Housman's verse.

The happy highways where I went
And cannot come again.

"Happy highway," Stratton repeated on a sigh. He enjoyed reminiscing about his land of lost content: when he'd been a three-dollar-a-day carpenter building cabinets and homes after the snows became too deep and the weather too brutal for him to lock away his saws, chisels, planes, and hammers in his tool chest, load up his pack mule and strike out for the high country, first in San Juan County and then in the District. Seventeen years of studying the composition of rocks, of the earth's strata when deciding where to prospect; of digging promising holes that turned out to be dry; of sharing drinks and meals over campfires with other grizzled seekers; of reveling in the isolation, the quiet, the haunting loveliness of the Rockies. Massive rock formations, valleys so steep you couldn't see the bottom; forests so dense you could walk for days, your boots a whisper on the fallen pine needles. Herds of big horn sheep, elk, deer and antelope. Wolves, coyotes, foxes, and mountain lions sunning on rocks. Black bears gorging on berries before lumbering off to their winter hideaways; beavers damming lakes so blue the sky might have tumbled into their waters. Stratton could identify bluebirds, chickadees, plovers—all the mountain birds—and recognize them by their song. He'd chased ravens and magpies from his camps, marked carcasses by circling turkey vultures, startled when bald eagles launched from their nests high in the treetops, and watched golden eagles carry dinner back to their eaglets safely tucked away in granite crevices.

Until becoming Cripple Creek's first millionaire.

Stratton had certainly enjoyed it, parts of it. The company of his ladies, whether the high-class prostitutes at the Old Homestead House or those residing in cribs. He'd appreciated being able to give key employees fifty thousand dollar Christmas bonuses and purchasing the mortgage on Denver's Brown Palace Hotel just because he could. Buying houses for friends and two million dollars' worth of Denver real estate, along with $1.5 million for a state-of-the-art trolley system in Colorado Springs. What he hated was the accompanying notoriety—megaphone-wielding hack drivers bellowing his name to gawking tourists; being forced to disguise himself when out in public, surreptitiously exiting establishments from back doors or into alleyways; compelled to hire carriages instead of walking to his nearby office lest he be mobbed. He'd been hauled into court by unhappy courtesans, wannabe business partners, and charlatans who gambled that Stratton would rather pay up than be inconvenienced by lawyers and affidavits and cross-examinations on the witness stand.

"Wealth changes a man," Stratton mused, sipping his drink.

"Does it? Or is it our nature?"

"Money doesn't change those who have it to begin with. Or so I've observed. They remain true to their class."

"Jimmy's good," Ronan said, referring to Jimmy Burns, a plumber who had struck it rich at the Portland Mine. "One of the few who's remained with his feet on the ground."

Here Stratton would inevitably retell one of his favorite anecdotes. It went like this: During the strike of 1894, mine owners had come to him and Jimmy, asking them to cut their employees' wages and lengthen their hours. Once their men fell in line, the owners told them, the smaller mines would follow. Owners would win, twelve hundred miners would lose and the WFM would be broken before it began. Jimmy and Stratton had responded by reinforcing an eight-hour day, allowing their miners to join the WFM, and reaffirming every worker's right to collective bargaining.

Were those "the good old days?" If James Peabody was elected governor and the mine owners decided they were powerful enough to try again, who would be the WFM's Stratton? Their Jimmy Burns?

"McParland's sniffing around again," Ronan blurted.

Stratton sighed. "Hardly surprising. What with wastrels like Horace Strank recently forming the Mine Operators' Association. And we know what the MOA is about."

"Smashing unions," Ronan said, the pleasure gone from their visit. "With the Pinkertons as their hammer."

Stratton shifted position until he was fully prostrate. His hands, cradling an empty shot glass, rested atop his waistcoat. "I fear...

since the Supreme Court declared corporations to be people with a person's rights, well, I fear we've taken two steps forward and centuries backward."

Stratton appeared to drift off. He reminded Ronan of a mine donkey so worn out it died in its traces. Quietly, he reached for his violin case and stood, readying to leave.

Stratton stirred. "'Til next month," he whispered, extending an arm for Ronan to clasp.

"Aye." How frail his hand felt, like the bones of a baby bird.

Swallowing back a wave of sadness, Ronan departed, knowing this would be the last time he'd be seeing Winfield Scott Stratton. At least in this world.

Ten

Last Sunday Ronan and I rode the Colorado Midland to South Park by way of Lake George and Eleven Mile Canyon. (Okay, it wasn't just Ronan and me, but Uncle Liam and Annie Fein and her girls. Timmy and Danny remained in Cripple playing baseball.) I told you how Ronan and I had quarreled, or I had kind of said the wrong thing about being on "my side," but he seems to have forgiven me. Or forgotten or never cared about it—or me—in the first place. Anyway, all along the way the train stopped so we could pick wildflowers. We picnicked on fried chicken and potato salad and drank Hires Root Beer, Dr. Pepper and Coca-Cola, all in glass bottles and tasting nothing like you and I know. Remember when we used to go kinda that route to ski in Breckenridge? The train's much more pleasant, though slower, of course. You would like it. Fairplay's another mining town—like so many that are now totally abandoned—and Lake George is just a railroad stop. In winter when the lake freezes over, men cut out huge blocks of ice for shipment to Colo. Spgs, etc., to keep perishables fresh.

Something, though, that's increasingly bugging me. Saint Paddy again. I don't even really like to talk to him beyond a "hello" and "How ya doing?" From watching him at the Pick-Axe, he seems to hoard a person's words in *order to hurl them back, or twist them as he sees fit at the most unexpected times. And he doesn't really contribute anything much beyond slogans and platitudes and tired jokes. The longer I'm here, the more I can't understand how Saint Paddy somehow emerged whole and rich enough after the strike to purchase Shamrock Ranch.*

Ronan gazed out the window of the Short Line's club car. Teddy Roosevelt had once declared that the route, which wound from Cripple Creek to Colorado Springs, was so beautiful it "bankrupts the English language." Ronan agreed. Tunnels carved through granite; the backside of Pikes Peak already dusted with snow; stands of aspen, pine and the twisted branches of Ute prayer trees; streams sparkling like fairy lights in the late summer sunshine.

Due to a fare war among the various railroads, even the poorest passengers on the Short Line were housed in elegant club cars, all red velvet and polished wood and brass. Ronan was pleased such luxuries were available for a mere four bits round trip. Not because he cared for himself, but because they were a reminder of how far he and his kind had come, at least here in this raw and rugged country.

The rhythmic clackety-clack of the train was enough to put a man to sleep, though he was distracted by the swaying of the car which caused his thigh to repeatedly press against Maeve Mooney's. Well, that might be inappropriate, but she was not the kind to mind or to think he was flirting. She was more the kind to dismiss it as an accident—which it was—or ignore it altogether. One thing he liked about his sometime music partner. She generally shrugged aside minor actions that horrified "respectable" women.

Seated on the opposite bench, Uncle Liam addressed him. "Not much like from where we came, aye?" Uncle Liam's eyes had been clear these past few months, his color healthy enough to shave a decade off his actual age. Beside him, Annie, wearing a straw boater and simple white shortwaist, knitted a scarf in black and gold, the colors of the WFM's logo.

Ronan nodded. He did miss the explosion of colors covering the Appalachians in the fall. And he supposed some could ascribe a certain perverse beauty to Pennsylvania's slag heaps and poisoned streams and dilapidated coal patches—if you could rationalize that their product fueled Andrew Carnegie's steel mills and America's trains; fattened the portfolios of the Mellons, Morgans and Rockefellers; altered Chicago, New York and San Francisco skylines; built seventy room "summer cottages" for wastrels and the children of wastrels to flee the heat of Fifth Avenue for Newport. In one way or another, one could trace every robber baron's riches back to his home state's coal mines. In return, those miners got black lung disease while their children got the privilege of gathering bits of coal fallen from passing trains to carry home and warm their hovels.

The car swayed again, causing his shoulder to brush Maeve's. In the window's reflection he studied Maeve Mooney, looking quite smart in her toque hat with its fancy scarlet feather, green walking skirt and jacket trimmed in the same scarlet. She might think to keep up the silly pretense of amnesia, though she often forgot her story from one telling to the next, but it was clear from her bearing and tastes that Maeve Mooney came from money. Or perhaps from a show business family. Whatever, it didn't matter. She was no different from most of the others who'd drifted to the District.

For her part, Maeve tried unsuccessfully to focus on the glorious view, which in her time would be replaced by a potholed four-lane highway glutted with cars and commuters, but Ronan Doyle made for an irresistible distraction.

"You know what I dream of?" Ronan leaned over, his voice so low that amid the hum of conversation, the rhythmic thwump-thump of train wheels, she didn't initially realize he'd been addressing her. When she turned to face him, they were separated by mere inches. The way it was with lovers.

"What do you dream of, Ronan Doyle?" Though Maeve's heart

began that silly hammering it so often did in his presence, she refused to pull away. No reason to reveal how he affected her, since he didn't.

Perhaps it was the imminent passing of W.S. Stratton, the looming election that caused his tongue to loosen enough to express sentiments that usually remained safely bottled inside. "I dream I'm an old man sitting on a bench in front of my home," he said. "With no one ever giving a thought to me. And I'm gazing out at passersby with all my past rolling around in my head and nobody the wiser. All anyone sees is an old man sitting in the sun."

If Maeve moved her head slightly, their foreheads would touch. Her pulse increased. How peculiar, this unexpected intimacy. And sad. For Uncle Liam often lamented that a short life was the Doyle men's curse, while Ronan appeared to hope he would be different.

"*They shall grow not old, as we that are left grow old,*" Maeve said, her voice husky. She suddenly felt on the verge of tears. "*Age shall not weary them, nor the years condemn.*"

Ronan frowned.

"You're not the only one who reads," she said defensively, though "For the Fallen" had not yet been written. "I'm not a total airhead," she added, her prickly armor firmly back in place.

"Airhead?" Ronan repeated.

"Ninny," she clarified. "Eejit."

He smiled. "Never said you were."

They stared at each other. There it was again. That overwhelming desire to weep at the thought of Ronan's fate. So many dreamed of more...more wealth, more power, more fame while Ronan Doyle asked only to live long enough to savor the sun on a summer's afternoon.

Already dead, already dead. She supposed that was true, but if this was 1902 and she was from the 21st century, couldn't she say that of herself as well?

Maeve reached up to tuck a strand of Ronan's hair behind his ear and cup the side of his bearded cheek. "I promise you this," she whispered. How brown his eyes. How flawless his features, how admirable—if deluded—his idealism. "When I'm an old woman walking past, I'll be the one who stops and sits beside you for a spell."

Something quickened between them. Maeve felt it and was sure Ronan felt it as well. He must.

"This changes everything, doesn't it?" she wanted to ask.

"What just happened?" he wanted to ask.

Instead, he favored her with the faintest of smiles and said, "I'll look forward to it."

"Well, what have we here?! As I live and breathe. What're you all doing recreating this fine Saturday morn?"

Maeve turned from her sightseeing to see Leprechaun grinning down at them. Upon settling into the empty high-backed bench opposite them, he reached for the pack of Chesterfields inside his shirt pocket.

"Hey," he said, "What's the only difference between an Irish wedding and an Irish wake?"

"Tell us," said Ronan agreeably.

"One less drunk," he said, slapping his knee.

All save Maeve settled into the usual small talk. One look at Leprechaun and she recognized he was on another bender. He could go from happy drinker to belligerent drunk in the blink of an eye, beginning with "I'll be having a wee tipple" and ending with "Aye, I've my snoot in in the schnapps, and what'll you be saying about that?"

After lighting his cigarette, Leprechaun said, "My *macushla*, my darling, and me're gonna picnic in the Garden of the Gods."

Was it Maeve's imagination or did the atmosphere immediately plunge to arctic levels?

"What a lovely idea!" Annie Fein said, but that was Annie. Kind to a fault and meaning every word of it.

Ronan's left hand, resting on his thigh, clenched.

Uncle Liam's lips turned up in what might have been a smile but was more a grimace.

Then there she was, Bridget Kehoe, frizzy hair crushed beneath a black straw hat, clutching a wicker hamper. When the train rounded a curve, she collapsed into the seat beside Leprechaun. "I'll be taking a stagecoach next time. I swear I'm seasick with all this swaying."

Mumbles from the men. Maeve nodded a greeting. Annie Fein said, "So nice to see you. The color of your jacket makes the green of your eyes sparkle."

Settling her hamper between her and Leprechaun, Bridget rearranged her cotton broadcloth skirt while scowling at them all.

"And what're you about today?" Bridget asked, directly addressing Uncle Liam. Liam removed his bowler hat, ran a hand through his thick hair, replaced it again and pondered the copy of *The Miners Magazine* in his lap, as if it might answer for him.

"Sightseeing, and a birthday present for Timmy," Annie said brightly, "though I'm sure Cripple Creek has everything he could wish for." After a sidelong glance at Uncle Liam, she reached down for the small carpet bag at her feet and stuffed her knitting inside.

Maeve realized Annie's friendliness was an act, that she was as uneasy as the others, though hiding it better. Why? They'd all seen Leprechaun and Bridget together. They knew the pair were betrothed in all but name. Maybe the Doyle men were simply uncomfortable being jammed into such close quarters.

More conversation, light enough, though Maeve imagined sharks circling beneath the surface, alert to the first scent of blood. She wanted to place her hand over Ronan's, force it to unclench, to soothe him for reasons she couldn't fathom...

"...fancy sleepers that offer champagne dinners on overnight excursions from Denver," Leprechaun was saying. Jaysus, he spent so much time decrying the rich, Maeve suspected he wanted to be one of them.

Leprechaun plucked a flask from inside Bridget's hamper, unscrewed it and took a swig. "Did you pack me some of your tea cakes, *macushla*?"

Leprechaun might not have existed. This time, she stared at Ronan as if she'd never seen him before.

What's going on here? Maeve wondered. It was like walking into the middle of a movie and having no clue.

Leprechaun retrieved a handful of tea cakes from the hamper and began munching on them.

Bridget turned her attention to Annie. "You've done well for yourself since your poor husband was crushed to death, haven't you? Thanks to the Doyle boys."

Annie gasped. Ronan and Uncle Liam looked stunned. Maeve blinked, as if that might clear what must be her faulty hearing. A seemingly oblivious Leprechaun continued stuffing his face.

"Of course, you're doing better," Bridget continued. "When that husband of yours was spending all his time at Crapper Jacks and instead of feeding his wee ones, he's wasting his money on their dance hall girls. Disgraceful, I'd say."

Annie's mouth opened in a shocked "Oh."

Ronan bolted to his feet. Two steps to the aisle, and his hand encircled Bridget's wrist. "Shut the feck up," he hissed, jerking her hard off her seat.

"Mind you!" Leprechaun sputtered. He stuck out his chin pugnaciously, before thinking better of it and confining himself to a scowl.

"After you apologize to Mrs. Fein for your rudeness, you and Paddy Mooney'll be taking your hamper and your own fine selves and finding a seat in another compartment."

Bridget's face had flushed red as her hair. She glared up at him. "You cannot be tellin' me what to do, Ronan Doyle."

Another jerk of her wrist; their bodies pressed close together.

Maeve watched in amazement. She'd never seen Ronan be violent with anybody, except for, well, there were the drunks at the Pick-Axe who had to be tossed out by the seat of their pants and the occasional admirer who tried to get a little too handsy during her shows. And those bare-knuckle fights at the Topic Theatre...

Across from her, Uncle Liam laid aside his magazine, unfolded his long legs and stood. Between the two Doyle men, they filled the space, and while Uncle Liam had always reminded Maeve of a child's teddy bear that had seen better days, his expression was as menacing as Ronan's. "Byrdie Kehoe," he growled. "Mrs. Fein is awaiting her apology."

Bridget glared at him, at Ronan, and back again. So many expressions flitted across her face, like a film at fast forward. Maeve couldn't decide whether she might scream, burst into tears, or throw something. A sudden slump of the shoulders, a dipping of her head in surrender. "I'm sorry. I should not have spoken," Bridget mumbled to Ronan's chest. After which, she pushed past him and stalked toward the exit, with a glowering Leprechaun scrambling behind.

Uncle Liam called after them, "Who keeps his tongue keeps his friends."

For Maeve, the word "magic" would never again conjure the phantasmagoric notions Nana Grace had stuffed inside her brain, or even her journeys through time. For her, magic would ever be this late August afternoon in Cheyenne Park—after they'd eaten roasted peanuts and drunk lemonade and she'd purchased a copy of *Alice in Wonderland/Through the Looking Glass* for Timmy Fein at one of the stores adjoining the Denver and Rio Grande Depot. In her memory, the entire experience would be bathed in a halcyon glow. Or maybe that's simply the way we imagine afterward, once our past has been imbued with the sorrow of knowing.

In 1902 the area was known as Cheyenne Park. Later it would be sold off to become part of the Broadmoor where Maeve would drive around and dream her dreams of riches and respectability. The trolley that had transported them from the Depot, as well as the park itself, was yet another gift from Winfield Scott Stratton. Not only had Stratton purchased the twenty acres, he'd overseen the landscaping, the baseball diamond, the rides and games, even the shuffleboard courts near the pavilion where on opening day John Philip Sousa and his band had entertained thousands.

The man himself might be dying inside his fortress on Wahsatch Avenue a handful of miles away, but his presence remained ubiquitous.

Maeve and Ronan had trailed Annie and Uncle Liam over a footbridge crossing Cheyenne Creek and along winding paths sheltered by scrub oak and cottonwoods. While Annie and Uncle Liam strolled arm in arm, Maeve dared not attempt the same with Ronan. Instead, she clutched her purse in one hand and in the other a bag containing Timmy's book so she wouldn't have to decide whether, yes, she should, or no, she shouldn't possibly annoy Ronan by attempting to loop her arm through his.

Their walk ended in a panoramic view of an emerald carpet containing all the park's entertainments. Breathtaking, just as Stratton had envisioned, though it was the people Maeve found most captivating—women in pale gowns and parasols; men in straw hats and sack suits; boys in knickers and girls in snowy white pinafores.

An Impressionist painting come to life.

Though that wasn't what caused the tableau to remain forever branded in her mind. At that moment, Ronan turned to her, his dark hair shining in the afternoon sun, his chambray shirt blue as the afternoon sky.

"Might I confess what I enjoy about your company?"

Maeve tensed. Ronan so seldom strayed into personal territory that she had no idea how to react. She suppressed the urge to grab his chin and pull his face close in order to study it. "What are you up to?" she would ask. "What is this really about?"

"I like that you don't look at me as if I'm a butterfly to be pinned on a board." He gazed down at her. "To be captured and kept. So many think an interesting pair of eyes or straight teeth or a full head of hair or a broad back will save them somehow or make them happy when it's simply a projection. Like the moving pictures they show here in the park in the evening. Almost immediately, they'll face disappointment. Which they blame on you rather than look to themselves."

Who did this to you? Maeve felt a piercing sense of shame for that other Maeve Mooney, who'd pinned all manner of butterflies. Only she'd never intended to keep them. Pin them, use them, remove the pins. And if the butterfly flew away or dropped and crumbled, she'd never given it a thought.

Had she wounded some man as deeply as Ronan had been wounded?

Maeve hesitated, seeking to say the right thing, fearing she'd do the opposite and he'd withdraw, as was his wont.

"You can't capture a moment in a bottle," she finally offered. "Though we think we can and turn our anger on the other when we can't."

With a sudden blinding intensity, Maeve realized she *had* captured this moment, that she would return to it with love and gratitude and a sense of wonder all the days of her life.

Had words not have been impossible, she would have said more. Instead, she stood on tiptoe, slid her arms around Ronan's neck and kissed him.

Surprised, and ever so thankful, when Ronan kissed her back.

PART FOUR

September 1902

❧

Love is a smoke and is made with the fume of sighs

— SHAKESPEARE, ROMEO AND JULIET

Eleven

Maeve felt like a teenager, stalking her first crush. Except, in real life she'd never had first crushes or any crushes. She hated the mix of euphoria and dread she felt at first glimpse of Ronan striding into the Pick-Axe, or when they shared a duet and he gazed into her eyes as if they were lovers when beyond that brushing of lips nearly a month ago, there'd been nothing more. Were they engaged in some peculiar mating dance where she was as clueless as when Timmy Fein had tried to teach her the two-step? Maeve's mind was a perpetual haze save for one coherent thought: Ronan Doyle. She didn't understand any of it. Whenever she and Ronan were together, she felt simultaneously comforted and distressed. Her chest hurt from all the silly pounding of her heart. Lest she constantly stare, she had to turn her back to him. Ball her hands at her sides to keep from reaching out to smooth his hair, trace his profile, touch his hand when it lay mere inches from her own. She wanted to weep and haunt graveyards in a long black veil. Dance round a bonfire on Midsummer's Eve invoking enchantment spells. Tear petals off daisies while intoning "He loves me." "He loves me not." Create execrable love poems, as she had when she'd been barely pubescent, and search the library for anthologies of romantic poetry to read late into the night when she ached for him.

I can't stand this. My heart is going to burst. My stomach... Maeve couldn't eat. She couldn't sleep. *At thirty-one, I'm a walking cliché.*

Pitiful, really.

When Ronan smiled at her or covered her hand with his or offered her his arm, she became convinced he was merely being polite, that he'd have done the same for any woman. That their day in Colorado Springs hadn't meant anything. Shouldn't her kiss have been an invitation to something more?

"He's quite religious," Annie Fein offered when Maeve confessed her frustration. Yeah, Maeve knew that. Most everybody, including her, attended Sunday Mass (though she skipped confession). That's just what your ancestors did. And all those religious necklaces, couldn't they simply be to make Ronan look sexier rather than a symbol of his faith, though Ronan Doyle didn't need any accessories to look sexy.

"Then there's that other," Annie added. "I don't believe I've ever seen Mr. Doyle in any sort of...personal way...with a woman." She looked troubled. Obviously, everyone in the District knew more about their fellow citizens' secret lives than Maeve did. "Both Doyles were badly hurt, you know."

"Tell me, Maeve demanded. Not really demanding, politely asking, but if Annie was a true friend, she'd spill so Maeve would know if Ronan was even capable of reciprocating her feelings. But if he wasn't, what would she do then? Try harder? Throw herself down the White Rabbit?

Annie patted her hand. "Be patient. Treat him as you would a skittish animal. Not a wild one, just one who's had the trust wrung from him."

She had no idea how this Maeve Mooney, who had once flirted and bedded whomever she pleased, felt so shy and awkward around a man who wasn't *that* much different from her previous dalliances.

But he was. So far above all the rest, not so much because of his physical beauty, but because of the purity of his beliefs.

Question to ponder: Why was it that when Padrick went on and on about unions and "which side are you on?" it sounded ridiculous, but with Ronan it sounded like holy writ?

Labor Day, like the Fourth of July, consisted of three days of celebration, though the speeches and activities revolved more around working-class solidarity and with the forthcoming election, reminders of the importance of voting. Surprised that women could vote, Maeve publicly pledged she would. After which she worried Ronan would think she'd never voted before—she hadn't—and criticize her for being politically lazy. On September 14, W.S. Stratton's death was proclaimed across the state—from the *Florence Daily Tribune's* blunt **Stratton is Dead**, to **Stratton, the Father of Cripple Creek, Passes to His Accounting**, via the influential *Rocky Mountain News*. Stratton lay in state at the Colorado Springs' Mining Exchange he'd built, and Ronan, with Maeve by his side (did that mean something?), passed by his coffin along with thousands of others.

"It's like trying to read tea leaves," Maeve whispered, later that night in her suite at the National Hotel. "And I'm not psychic."

On September 17, 1902, the harvest moon arrived, round and orange as a Halloween pumpkin. How else could Maeve celebrate it but by ending her set with Neal Young's "Harvest Moon"? When she'd worked at the Golden Bee, she'd often played it when the night was winding down and customers waxed nostalgic. She would close her eyes, allowing her fingers to find the keys of their own accord, the lyrics flowing from her with such longing, for wouldn't it be wonderful to dance under the moon with the man who loved you, who'd always loved you? Until she'd gotten tangled up with lowlifes like Beau Strank and realized such sentiments had less substance than the fevered dreams of an opium eater.

Still, tonight as Maeve played, she pictured Ronan and her dancing in a meadow—perhaps the one outside her bedroom window at Shamrock Ranch—their bodies limned in the light of a moon round as a golden coin and gleaming just as bright. She gazed up at the actual Ronan, who'd left his place behind the Pick-Axe's bar where he'd been polishing glasses, leaned against the piano the way he did after finishing a duet, watching her. Was he intrigued by an unfamiliar song? Captivated by its lyrics? Realizing this was another of her delusions, Maeve's voice broke on the final line. Ronan Doyle wasn't in love with her, not now, not in the past, not tomorrow. Not ever. Without putting away her music or acknowledging the crowd's applause, Maeve bolted out the door.

I can't do this. Tomorrow I'm going home, she vowed as she hurried along streets that were a chiaroscuro of moonlight and shadow, toward the National Hotel. *No procrastinating.* And if she died on her return, wasn't that preferable to the perpetually open sore that was her heart?

Once inside her suite, she switched on the Tiffany lamp beside her bed before crossing to the lone floor-to-ceiling window that in future Cripple Creek would never pass a safety inspection.

Resting her cheek against the cold glass, she whispered, "You're not a good person. This is exactly what you deserve." How stupid to cry, when she didn't actually *love* Ronan Doyle. He was a conquest, no different than any of the men she'd targeted to advance her career or because she was bored or had decided being first lady of Colorado might be fun. Now she was pouting like a spoiled child. When the world was awash with tragedy and loves forever lost and pain so intense some died of it, Maeve, delusional, self-absorbed Maeve, had decided she must be the heroine of some romance novel simply because she wished it.

The moon, now bleached diamond-white, had climbed halfway across a darkness pricked with stars. Not the most spectacular display she'd seen. When Maeve had been little and an early winter storm was predicted, her dad would prop her beside him inside his tractor cab, after which he and Padrick and Granda baled hay under moons red as blood; moons so immense they seemed to swallow the sky; moons that set the surrounding clouds on fire.

What are you doing tonight? she wondered. *Did you plant hay this year? Is it September 17th in your world? When I return...will I return...will something go wrong? Will I die?*

A loud knock caused her to jump. Room service wasn't really a thing yet and Maeve was in no shape for visitors.

"Go away!"

A second, more insistent. How rude when Maeve planned to spend the rest of the night wallowing in her misery. Hurrying to the door, she flung it open.

"Jaysus, Maeve," Ronan said. "Didn't you hear me call you? I made enough noise to raise the dead."

If she'd been another Maeve, she'd have grumped, "What are you talking about?" Or flirtatiously batted her eyes and said something wittily provocative. Instead, she simply stared.

"You forgot your coat." Ronan held out a broadcloth wrap with mutton sleeves.

Maeve snatched it and clutched it wordlessly to her chest.

"May I come in?"

She hesitated before stepping aside. *What is happening? How can you be here? Why are you looking at me like that?*

"You seemed sad earlier. What's made you unhappy?" When she merely shook her head, Ronan attempted a tease. "You usually have more sass, Maeve Mooney. I'm not sure what to make of this."

Maeve continued to gawp, as if she'd lost her senses. 'Twas true his Maeve was a quirky creature, but, despite his better judgment, Ronan had grown fond of her. "Tell me, Maeve. What's troubling you?" He raised her chin with two fingers, forcing her to meet his gaze. She shook her head before looking down at the floor. Why was bold, self-assured Maeve Mooney suddenly acting like a shy schoolgirl?

Turning away, Maeve retreated to her former post at the window. With Ronan's touch, her heart rate had increased to its usual marathon rate. Surely, he must hear it, must realize how she felt. Was he toying with her? Had bringing her wrap been an excuse? But an excuse for what? He'd passed up a thousand opportunities to initiate "intimacies," so why was he here?

Ronan crossed to stand beside her, close enough that it seemed natural for him to reach over and hook his little finger in hers. Moonlight illumined their faces, creating ghostly patterns on the oriental carpet. Below, a trolley rumbled past; a jangle of noise and music rose from saloons surrounding the National, plus the string band entertaining in its first-floor Dining Room.

For Maeve the silence was excruciating. For Ronan, a memory flashed of him tucked away in the copse behind his uncle's boarding house, gazing up at another full moon, this one dulled by pollution, and wondering where life would take him.

"My mam used to tell me that, in the auld sod, fairies came out on nights like these, magical nights where they'd dance upon the dew."

Maeve thought of the fairy ring beyond the White Rabbit, thought of the magic that had brought her here. But how to respond? "Have you been to Ireland then?" An innocuous question. Fitting for an idiot.

Ronan shrugged. "Does it make a difference? It's in our blood regardless, isn't it?"

Maeve gazed up at him. Impossible to believe such a man stood here beside her, his finger linked in hers, close enough that with the slightest repositioning, they could embrace. If she spun *that* out, if she were the old Maeve Mooney, she knew what would happen by night's end...

Ronan grazed her cheek with his fingertips, noting the hitch in her breath, the longing in her eyes. How often had he been irritated

THE GOLDEN PROMISE OF CRIPPLE CREEK

seeing such looks from other women? With Maeve, it caused his pulse to quicken in a way that, after all these years of abstinence, was foreign.

"Like children sleeping so we could dream the night away," he whispered, paraphrasing a line from "Harvest Moon." "'Tis a gentle image and fit for a night like this." When was it he'd decided Maeve Mooney was worth deconstructing the wall he'd built around his heart? At least making the attempt? It had happened so gradually until now here they were, on the precipice of something grand or frightening or destructive, he had no idea which.

"Gentle," Maeve echoed.

Ronan studied her. Tonight, she had done that thing where she piled her hair atop her head and threaded strategic strands with rhinestones. In the moonlight, they winked like the fireflies he'd once chased during Pennsylvania summers.

"I like your hair like that."

Maeve made a strangled noise. Ronan didn't know whether to tease her because of her very un-Maeve-like behavior, soothe what was apparently a case of nerves or do what he wished and take the next step.

"Might I take it down?"

Maeve's eyes widened. She did not respond for so long that he feared she might have fallen asleep like a horse, standing up and open-eyed.

"Maeve?"

Could this really be happening? To go from misery to euphoria in the space of minutes? But what Maeve was feeling was more akin to terror. She was new at this, had no idea how to act, whether one false move would cause him to flee forever. "That Maeve Mooney, she's not worth it," he would tell everyone.

"Yes," she whispered.

Leaning down, Ronan carefully removed various strategically placed hairpins. Simple enough since he'd often watched her fix them during performances. Once loosed, her hair, dark and shimmery, cascaded down her back.

"Magical," he whispered, running his fingers through it, catching threads of tiny jewels. Maeve shivered at his touch. "Like the faeries," he said, handing the threads to her.

Maeve's laugh came out as a strangled cough.

Face to face, mere inches apart. "Are you fearful? Would you like me to stop? To leave?"

In answer, she clasped one of his hands, brought it to her lips and kissed each knuckle. *Is this a dream?* Some sort of cruel joke ending with the punchline, "You're not what I want, not at all?"

"I want you to tell me something," Ronan said. "The truth."

Maeve swallowed. "About what?" "*Where are you really from? Are you a time traveler? I always sensed you don't belong here.*"

"I no more believe you've amnesia than James Peabody has a soul."

"Oh! That. Well—"

So, if you've a husband you're hiding from or who could turn up any time, I need to know."

"There's no one." A truer statement than Ronan could know. The men she'd slept with had been chosen by another woman, and that woman had become a stranger. She approached him virginal, and in a way that left her feeling unbearably vulnerable. "Please don't hurt me," she wanted to say, where the old Maeve would have said something like, "Wanna fuck now or after we eat?" She wanted to ask him to make love to her, for that's what this would be, but the words refused to emerge from her mouth. Still, Ronan must have understood, for when he bent over and kissed her, it wasn't a mere brush of the lips. Full-bodied, and yet tender somehow. Maeve allowed herself to melt into him and give herself, body and soul, to Ronan Doyle.

∾

A love poem. Maeve felt she was that—a creation of all the words poets inked, striving to capture "love." And never succeeding, for who can capture the remains of an ancient dream? Perhaps that was why her mind was a tornado of thoughts and emotions, unable to find the calm at its center where the ability to fully experience these moments with him—with Ronan—was possible.

"Shh," Ronan whispered, feeling her tension. "Lie back and let me love you."

He undressed her, undressed them both, slowly, deliberately as if they had all the time in the world rather than a handful of hours. Maeve alternated between staving off a panic attack and melting into the mattress. But when Ronan embraced her, skin to skin, and she felt the soft fuzz of the hair on his chest and thighs, could trace the muscles on his back, inhale the faint scent of Florida Water and Ivory soap, she drifted back to earth.

"You are the lark-song/calling me home."

"Relax," Ronan breathed against her ear. "I'll not hurt you."

Turn off your brain. Stay in the moment. Maeve narrowed her concentration to his lips whispering beneath her ear, following the curve of her jawline, trailing to the flesh above her collarbone; to the calloused hands that trailed her body, marking its curves.

"A love like this can know no death."

But even as her body surrendered, her fears whispered: How could you willingly hand over the power to shred your soul to this man? To any man?

"I'm afraid of how you might destroy me," she whispered. "I've never been here before. It's terrifying."

"I have spread my dreams under your feet/Tread softly because you tread on my dreams."

Ronan raised up on his elbows to study her. She was so exposed, so vulnerable, he felt such a tenderness, a primal instinct to protect her. But because he prided himself on being an honest man, he could only promise, "I'll do my best to cherish you as you deserve."

The warmth of his breath upon her skin, the silken strands of his hair. Patiently, his body wooed hers until every centimeter of her skin finally caught fire. Her doubts, her inhibitions rose like smoke toward heaven.

Here. We two. She didn't need to believe him, or question him, or worry what would happen afterward. How beautiful, how perfect this moment, how blessed she was. She didn't need to whisper, "I love you," in order to sanctify the experience, though she felt it. Flesh, blood and bone transformed to something sacral without the need for words.

Ronan smiled down at her, his hair a dark frame against his face, his necklaces gleaming in the moonlight, as he entered her. It was slow and tender, so perfect that the moment didn't seem quite real. *So many times I imagined...but not like this, nothing like this.*

"All that we see or seem/Is but a dream within a dream."

"I'm glad you found your way to Cripple Creek, Maeve Mooney," Ronan whispered afterward, brushing strands of tangled hair away from her face and kissing her forehead. "My world would be less without you."

"I wasn't alive before I knew you," Maeve whispered, too sated to guard her feelings. But there'd never been such a time, not even when in the womb. Since God had first breathed life into His creation, she'd been searching for her other half.

When Ronan fell asleep, she rested her face against his chest. The beating of his heart beneath her ear lulled her into her own dream within a dream, where past, present and future all mingled together.

"And yonder all before us lie/Deserts of vast eternity."

PART FIVE
March–August 1903

Looking back, I trace the beginning of our end to the demise of Winfield Scott Stratton. He was the workingman's protector, our Jesus, far better, as it turned out, than our very own priests and bishops, who like Judas, betrayed us in the end. Because of Stratton's staggering wealth, Penrose, Tutt, Moffatt, Hagerman and the rest of the robber barons had to listen to him. Now the cracks in the levee that had always been there, began leaking. We watched and worried and marked the changes, though when the mine owners expanded their mining-related businesses, we approved. More successful projects for them meant more secure employment for us. They built smelting and reduction facilities in order to refine and separate the gold from the ore, thus controlling the process from start to finish. We could not know that the Standard Mill, an ore-processing facility down in Colorado City, would be the snowball that eventually became the avalanche, burying us all. In the fall of 1902, the WFM organized the Standard's mill workers, who'd long been treated like indentured servants. Simple enough. Only it wasn't. The company refused to negotiate. Period. I would like to say I realized the importance of the Standard Mill standoff, but most of us were distracted by the election of James Peabody. In his inaugural address, Peabody pledged to be Colorado's law and order governor and vowed, "Colorado will be run like a business."

Interpretation: No unions since unions threatened the social order and the traditions upon which all successful businesses rested.

We'd heard it so many times before... A threat to class interests, to private property, to democratic institutions, to the nation itself. Socialists, anarchists, Vandals, Huns...

But this time the slander and slurs felt more dangerous. On the heels of his inaugural speech, Peabody ignored a constitutional amendment, voted in by a 72 percent margin, mandating an eight-hour day. We'd been ecstatic at its passage, never dreaming Peabody and the legislature would ignore the voice of the people. Or that outside corporations, headquartered in places like Chicago, New York and Boston, had already begun pushing their way in. It was their voices the politicians would heed.

A decade after we were crushed, John D. Rockefeller, one of the industrial titans you'll recognize to this day, orchestrated the Ludlow Massacre in which national guardsmen gunned down twenty-one people, including miners' wives and children, in their tents. The Ludlow Massacre is what historians remember. The Colorado Coalfield War led to the implementation of child labor laws and an eight-hour workday.

While the Colorado Labor Wars resulted in ghosts and
ghost towns and those of us who survived being ostracized
or drifting around like the ghosts we left behind.

INTERVIEW FROM FORGOTTEN VOICES
FROM COLORADO'S LABOR WARS

Twelve

I t was early March of 1903 when Horace Strank awaited his guest in the reading room of Colorado Springs' El Paso Club. While firearms and intoxicants were forbidden in the exclusive establishment, smoking was not, so Strank puffed on one of his beloved Havanas. And it was easy enough to sneak a sip from the flask of Macallan Whisky tucked away in an inner pocket of his suit coat. *Need to watch that, old boy,* he silently chastised himself. Between the drink, chasing the dragon in Myers Avenue's opium dens and enjoying the pretties at the Old Homestead House, he might be overindulging. He could just hear his sour-as-a-pickle Calvinist grandfather lecturing, "Nothing is more dangerous than to be blinded by prosperity." But that's because, galumphing from one failed business venture to another, his grandfather's vision remained perfect up until the day he died.

Besides, God was for mackerel snappers, holy rollers, and idiots. By the twenty-first century, man would be too enlightened to believe such drivel.

Horace Strank swore he could feel his head buzzing, his blood thrum. *It's the stress, the worry.* He was overextended, particularly since Strank's Manse was a goddamn money pit and the balance sheets on all his endeavors were precarious. Still, so long as the WFM refrained from striking, the money would continue flowing from the District to Colorado City and into his pockets. Like Spec Penrose, Strank's dad had been a doctor. But unlike Spec, Horace did not come from wealth. He was a self-made man with no intention of being pulled back down into the plebian muck from which he'd scrabbled.

Strank's gaze wandered around the otherwise empty room with its ceiling beams, plush oriental carpet, long table with neatly arranged newspapers and magazines and the enormous stuffed elk head perched above the fireplace.

Maybe I should go on one of those hunts like Teddy so loves. Roosevelt was talking about returning to Colorado to hunt bears and big cats. *Might just go with him. Bag a griz, have it stuffed and display it in the entryway of the manse.*

The El Paso Club was a prime meeting place for Horace Strank and Cripple Creek's other newly minted millionaires. Colorado Springs took pride in its nickname "Little London," and the club certainly emulated the look and feel of English aristocracy. For a moment, Strank fancied himself in a scarlet coat and black cap, galloping across English meadows and woodlands, trumpets blowing, hounds yapping on the trail of some mangy fox.

Cripple Creek had its share of foxes. And a few years back the nearby town of Gillette had hosted a bullfight.

Hmmm...

Anyway, Strank enjoyed being greeted at the club's front door as if he were royalty. Discreetly, of course. Everything about the club was discreet. Which was a primary reason great men enjoyed its environs. Ulysses Grant had played poker here and Oscar Wilde had visited. (Strank had never been a fan of *The Picture of Dorian Grey*. It struck him as possessing perverted undertones. But then, what could one expect from a Mick?) He'd even introduced himself

144

to Nikola Tesla when the inventor had dined there. Peculiar fellow with a bit of an accent, but pleasant enough.

Strank leaned forward, idly perusing the offerings on the reading table. Headline from a New York Times article: **Bill to Forbid Child Labor: South Carolina has Passed the Marshall Bill**.

"Good luck with that," he muttered, though Strank wasn't a fan of sending them below too young. The unions were big on educating their offspring, which was fine by him. Truth was, until recently Strank had never had a problem with labor, even the Western Federation of Miners. He particularly enjoyed Leprechaun and his tall tales and the conviviality of the Pick-Axe when that lush songbird performed. The Victor bunch was more radical because, with their Battle Mountain being the richest hill on earth, they could afford to be. Nevertheless, the District generally ran like a well-oiled hoisting sheave.

Still, with the rise of militant unionism, the founding of the Mine Owners Association and Citizens' Alliance had been a necessity. As he'd told members of the Denver Chamber of Commerce during a recent speech.

"Labor unions are a natural result of conditions, and they consist of a lot of people who are not as bright as they might be. These are led by a lot of tricky fellows who break into the legislature instead of the penitentiary."

"Mr. Strank!"

Pulled out of his imaginings Horace jumped, quickly recovering as he rose to greet his guest.

"Ah! Mr. McParland!" Horace clasped the smaller man's outstretched hand. He rather admired James McParland. He got the job done. And Strank was afraid the Citizens' Alliance was going to need the job done more quickly than they'd planned.

They settled in a pair of leather wing-backed chairs, bringing one closer to the other. Even though the El Paso Club was renowned for its privacy, allowing members to speak freely without worrying their remarks would appear on the front pages of the

Victor Daily Record, a man could never be too careful. After pleasantries, Strank, ever a direct man, asked, "What do you propose, McParland?"

"It's easier to keep a union out than to root it up once it takes hold," said McParland, crossing one leg over his knee in a faux relaxed gesture. "But the Pinkertons are well set for the task."

"And you in particular," Strank said, attempting to blow a smoke ring. Damn difficult if the tobacco wasn't packed just right. "Lots of Micks among the leaders. I suspect you'll take great pleasure in breaking Ronan Doyle the way you did his uncles."

McParland maintained his face in its usual mildly agreeable expression, which would never give away what he was really thinking, which was that he didn't much like or respect Horace Strank. Too many vices, too deep in debt, which led to impetuosities. Fortunately, other members of the MOA and Citizens' Alliance were cut from finer cloth.

"Shall we get down to business?" He knew he'd have to lead Strank gently but firmly to his conclusions, as he would Penrose, Tutt, and the others. Forget Jimmy Burns of the Portland. Misplaced loyalties would be that one's downfall. Unfortunately, the District's tycoons remained largely content with their workers. Complacent in their prosperity, they cheerfully acquiesced to union demands. Encouraging their thuggery. The WFM itself was responsible for every case of theft, accident, arson, and murder, not to mention every mine explosion throughout the western states. At least in McParland's telling. The Pinkerton playbook was to magnify, vilify, and persecute its enemy. Define who the WFM—all the unions—were. Eventually, an ignorant populace would be convinced, leaving McParland free to achieve his goal. Which, in this case, was the annihilation of the Western Federation of Miners.

"We've got our operatives embedded at Cripple Creek's highest levels, as we've done in Colorado City," said McParland. "We've sabotaged the smelterers for months now. They'll never get a contract that means anything."

True enough, the mill and smelter employees lived in deplorable conditions—over-worked, underpaid, clad in rags, and half-starved. Such did not stir McParland's sympathies. He himself had been a laborer, a policeman and the hardworking owner of a liquor store that had burned to its foundations, leaving him worse than penniless. Had that defeated him? No. If others were so feeble-brained that they turned to socialism, they deserved the holocaust that would soon engulf them.

"Fortunately, the bosses are having none of it. That's where we came in. One of our operatives was even elected union secretary. So far we've had forty-two dangerous union agitators fired, without our fingerprints anywhere on the deed.

"Yet on Valentine's Day, the mill workers still struck," Strank countered. "And now the WFM's demanded all mines refuse to sell ore to the ore mills in Colorado City. So far there've been twelve mines that have struck and they're threatening all the rest if they refuse to cooperate. A 'solidarity' strike, they call it." Strank could barely utter the words without his throat constricting.

"Their bosses are as predictable as they are stupid," McParland said companionably. "I eagerly anticipate the moment they call it." He would exterminate the WFM the same way he'd exterminated the Molly Maguires. And make no mistake, it had been James McParland who'd led the Mollies to the gallows.

A waiter entered with a tray containing iced lemonade. McParland poured himself and Strank a glass, after which he sipped the beverage in silence, allowing his companion time to simmer in his private terrors. McParland's job was to till the soil, plant the seeds and lovingly tend the plants until, voila, you had a bountiful harvest.

"I'll be dining with Spec Penrose, Tutt, Carlton, and the others this evening," Strank said finally. "What would you have me say?"

McParland placed his glass on a side table and stroked the ends of his handlebar mustache, as if in contemplation. The truth was he could execute this particular plan in his sleep. Play upon the mine owners' fear and greed.

"'Industrial conflicts cannot be settled by arbitration,' you tell them. Urge your clients to stand firm, reinforce their mistrust of labor's motives and actions until mistrust hardens into hatred. Assure them that if they follow your guidance, they'll emerge victorious."

No union. Docile workers. Chests of gold. Riches stacked halfway to Pikes Peak. A castle in Scotland like Andrew Carnegie's. The Hope Diamond. A fleet of those new-fashioned automobiles. It didn't matter whether you bought anything so long as you knew you could.

"'Tis a matter of good vs. evil," he said aloud. "God the creator casting Lucifer into hell for the salvation of capitalism. Tell your brethren the truth of it."

Looking puzzled, Strank studied the tip of his Havana. "I'd prefer to leave religion out of it," he finally said, leaning forward to place his cigar in a nearby ashtray.

"Union men are vermin. They must be exterminated."

Horace wouldn't go that far. He enjoyed a rapport with many of the locals and attended their picnics, parades and bare-knuckle bouts at the Topic. "Symbiotic relationship" was a phrase he'd heard Ronan Doyle use during his speeches. Fancy words coming from a pretty boy who'd never finished eighth grade. Though it hit the nail on the head, Strank had to admit.

Sensing his target's hesitation, McParland leaned forward, his expression sincere. Sincerely alarmed.

"There's a secret inner circle in the WFM composed of its head officers." He'd made this particular claim so many times, he some-times believed it. "Outlaws, the lot of them, dynamiting and destroying property and threatening your very lives, the lives of your loved ones. And all the while masquerading as ordinary union men."

"You're not meaning those officers in our District? I know all of them and they're—"

"Bloodthirsty radicals. Socialists, the lot of them!"

Horace wished he could tip his flask. McParland's accusations made his palms sweat. He frequented the Pick-Axe and its proprietor, Ronan Doyle, had always treated him with a distant politeness. (Which might masquerade for contempt. He wondered about that sometimes.) You might call Doyle and the rest "fiery" at times, but bloodthirsty?

McParland leaned forward. "And their national treasurer, that Big Bill Haywood, if he could murder every man in a suit better than his own, he would without a care." Within the last three years, the Pinkerton's Denver office had done more business eradicating the infestation of Colorado labor unions than the other five agencies in other states combined.

"Murder?" Strank echoed weakly. He imagined Cripple and Victor razed as thoroughly as during their fires. Only this conflagration might destroy his—everyone's—livelihood.

Now that he had his prey sufficiently agitated, McParland maneuvered in for the kill. "Not only have our top spies infiltrated the mill workers, but we've also got Colorado Springs' sheriff attending to our needs. Just this morning Governor Peabody signed an executive order sending three hundred National Guard troops to Colorado City." McParland had personally informed the governor of the mob violence there. Good men being beaten, property destroyed and armed bodies of men patrolling the territory like Quantrill's Raiders. Didn't matter that the locals disagreed, saying none of that had happened and events remained peaceful.

"All that takes money. Explain that to your associates. We're in the beginning stages of this particular campaign, and the owners can't stint on their funding. Leave it to the Pinkertons and we destroy Big Bill and his communist comrades so thoroughly they'll never dare show their faces again anywhere in this hemisphere."

With that, James McParland rose and took his leave, leaving a horrified—and sweaty—Horace Strank fulminating over the socialist threat that had been so cleverly hiding in plain sight.

Thirteen

Governor Peabody quickly brokered an end to the strikes; for a few weeks it seemed the hurricane had changed course. District gold miners, who wanted no part of a strike, were so relieved they set off fireworks, rang church bells and blew mine whistles, while marching bands paraded along Bennett and Victor Avenues. But soon, the vice-president of the refining company reneged on his promises. Deciding a massive show of union force was in order, Big Bill Haywood finagled quite the clever move, so that when the strike call came down on August 8, 1903, blindsided union members were furious at him and the rest of WFM leadership. And the reason Ronan found himself at Denver's national headquarters, confronting the WFM treasurer. Even seated behind his cluttered desk, Big Bill was an intimidating figure. Hands the size of hams, shoulders wide enough to remind a man that while he'd once been a miner, he'd always be a brawler.

But Ronan represented his local, and he'd faced worse than a one-eyed behemoth, no matter their common cause.

"*You* just can't call a strike. The members must vote yea or nay. A union officer can't be ordering his brothers as if he were a capitalist running the Gold Coin or Independence and his men need to do what the feck he tells them to."

Haywood leaned back in his chair, causing it to squeak in protest. "This year's convention delegates passed a resolution granting our executive board the right to call a strike and never mind voting by the rank and file." He paused. "You should know about the resolution, Adonis. You attended the convention, if I recall correct."

Aye, Ronan had, but so had Maeve, staying at the 11th Avenue Hotel on the outskirts of Denver, so he may have been a bit distracted.

Rather than remind Big Bill how much he hated that ridiculous "Adonis" nickname, Ronan said, "The District's in no mood for a strike. Particularly when they weren't allowed a vote. And they'll not take kindly to being told they should've read the fine print, that the executive board suddenly gets to call the strike while their wishes are ignored."

Haywood fixed his gaze on Ronan. Well, one eye because his right eye had been lost in a childhood whittling accident. "We've gotta organize Colorado City's smelterers. Break their bastard vice-president, who refuses to rehire good union men."

Nine men in total, laid off smelterers who didn't even want to sign a union card. And for such small stakes, Haywood was willing to engage in a pissing contest that might paralyze the entire District?

"Remember, Adonis. One Big Union."

There it was, Haywood's dream, but Ronan's as well. When all the craft trades combined with common laborers, with every working man and woman under one giant umbrella. Currently, organized labor was no different from the capitalists who pitted carpenters against draymen or muckers against maids, saying some should be paid more and others less.

Dividing the classes so we'll fight each other rather than our oppressors.

Haywood finished with a well-worn phrase: "If we workers are organized, all we have to do is to put our hands in our pockets and we've got the capitalist class whipped."

Ronan felt the enormity of it, condemning his members to months, maybe years, of hardship with no guaranteed outcome.

But we won the 1894 strike. We'll win again. We have to.

"So be it," Ronan said, meeting Haywood's gaze. "We'll be riding this train to the end of the line. I just hope it doesn't end up plunging us all into the abyss."

Even while we were well aware that America had always exploited its working class, we believed we would beat the odds. That our strike would be remembered as another milestone along the way toward the time when "All men are created equal," and "No one is above the law" were other than slogans.

Our age was one of great industrial unrest, though that's been largely forgotten. Those in charge will not be handing over the blueprints once used to fight them. Far easier to pretend working men and women always kept their heads bowed, always cheerfully went to the slaughter.

But that's never been so. No one remembers the Homestead Steel Strike, or the Haymarket Riot or the Pullman Strike, where workers fought back and were shot dead or executed seeking a better quality of life for future generations who neither know nor would care if they did know.

Nor do you remember what happened here in the District. But it happened all the same.

One of the men we hated most was Sherman M. Bell, adjutant general of the Colorado National Guard, and the man in charge of enforcing martial law. Some might call Bell handsome, with his dark, slicked-down hair and button eyes, military mien, and fancy way of dressing. His custom-made

uniform, which had cost him a thousand dollars—all gold
lace, cords, and tassels—was an affront to good taste.
Sherman Bell was a man who knew everything and never
wavered in that belief. Bell, who was also a mine manager,
often referred to Peabody as "His Excellency the Governor
of Colorado," and was confident that "Me, God, and
Governor Peabody" would destroy the "damned anarchistic
federation" that was the WFM. And, as he went about doing
precisely that, he justified his reign of terror as a "military
necessity, which recognizes no laws, either civil or social."
The second was General John Chase, a Denver oculist who
was Sherman Bell's field commander. While Chase wasn't
quite fifty years old, with his white hair, bushy white
mustache and portly build, he looked far older. His preferred
uniform was a duster coat, high-topped boots and a battered
campaign hat. Another belligerent, who preferred shouting
to speaking. During the strike, Chase ordered mass arrests,
many without charges, and imprisoned strikers in deplorable
conditions, along with anyone who spoke too publicly in
favor of the miners. All of it was unconstitutional. Chase
was ultimately court-martialed for his actions, but no matter.
Governor Peabody immediately reinstated him as
commander of Colorado's National Guard.

After it was all over and we were spread like ashes in the
wind, I used to pray that everyone involved, even those like
James McParland who weren't mentioned here but played
their part, would die terrible deaths.

They didn't. Several went on to participate in the Colorado
Coal Wars and the Ludlow Massacre.

All went on to enjoy long, prosperous lives.

ANONYMOUS UNION OFFICER INTERVIEW FROM FORGOTTEN
VOICES FROM COLORADO'S LABOR WARS

PART SIX

August–November 1903

*The United States has had the bloodiest and most violent labor
history of any industrial nation in the world.*

— PHILIP TAFT AND PHILIP ROSS, "AMERICAN
LABOR VIOLENCE: ITS CAUSES, CHARACTER, AND
OUTCOME"

Fourteen

W hile Maeve was sometimes frightened, sometimes indignant, sometimes despairing with each new horror, she never thought of abandoning Ronan for the safety of the twenty-first century. Even knowing the ultimate outcome of this war, she erased the knowledge, not by pretending, but by ignoring it. The way most of us do with death. Intellectually, you understand its inevitability, but you don't actually believe it will come, not for you. Yet, in the stillness of night, wrapped in Ronan's arms, listening to the steady beating of his heart, Maeve lay awake, reminding herself, *This moment. I will hold it close and not ask for more.* After the strike was called, Ronan began spending the night at the Gold Nugget boarding house where she was staying rather than at the National Hotel, which seemed inappropriately extravagant. "I'm concerned for your safety," he'd said. The WFM had built up an impressive strike fund for its miners, but everyone remained nervous, anxious to return to work and the District to return to "normal." When local merchants declared they'd only accept cash payments for goods, the WFM organized co-operative stores.

That's the way it worked. Mine owners made a move on the chess-board; the miners checked it.

While Maeve couldn't sleep, knowing, yet not really knowing what was to come, she knew Ronan didn't sleep any better than she did. She experienced such a tenderness toward him for pretending he did so she wouldn't worry; for willing himself to stay still lest he disturb her; for forcing himself to pretend that his mind wasn't aswirl when his thoughts were written upon the darkness: his fears; his plans and schemes to anticipate the MOA and Citizens' Alliance's next move, to somehow keep his members and their families, all the working men and women of the District, safe. To outlast the mine owners and win this strike. Without violence, as he and the WFM leaders stressed from the beginning. At the end of each union meeting, miners recited a pledge promising to remain peaceful. "Give them no reason to arrest us," was Ronan's new mantra.

Not that Ronan was opposed to violence. She was not so naïve as to pretend otherwise. Recently, Maeve had come across him, Uncle Liam and Leprechaun in the back storage room of the Pick-Axe, with an old rug pulled back to reveal a trap door. Around them, an arsenal of weapons, including a wooden box marked "dynamite."

Ronan looked up, startled. "I thought you locked the door," he said to Leprechaun.

"You've not seen anything, sweetheart, have you?" Leprechaun said to Maeve with a wink.

As if this were all a joke.

The month of September reminded Maeve of those Advent countdown calendars where each flap reveals yet another surprise until reaching its happy destination. Only there would be no happy destination at the end of this calendar.

On September 4, Governor Peabody sent in the National Guard, even though no violence had been reported. On Labor Day, five thousand members of organized labor, all carrying the banners of their particular union and various lodges, paraded along Bennett Avenue, so many that it took an hour for the entirety to walk from one end to the other. Immediately afterward, the National Guard—whose salaries were paid by the business community rather than the State—began arresting union officers and those known to be most vocally sympathetic to the cause.

Enormous searchlights were brought in and placed on the mountains surrounding various towns. Telegraph stations were set up, as were field telephones to provide communication with Denver and the rest of the United States, all the way up to President Roosevelt. The National Guard hauled in a Gatling gun and armed its troops with a thousand Krag-Jorgensen rifles—a repeating bolt-action rifle—and sixty thousand rounds of ammunition.

By September 13, the military was in complete control of the District. Troops established a bull pen, their version of a military prison, in the mining camp of Goldfield. Union meetings were broken up; their members harassed or imprisoned without charges. In the dead of night, miners were removed from their homes and carted off to the bull pen. Since no charges were ever proffered, the miners had no way to defend themselves.

For its headquarters, the Colorado militia commandeered the Mining Exchange building, where miners purchased their supplies, where their gold was weighed, tested, and sold to the highest bidder, and where more shares were traded than any other exchange in the world.

Right in the heart of Cripple Creek.

In this poisonous climate, a misinterpreted look, a heated exchange of words might lead to an explosion. With each breath, you inhaled the tension along with the fall air. Fear, like some chronic illness, took up residence in Maeve's very bones. Women conducted their business with heads down and gazes averted to avoid antagonizing soldiers, who weren't shy about brandishing their bayonets. Children were kept close. Hostility emanated from the muckers, timbermen, pick boys, powder monkeys, every man attached to the mines, but they kept to their pledge of non-violence.

The first strikebreakers, fifty-one in all, were shipped in, some from as far away as Michigan. Flanked by troops, they were marched down Bennett Avenue to cries of "Scabs! Scabs!" When one, a Dane named Emil Peterson, yelled to his fellow strikebreakers, 'Don't go to work,'" soldiers opened fire.

That evening as Emil Peterson was recounting his story to a packed union hall, troops barged in and approached Ronan, who'd been overseeing the meeting from the dais.

"Ronan Doyle," barked the commanding officer, "come with us. You're under arrest."

Ronan was taken to the bull pen, a filthy, squalid tent without blankets or bedding or other comforts, where he was greeted by three other union leaders.

The armed thug who'd pushed Ronan inside the pen warned, "You so much as appear an inch outside the entrance, and we'll blow your head off."

After which the four union men settled in to wait for whatever came next.

On Monday, September 21, when Ronan and the other three prisoners were scheduled to appear in court, sharpshooters watched from atop the cupolas fronting the National Hotel where Winfield Scott Stratton had once booked an entire floor for his lodgings. Gatling guns were positioned in the center of Bennett Avenue, muzzles pointing toward Midland Depot, awaiting the prisoners' train. As the scheduled time of 1:30 neared, trumpets blared and mounted troops dashed along the avenue, ordering people to

"Halt!" and "Clear the street!" while soldiers prodded bystanders with bayonets.

After Ronan and his three companions disembarked from the train, they were marched to Cripple Creek's courthouse flanked by two files of infantry. More awaited at its entrance.

Accompanied by Uncle Liam, Maeve had arrived hours earlier in order to get a seat. As they pushed inside, Uncle Liam's hand in the small of her back helped ground her. She seated herself in the front row, next to the other prisoners' wives, a silent acknowledgement of her position. Even though she and Ronan had been discreet about their relationship, there were no secrets in the District. Maeve was secretly proud to stake her claim, even though love was nothing like a mining claim and Ronan Doyle probably had no idea he'd been "claimed."

Despite the open transom windows, the afternoon air was unpleasantly warm with the smell of too many bodies, of Uncle Liam's pomade, tobacco and (Maeve hoped she was wrong), alcohol. But as soon as Ronan and the prisoners arrived, she forgot everything but her beloved. Since Ronan stood a head above the others, he was clearly visible. Even in his disheveled state, with his hair tied in a careless knot at the nape of his neck, his white shirt streaked with dirt, his Levi's stained, his hands cuffed in front and shackled to the others, Maeve likened him to a king among his subjects. (Ronan would have lectured her about the whole "king" analogy, reminding her no man was above another.) Her heart swelled with pride, love, and even awe. She'd seen this transformation on the Fourth of July, the moment when Ronan became something more than a man, when he seemed infused with a supernal power.

Judge Seeds presided over the hearing. Seeds had a reputation for fairness, though like so many, he was a union man, which didn't sit well with white-haired, white-mustachioed General Chase.

Seeds first demanded that Chase produce a writ of habeas corpus, explaining the charges against each of the prisoners.

Chase refused.

Which caused Judge Seeds to quote the U.S. Constitution: "The privilege of the writ of habeas corpus shall not be suspended unless when in cases of rebellion or invasion the public safety may require it."

Chase refused again on Tuesday. On Wednesday. Prisoners marched in. Marched out. Soldiers remained. Gatling guns remained. Sharpshooters remained.

On Thursday, Chase warned Judge Seeds, who had arrived at the end of his patience, "Whatever the decision, I will return the prisoners to Camp Goldfield unless otherwise ordered by Governor Peabody."

Judge Seeds ordered the prisoners released. Immediately.

General Chase marched Ronan and the others out of the courtroom and back to the bull pen.

"How can this be?" Maeve asked Uncle Liam.

"However long the day, the evening will come," Uncle Liam said, smiling his Ronan smile.

Which might have been more comforting had Maeve not suspected Uncle Liam had once again succumbed to the siren call of demon rum.

Two other events took place before September mercifully gave way to October. On September 29, the offices of the *Victor Daily Record*, the lone mouthpiece of the Western Federation of Miners, was raided and its employees marched off to the Goldfield bull pen. At this time, one of the heroes of the strike made her first appearance. Emma Langdon, a dark-haired, dark-eyed beauty, was a linotype operator, as was her husband. After soldiers arrested him and the other male employees, Emma barricaded herself in the Daily Record office, and with the aid of two helpers, produced the morning edition. The headline, which would later become famous, read: **SOMEWHAT DISFIGURED, BUT STILL IN THE RING.**

The following day an even more devastating blow occurred. The Gold Coin Mine and Economic Mill, both properties of the Woods Investment Company, were forced to shut down. As the miners exited work, they were met by Mr. Woods, who apologetically stated they'd have to drop their WFM membership if they wanted to continue working. All declined.

Soon after, The First National Bank of Victor was declared insolvent after striking miners withdrew their funds to flee the District. All local projects were put on hold or abandoned, quickly driving the Woods Investment Company into bankruptcy. The Woods family, who had done so much to create the town of Victor, never recovered. By the time the last Woods brother died in 1932, he was so poor his friends had to raise the money to bury him.

Fifteen

I wish you were here so I would know. *It's like you've got a destination in mind without a map to put in all the side roads and small towns along the way. Here we are with Ronan in those bull pens I remember seeing in photos. Little white tents? But they didn't mean anything. Just black and white images of buildings and moonscapes and grim-looking miners, but now it's in technicolor, all around me, and it means* something. *I wish I were a fortune teller, not to predict the future, but to change it. So many of the people I've met. They aren't asking for much, but they deserve a little, don't they?*

Which brings me back to our sainted ancestor. Do you ever wonder how Saint Paddy ever made enough money to purchase Shamrock Ranch? When I compare him to Ronan, to a lot of the others I've met, I can't see how he ever became a hero. He talks a good game, but does he actually do anything? And he's always lurking about, speaking when he should be silent. Is he, with spies everywhere, giving away secrets with his big mouth?

Is "The Tale of Saint Paddy and the WFM" documented, or just family lore?

I hope you're getting my journals, that they're not hanging out in the ethers somewhere. I'll write more often. Don't worry. PLEASE! I can't leave, can't even think of leaving... Abandoning Ronan right now wouldn't just break my heart. It would shred my soul.

~

When Ronan appeared in the doorway of the Pick-Axe as Maeve was readying to perform, she burst into tears. Running to him, she flung her arms around his neck. He looked exhausted, dirty, and after Leprechaun and the few customers cheered him and crowded close in order to touch him like some giant good luck charm, maybe a bit pleased with himself. "Are you enjoying this?" she wanted to snap. "When it's killing me, all of us?" Instead, she buried her head against the roughness of his shirt, inhaling his smell as if it were the finest perfume, until well-wishers had retreated, and her emotions had slowed from a torrent to a stream.

After releasing her, the first thing Ronan whispered in her ear was "I need a bath."

After they retreated to his upstairs apartment, Maeve helped him undress and scanned his body, that flawless, exquisite body. He'd lost weight; bruises ringed his wrists and ankles. She ran her fingers lightly along an ugly discoloration on his right side that looked as if it could have been delivered by the kick of a boot or a rifle butt. Imagining the scene she blinked back tears, but she didn't question him. He appeared exhausted, like a music box wound down to its finish. Easing himself into the steaming tub with a satisfied groan, he soaped up a wash cloth and scrubbed away nearly two weeks' worth of grime.

After he finished, Maeve knelt behind him, where he rested his head, and asked, "May I shampoo your hair?"

When he nodded, she felt as if she'd been granted a prize. Ronan was usually so loathe to accept help from anyone, as if he must always be strong, always act the part of Ronan Doyle, WFM president. A symbol rather than a man. After washing and rinsing his hair, she massaged his scalp, causing him to sigh with pleasure.

I wish bubble bath was invented so I could create clouds of bubbles for you. Or maybe scented oils, rose petals, rubber duckies? Anything...

She continued circling Ronan's scalp with gentle fingertips, grateful she could touch him with purpose, not because she was needy, though in truth she longed to run her fingers the length of his body, caressing the planes of his muscles, the swell of his chest in gentle exploration, as if caressing a working man's version of Michelangelo's *David*.

Heaven. Exquisite pain. Hell.

Ronan's breathing deepened, the dark hair on his incomparable chest accentuating its rise and fall. If he dozed off, she could devour him with her eyes as much as she pleased without embarrassment. Her fingers itched to trace the outline of his perfect profile, which she often did when they made love, as she ran her fingers through his hair and caressed him in the act. But this was different somehow. Inappropriate to be so hungry for him outside of lovemaking.

"I could sleep for a week," Ronan murmured, when she moved from his scalp to his neck and shoulders, careful not to disturb his necklaces. "We had no blankets and our bed was the ground. We ate 'slop on a plate,' we called it. With our fingers. It wasn't pleasant."

Maeve was indignant for him and protective, telling herself she'd rather suffer this than him. And at that moment she meant it.

I love you, she thought, the declaration so loud in her head she was sure he would hear. *If I could give you the world, I would.* She was glad she'd never fallen in love before; this feeling was an ache that made it hard to swallow, at times, hard to breathe.

"Have you ever been in love?" she whispered, and she was immediately appalled that something so close to her thoughts had been uttered. How selfish when she should be concerned only with caring for him. His breathing remained steady and she hoped he'd dozed off.

Ronan rolled his head from side to side. "Once, a long time ago," he said softly.

Maeve felt it, that expanding lump. Not "Aye, with you, Maeve Mooney."

Her fingers continued their massage. "What happened?" she managed through her disappointment.

"She wasn't who I thought she was," he said. It was little more than a mumble. He might be talking in his sleep.

And if Ronan knew who Maeve truly was, what would he say about her?

Sixteen

M id-October, Leprechaun and Bridget Kehoe married. Maeve was surprised that that Harry Orchard character rather than Uncle Liam or Ronan served as best man. But considering Uncle Liam had fallen off the wagon and Ronan was boycotting the Catholic Church where the Ceremony of Matrimony was being performed at this very hour, perhaps that made sense.

"We can still catch part of the Mass if you'd like," Maeve said. They were in Ronan's room where Ronan was bent over his desk, scribbling notes from his latest phone call with Big Bill. Wouldn't it be a trick to write her family about their great-great-grandparents' wedding? Still, chronicling personal events seemed self-indulgent, even petty. Her entire being was focused on staying close to Ronan, to comfort him with her presence, if that were possible. The strain, the sleeplessness, the times he looked utterly devastated, made her want to weep. Instead, she did what she could to telegraph she was confident of victory by joining the Women's Auxiliary and throwing herself into strike-related activities.

Ronan ran a hand over his hair, unbound in the privacy of their room. "I'll not set foot in a church until after we've won. Not when Bishop Matz so publicly condemned the strikes. He called socialism and the WFM godless, when he is Satan himself, topped by a mitre."

Nicholas Matz was the Bishop of Denver, which made him one of Colorado's most powerful prelates. His words, his condemnation would strike many of his parishioners as the direct voice of God.

"It was dreadful," Maeve agreed. She'd been beside Ronan when Father Volpe had read Matz's letter from the pulpit. Ronan's face had paled; his hands had clenched into fists. He'd leaned forward as if readying to rise, so she'd placed a warning hand on his thigh. What would they call it in the twenty-first century? The optics of the situation? Don't do anything that could be used by the Citizens' Alliance. *Ronan Doyle has a dangerous temper. Ronan Doyle is cracking under the strain. Ronan Doyle is godless. Ronan Doyle is violent. Ronan Doyle is a socialist.*

"Matz came out on the side of the owners. So much for 'Blessed are those who hunger and thirst for righteousness, for they shall be satisfied.'"

Maeve's gaze drifted to the rosary on the stand beside Ronan's bed. He often ran his fingers over each of the decades as if they were worry beads. She knew the psychic cost to Ronan of breaking with his religion. Another betrayal. Which made her even more determined to be his refuge.

"He said it's sinful to seek heaven here on earth rather than in the hereafter. When if we only wait until we die, the roles will be inverted, and the poor, the afflicted, will become the landlords."

"That's just one man's opinion," Maeve responded helplessly, foolishly. She might no longer fully believe, but Ronan did. Stepping up behind him, she massaged his shoulders, trying to transfer her love, her confidence, her belief in him through her touch.

Ronan gazed at the print of the Sacred Heart he'd placed next to the tintypes of his parents. Jesus, His pierced hands outstretched, His scarlet heart radiating outside his vestment, His expression placid.

"Wonder how Bishop Matz would like mucking ore eight hours a day? Wonder how he'd like eating hard-boiled eggs from a dinner pail with filthy fingernails and cracked hands rather than dining at the Brown Palace with Spec Penrose and Horace Strank?"

Maeve bent over to kiss Ronan's ear; her hands continued their gentle kneading. Never had she felt so inadequate; never had she wished she could bargain with God, sacrifice what? Her life, her soul, to change the outcome of the strike? Or if not that, to ease Ronan's pain? What a misery to be in love.

When I was one-and-twenty
I heard a wise man say,
"Give crowns and pounds and guineas
But not your heart away;

Thirty-two years old and she'd forgotten A.E. Housman's advice. If only she could snatch back her heart, return to the before time when she didn't believe in love, when she didn't need love because she had no glimmering of what it was...

Ronan sighed and leaned back against his chair. "'Tis a bleak time just now," he whispered, as if others might be listening outside the door and would herald his confession across the District. "Mines reopening with some of our men slinking back. If they break us here, it's all over for the rest of the state."

"It will get better," she murmured. "Right will prevail in the end." Knowing it was a lie. Still believing it.

"Sometimes, I wonder whether the WFM, me and every member of the industry, are anachronisms. Like John Henry, the steel driving man. Who beat a steam drill only to die afterward. Is that what this is all about? Fighting a battle we've already lost?"

Ronan stood and shook himself, like a dog shedding water. "The wedding must be over by now." He kissed Maeve on the forehead and smiled down at her, a smile that was as bone weary as it was false. "Let us go celebrate the union of the battling lovebirds."

Leprechaun and his bride arrived to great applause, after which they took their places upon the dais where Ronan usually conducted meetings. Leprechaun was dressed in a highfalutin blue suit complete with waistcoat and silk cravat while Bridget was swathed all in white. Aye, and wasn't white the height of irony after the years she'd spent in the dance halls after Uncle Liam had cast her out?

Ronan would bet the moon that Bridget Kehoe was in a family way. She'd never have married Paddy Mooney otherwise. Obviously, her latest scheme had failed to bring Uncle Liam scurrying back, though some misadventure had found him seeking the bottle.

Toasts from the dais. Harry Orchard, freckle-faced and grinning, bowler tipped jauntily over one eye, stood to raise a glass. Facing the newlyweds, he said, "May peace and plenty be the first to lift the latch to your door and happiness be your guest today and evermore."

Everyone cheered. Beside him was his own bride, for Orchard too had recently married—which made him both a bigamist, for he had a wife in Canada, and a fool, thinking one could hide their secrets in the District. Ronan suspected he was one of those relaying WFM business to the Pinkertons.

One of many.

From her position on the dais, Bridget Mooney nee Kehoe bared her teeth in an ossified smile, but inside she was screaming. It wasn't fair, none of it. How had she ended up here with an alcoholic midget, when she'd been Pearl de Vere's most popular girl and it had only been a matter of time before one of Pearl's wealthy "johns" would marry her and set her up in a mansion on Denver's Capitol Hill. Until that business with Horace Strank when Byrdie hadn't stolen anything... Strank had simply misplaced his wallet...

Paddy bumped his shoulder against her and leaned in to whisper against her ear. "Have I told you, *macushla,* this is the happiest day of my life?"

Paddy's breath reeked of alcohol. If there weren't a hundred pairs of eyes on them, Bridget would have slapped him alongside the head the way he deserved. Instead, she turned her ossified smile in his direction, not meeting his gaze, and wished herself far away. Not back to her months in Pearl's brothel, or that awful April day when Cripple Creek burned. Yes, she'd been in a room above the Central Dance hall, just as people said, and yes, she'd fallen on hard times, and she might have been entertaining a "friend," but no one would have believed the way some crazy old hag in a sack dress and braids wrapped around her head had come barging into her room screaming about poisonous lineages and dipsomaniacs and she'd been the one who'd knocked over that gas stove, not Bridget, the way so many accused. A stroke of luck that a second fire four days later had been much worse, leaving a third of Cripple homeless and no one concerned about Byrdie Kehoe.

"Mr. President," Leprechaun yelled, waving his half-empty Coors bottle in the direction of the dance floor. "Come up and toast our happiness. And then to the golden future of Local 40 and the Western Federation of Miners!" Ever the fool, he was gloating over his triumph—that it was he, Padrick Sean Mooney, rather than a Doyle, who'd put the two-dollar (and far from impressive) ring he'd purchased at Raine's Jewelry on her finger.

Bridget didn't miss Ronan Doyle's flinch, the shake of the head, then acquiescence as the crowd cheered, leaving *her* side to approach the dais. Once there, Ronan faced the guests with his back to her. Deliberate, as if he thought she wouldn't notice. But she knew what that meant. He still loved her. Feigning such indifference to hide his true opinion.

"May your home be filled with laughter. May your pockets be filled with gold..."

He was mocking her, of course. And probably yet brokenhearted, though he'd had the courtesy to at least show his face at her nuptials. Not like the other Doyle, who was a coward to the core.

Surreptitiously, the former Bridget Kehoe laced her hands over the silk material on her stomach and cursed the unfairness of her fate.

"They look happy, don't they?" Maeve asked after the tables were being moved aside for dancing.

More smug is how Ronan would have described Leprechaun, at least, for he'd be believing he'd bested the Doyle boys. Truth was Ronan could scarce remember the lovestruck noddy he'd once been, and he suspected that was why Uncle Liam was drowning his past mistake in a barrel of Jim Beam. Accepting all the blame for succumbing to the charms of a young woman supposedly engaged to his nephew. When "Byrdie" Kehoe had played them both.

So odd he'd once believed Byrdie to be a porcelain figurine, exquisite as a Fabergé egg. What a fool he'd been! Reciting poetry —Shakespeare, Burns, Byron, Browning—because he despaired of capturing the magnificence of Bridget Kehoe's eyes, the meadow of wildflowers that was her scent, the dazzlement of her body pressed against his, which left him tongue-tied and moonstruck. *"She walks in beauty, like the night..."* In the end she'd overplayed her hand. Aye, he and his uncle had both ended up loving her, their Lady Macbeth of the Mountains. Ronan had long ago forgiven Uncle Liam for his betrayal, though Liam had not forgiven himself. And "Byrdie" had ended in the dance halls and on her back where she belonged. Until reinventing herself a time or three...

Leprechaun guided his new bride, she of the rictus grin that never reached her eyes, onto the dance floor, while Ronan, Maeve and their fellow band members played "When We are Married." Ronan silently charted the course of their union and its inevitable outcome. What Padrick Mooney and Bridget Kehoe had most in common was their mutual animosity. If they did not murder each other, then pity the offspring of such a vipers' union. For the thousandth time, Ronan was grateful he was not tonight's groom.

And while she might be able to fool her present audience, Ronan knew what was left of Byrdie Kehoe's shriveled pit of a heart was with Uncle Liam, passed out in the Pick-Axe's storeroom.

A pall had settled upon the entire District, as surely as the pollution belching from countless smokestacks—another reminder that the mines themselves were running at near capacity. Still, November of 1903 started off on a hopeful note with a prominent union member being elected Teller County assessor. "It's a sign we can win at the ballot box," Ronan told his members following the vote count. "As we will win the strike."

Ronan's optimism was misplaced. Terrorism arrived on the winter winds. Night riders roamed the District. Some, dressed in white robes similar to those of the KKK and nicknamed whitecappers, dragged miners or union leaders from their shacks, beat them up and threw them in Goldfield's bull pen. Union meetings disrupted. Women's Auxiliary meetings disrupted. An eight-thousand-book library destroyed. The handful of people who dared linger on city boardwalks spoke in hushed tones, continually swiveling their heads, as if their conversations would cause soldiers to spontaneously appear and cart them off to Goldfield. While saloons remained open, with restricted hours, there was none of the former raucous laughter and high spirits. The youngest and prettiest painted ladies fled the District.

Maeve flung herself into duties at the Women's Auxiliary. She helped raise bail bonds, feed imprisoned miners and distribute strike relief. She organized various entertainments, sometimes for harried mothers, sometimes for children, sometimes for the entire family. To raise relief funds, she gave a free concert at the Topic Theatre, which was filled to the upper tiers. She and Annie Fein had taught the children, with Timmy in the lead, to sing "America the Beautiful," which was greeted with a standing ovation. Emma Langdon, who had been responsible for publishing the *Victor Daily Record* with its famous headline back in September, gave lectures on labor history and insurrections such as the French Revolution and the English Peasants' Revolt of 1381. While Langdon had once declared, "A woman's place is in the home," her new nickname was "Labor's Joan of Arc." Even national officers of the WFM began consulting her concerning local conditions.

No matter how exhausted, Maeve remained awake in her room at the Gold Nugget until she heard the key in the lock and Ronan slip inside. Imagining all sorts of horrible things: Ronan being commandeered by whitecappers and hanged from one of the few remaining trees in the District that hadn't been chopped down for buildings or firewood. Or being tortured on yet another trumped-up charge by that horrible General Chase with his enormous white mustache and scruffy canvas duster.

Snuggling against Ronan's warm body, she would murmur, "Missed you." Before they drifted off to sleep, she'd make sure to speak only of inconsequential things. Never about the latest typhoid outbreak or Annie Fein's neighbor who'd slunk back to work at Victor's Gold Coin Mine.

Ronan had enough challenging news during the day.

"Let me be your refuge," she prayed.

If only for a handful of hours.

PART SEVEN
Winter 1903 – January 1904

❧

There is no period in American labor history where violence was so systematically used by employers as during the Colorado Labor Wars.

— PHILIP TAFT AND PHILIP ROSS, "AMERICAN LABOR VIOLENCE: ITS CAUSES, CHARACTER, AND OUTCOME"

Seventeen

❦

As fall slid into winter of 1903, all the western slope, much of Colorado was aflame—Idaho Springs. Telluride. Durango. Denver. Places so beautiful your breath caught in your throat at the looking. Monstrous slabs of granite, ravines running down their surfaces like tears in an ancient face. Waterfalls and streams teeming with trout. Lakes bluer than the cerulean sky reflected upon their surface. Old growth forests, meadows riotous with wildflowers, scarlet and gold aspen in autumn, now winter bare. Amidst all that natural splendor were slapdash towns clinging to mountainsides; shacks and tents; Tipples; headframes; smokestacks; effluvium smearing crystal skies; tailings, roads scratched into the sides of mountains, into the hearts of those majestic forests. Hundreds of thousands of tunnels burrowed into the earth as if made by gigantic gophers.

Desperate miners and their families vowed they'd not succumb to the militias and the owners. They'd not break the strike. Because you can't eat scenery and you can't buy much with scrip. And winter had arrived in the high country, hard and brutal as Colorado winters are.

But the miners were as hard as the winters.

On November 8, 1903, coal miners went on strike in the southern and northern coalfields. Mother Jones, the famous United Mine Workers' organizer, arrived in Colorado. As a young woman, Mary Harris Jones's husband and four children had died of yellow fever. Four years later, her dress shop had been destroyed in the Great Chicago Fire of 1871. She'd spent the rest of her life facing down presidents, politicians and business owners on behalf of the impoverished. While she sent encouragement to the District with slogans like "Pray for the dead and fight like hell for the living," she hopped a train for Trinidad and the coal fields.

Temperatures were bitter there; snow blanketed the plains and mountains and the winds howled like wolves begging for entrance. Miners were evicted from their company-owned houses and relegated to tents. Forced to survive on strike benefits of sixty-three cents a week, many were reduced to tying their feet in gunny sacks and parceling out rapidly dwindling rations. Their demands were the usual: eight-hour day, a check by a weighman representing the miners, payment in money rather than scrip. To make sure their men wouldn't be tempted to return to work, union officers sent thousands out of state where conditions, wages and working hours were far more favorable.

Governor Peabody and Colorado's citizens quickly turned their attention from the gold fields to the coal fields. It was one thing to be inconvenienced by a disruption in precious metals, but without coal how could Coloradans heat their homes?

On November 11, a conciliatory Governor Peabody told reporters:

"I hold that every man has a right to work, whether he is union or non-union. When a man is ready and willing to work and is interfered with, I will furnish him the protection that he, as an American citizen, is entitled to."

On November 19, President Theodore Roosevelt denied Governor Peabody's request that the president supply such troops as needed to preserve order in the Telluride district, where many of the coal mines were located.

Soon after, the coal strike was settled.

Events in the District were about to escalate.

Maeve wouldn't understand the importance of one seemingly innocuous slip of paper until after the crime.

She and the entire Fein family had been crammed into Uncle Liam's small bedroom off the Pick-Axe kitchen and storage area, where he was still recovering from his latest bender.

As a treat, Maeve had purchased three Black Cows—root beer floats—from Cripple Creek Brewing. It amused her that the creator of what would become an institution had been inspired by a moonlight view of snow-capped Cow Mountain. Add a scoop of ice cream to a glass of Myers Avenue Red Root Beer and *voila*! And since such treats were too expensive for the Feins and Maeve's bank balance remained plenty healthy, she'd happily splurged.

While everyone savored their treat, Maeve had picked up the copy of *Alice in Wonderland* she'd bought Timmy for his birthday. Timmy was enamored of many books, such as *The Call of the Wild*, currently being serialized in *The Saturday Evening Post*, but Maeve liked to think *Alice* remained his favorite because she'd purchased it for him and he yet retained a bit of his former crush.

Idly, she flipped through the contents. On the first page, Timmy had circled eleven letters scattered throughout the text, for what reason she had no idea. Beyond that, she flipped through the chapters and drawings when she noticed a slim piece of paper, no more than two inches long tucked into the middle of a page. What caught her attention was the handwriting, which she recognized from invoices and WFM notes she'd seen Ronan peruse. Maeve removed the paper. **"16 11 Outside Anaconda Spikes"** was written in Leprechaun's distinctive handwriting.

Huh? Maeve frowned. Timmy must have picked the slip up somewhere to use as a bookmark. But what did it mean? The name of a brand of whiskey or beer she'd never heard of? Or maybe Leprechaun had simply been doodling.

She returned the piece of paper to *Alice* and promptly forgot it.

Until the Florence and Cripple Creek train was nearly derailed.

~

The sky was a black bowl, the stars and moon erased, the crust of snow beneath Ronan's feet silver and shadowed. He followed far enough behind the pair that he needn't worry about discovery. Besides, the two men would be following the F.& C.C. tracks, making them in no danger of vanishing. Ronan just wasn't sure what they were up to, though he had an idea.

As he crept along, Ronan's mind jumped to the bleak Dartmoor moors and the baying monster of death he'd been reading about in *The Hound of the Baskervilles*, recently serialized in the *Strand*. "Presume nothing," Sherlock Holmes had warned, which was good advice, though like most Englishmen, Holmes was a bit of a ponce. Ronan pushed away images of a great glowing dog bent on murder for, as Holmes had mused, "The devil's agents may be of flesh and blood."

And carrying themselves about on two feet.

For weeks, Ronan had suspected someone close to him was on the Pinkerton payroll. It was simply a matter of sorting out the traitor—or traitors'—identities. Ronan had kept his own counsel, planted false stories, noted suspected individuals' schedules, when they appeared and disappeared, the times their remarks did not quite add up or his gut warned something was off. He could not afford to trust anyone.

The night air sliced Ronan's lungs, but it kept him awake. Not that he could sleep much anyway. His footsteps crackled softly with each step, the only sound in a world frozen to silence. It was that time between shift changes and since night raids had diminished, guardsmen were largely keeping to their tents. Rail walkers would be inspecting the tracks, but dozens of lines crisscrossed and meandered so there would always be places to hide. His quarry didn't seem all that concerned about being discovered. Might be the liquid courage they'd undoubtedly downed.

Near a high embankment outside of the town of Anaconda, Ronan halted neath the trunk of a lone pine to watch the pair. More blurs in the dark than anything else, they seemed to be bending over the tracks near a bridge and moving about. Scrapes, whispers carried easily in the still air. Were they sabotaging the tracks? If they were thinking to further damage the strike by derailing a train, causing it to tumble three hundred feet into a canyon, thereby bringing the wrath of the entire state down on organized labor, Ronan would deal with them himself. Nor, despite the stain on his immortal soul, would he suffer a moment's sorrow. Life was cheap. Life was fleeting. Didn't matter whether you possessed a safe full of gold bullion or a pocket of scrip. Didn't matter if you were Pope Pius X or James Peabody. Every living creature ended the same way. If it came to that, Ronan wouldn't flinch from what needed to be done. A bullet to the head? A tumble down an abandoned shaft? Pummel the traitors to death with his fists?

If those two eejits think to destroy the rest of us, I'll personally send them to the devil.

Which was why when word came down that railroad detectives had warned the F. C.&C. engineer they'd discovered several spikes and bolts had been removed from the rails on a particularly high embankment outside Anaconda, Ronan received his answer.

And that broke his heart.

On the morning of November 16, before three in the morning, the F. C.& C, carrying forty union and non-union miners from work to rooming houses in Cripple Creek, averted catastrophe by stopping mere yards from damaged tracks.

All the newspapers reported some version of the following: The train's engineer, William Rush, claimed he'd received an anonymous "tip." After conducting an investigation near the designated spot, Rush had discovered a loosened rail with all the spikes removed. Or had rail detectives uncovered the sabotage? Stories differed. Regardless, after the incident had been reported to Sherman Bell, and his troops had spread through the camps, two union men were arrested and confessed.

When Maeve told Ronan about the piece of paper she'd come across in Timmy's book, "**16 11 Outside Anaconda Spikes,**" the message was easy enough to interpret. Remove spikes outside the town of Anaconda on November 16. Warn the engineer beforehand? Blame the union?

Conveniently, the wrong men had been arrested and were released. Meaning Leprechaun and Harry Orchard were in the employ of the Pinkertons and therefore untouchable.

No one was ever convicted of the sabotage.

Eighteen

~~~~~

O n November 21, 1903, two management employees, a
superintendent and shift boss, were killed by an explosion
at the six-hundred-foot level of the Vindicator Mine. Newspapers
immediately blamed the union. An "inner circle" of WFM agitators
was universally mentioned. Since "inner circle" was one of
Pinkerton James McParland's favorite phrases as he wove his
conspiracies about the nefarious union, he was obviously one of the
reporters' main sources.

Ronan stayed in close touch with Big Bill and Denver headquarters. Easy to see the spin: violent union, lawless strikers, godless
anarchists. All of which anyone with a thinking brain would disre-
gard as nonsense. It was true the Vindicator was an ugly, sprawling
mess of buildings and pilings, employing three hundred men and
with two shafts providing accessibility to five miles of underground
workings. Easy enough for somebody to haul in dynamite and rig
some sort of death trap. However, the Vindicator was under military guard, only non-union men were employed there and no union
members could enter by the shaft where the explosion took place.
Irrelevant, of course. The WFM and other unions could only relate

their version of events to the few remaining sympathetic reporters and brace for the fallout.

"Who had the most to gain from the explosion?" Big Bill asked Ronan over the phone line recently installed in Ronan's room. "As if we don't know."

"A stroke of luck for the mine owners since they can shape their tale like feckin' pottery clay."

"Well, it's up to us to change their luck then," responded Big Bill.

Ronan entered the Pick-Axe near sundown. Without speaking he stalked behind the bar to pour himself a shot of Jim Beam from the bottles arrayed in front of its gigantic mirror.

Seeing his face, Maeve rose from her seat on the piano bench to lock the front door. The saloon was nearly empty, a common enough state these days.

Ronan ignored Leprechaun, also behind the bar, refilling a crock of pickles. "Sherman Bell and his devils have spread across the District, arresting anyone they can think of for the Vindicator explosion," he said after downing a shot. Maeve had seldom seen him drink so much as a beer. "They've found footprints—size eight, so they say—in the area of the explosion so they'll be rounding up anyone—"

"With dainty feet," Uncle Liam interrupted. "Sounds more like a lassie's shoe." Uncle Liam had his cherry phosphate soda, his favorite drink when sober, beside him and his Solitaire deck spread out on one of the faro tables.

"Or Leprechaun's," Ronan said, his voice flat. Leprechaun snorted and opened his mouth as if to make a joke, but seeing Ronan's expression, ducked his head and concentrated on filling the crock.

Ronan stepped away in order to distance himself from

Leprechaun. First trying to derail a train. And now, had he and Harry Orchard blown up the Vindicator? Odd when the possibility tumbled round in his brain that he felt nothing. No, that wasn't true. He felt a white-hot rage so icy, it felt like numbness, like nothing. He wished the ghosts of his dead uncles would rise from their graves to torment Mooney. Or demons poke his backside with pitchforks in a foretaste of what he'd suffer once he was consigned to the ninth circle of hell where all traitors resided.

Patiently waiting for Ronan to impart further news, opinions or frustrations, Uncle Liam continued his slap, shuffle, slap, shuffle, rearrange, repeat. Leprechaun turned his back and began polishing shot glasses. Maeve's fingernails bit into her closed fists. "Such a tragedy," she offered into the silence because she could think of nothing else to say.

After downing a second shot, Ronan snarled, "Are you wanting me to weep for those two boss boys?"

Maeve was taken aback by his unaccustomed belligerence. Eyeing the rows of whiskey bottles, gleaming in the artificial light, she imagined drowning herself in a beer butt the way that English duke had been drowned in a barrel of malmsey wine for committing treason during the Wars of the Roses. She could understand it now, the welcome relief when the wine filled your lungs; sinking into unconsciousness, not having to worry about the future, about nothing beyond the moment when you drifted into the hereafter...

"It's just any death is a tragedy and with tensions so high—"

"Aye, and I've got a list here—" Ronan tapped his temple— "from Gunnison to Custer to Park County encompassing only the last several years and I've not heard anybody weeping or calling on our politicians for justice when some poor bastard is blown to bits or crushed in a cave-in."

"I know that but—" She hated seeing Ronan so upset. Not outwardly upset but so cold, which was worse than if he were screaming and yelling and smashing up the bar. She searched her mind, dulled with nerves, to find words that might soothe him.

"How about this list?" Ronan held out his arms in front of him. One by one he ticked off on his fingers: "Fifty-nine killed in a gas and dust explosion ignited by a lamp; another ten burned to death in an explosion and fire."

He tapped a third finger and then a fourth. "Water floods a shaft, ten killed; twenty-four killed in another gas and dust explosion; another explosion with forty-nine blown to smithereens; same type of explosion ignited yet again by a lamp with twelve killed and then, fancy that, another thirteen."

"Don't forget the Smuggler Union Mine in San Miguel County," chimed in Uncle Liam. "That fire burned twenty-eight."

"Do you sense a pattern here, Maeve?" Ronan said, his gaze fierce, as though blaming her for the deaths. "A pattern the mine owners can't seem to see or care about because what's a few lives to keep the union out with all our gabbling about safety conditions?"

She knew he wasn't expecting an answer she didn't have. Because he was right. And it made no difference.

"Would ye have me continue?" Ronan's manner was relentless. Leprechaun pulled out his ubiquitous pack of Chesterfields, lit a cigarette and continued his task. "How about closer to home? James Drury in the lower slopes of the Hull City Mine. Head blown away when he drills into a shot that had earlier failed to explode. Or last year one of ours is riding in a cage down the shaft, sticks his head out only to have his skull crushed and his neck snapped by a passing timber."

Maeve wanted to cover her ears, to retreat from the Pick-Axe until she could find the proper words to soothe Ronan's rage or somehow rectify all the wrongs.

"Don't forget John Williams," Uncle Liam said, pausing in his spread to tip his head back and drain the remainder of his soda. "Rocks from a bucket drop upon him." He slammed his glass upon the table. "Just like that. One moment alive and the next Johnny's facing our Maker without benefit of Extreme Unction to save his soul." Uncle Liam fixed his eyes, dark as Ronan's and filled with his pain, on her. "My advice, *ceann beag*, is don't go breaking your shin on a stool that's not in your way."

At that moment, someone rapped on the front door. Maeve jumped. They all turned to see several soldiers framed in the front windows, peeking into the interior.

"Feckin' hell," Ronan muttered, folding his arms across his chest. Maeve imagined him refusing to open the door, being shot by troops or members of the National Guard or whatever they were, right where he stood.

"You don't need to let them in," Leprechaun said, stubbing out his cigarette with the toe of his boot. "They've no right."

"Shut the feck up," Ronan snapped.

Maeve hurried to unlock the door.

One of the nameless, faceless number they passed every day on the streets or saw patrolling the roads or swarming the various camps, stepped inside.

"Ronan Doyle," the man said. "You're under arrest."

Uncle Liam gathered up his cards. He and Ronan exchanged glances. It was all there—all the other men who'd been hanged or blown up or otherwise disposed of by mine owners paying the likes of these pissants with their double rows of shining buttons, dusty knee-high boots and bayoneted rifles.

Without a word, Ronan and his size twelve boots followed the guardsmen out the door.

Ronan was released three days later without charges.

On December 4, Governor Peabody declared Teller County to be in a state of insurrection and rebellion and placed it under martial law. One thousand National Guard troops were shipped in to occupy the Gold Camp.

Sherman Bell immediately announced, "The military will have sole charge of everything and those whom the military think ought to be arrested will be landed in the bullpen. If an order is issued to arrest all socialists, they will also be landed in the pen."

Governor Peabody's proclamation of martial law was read out at the corner of Third Street and Victor Avenue by two majors leading a detachment of fifty cavalry. They repeated the proclamation in all surrounding towns. Local police were deposed. National Guardsmen began patrolling Victor, Altman, Independence, all the camps.

The following day, Ronan readied to travel to Denver and a meeting with Big Bill Haywood. "Do you want to accompany me?" he asked Maeve.

Under different circumstances, she would have loved to visit turn-of-the-century Denver. On their first trip, they'd spent the day in a comfortable railroad car enjoying scenery unmarred by congested six-lane highways and sprawling suburbs, ending in a city big enough for comforts but small enough to remain charming. She'd imagined herself similar to a musical montage à la Butch, Sundance, and Emma enjoying New York City in *Butch Cassidy and the Sundance Kid*. Laughing in front of the Denver Club, which wouldn't allow women inside for decades; attending a vaudeville performance at the Tabor Grand Opera House; pausing at the grounds in front of the state capitol to gaze awestruck at its copper-plated dome (soon to be gilded in gold leaf courtesy of the Cripple Creek & Victor Mine). Watch them strolling arm in arm through Elitch's Zoological Gardens! Maeve carries a parasol, her long skirt trailing behind like a peacock's tail. Ronan is impeccably tailored in top hat and morning dress, clothes he'd never ever possess in reality. Candid snapshot of them screaming at the top of Elitch's roller coaster, after which they dash to its carousel where they snuggle into a chariot drawn by two fierce-looking horses (years before both the roller coaster and carousel are actually built). Final pose: faces glowing in candlelight as they enjoy boiled lake trout dinners—and each other—at the Brown Palace.

"Maeve? Is something wrong?" Ronan waved a hand in front of

her face. "I was saying I'll be at headquarters and we'll not be able to enjoy ourselves as we did before, but—"

Maeve blinked herself back to reality. No musical montages, no happy interludes. "I'm needed here," was all she said.

The Mining Exchange Building was an impressive seven stories with a twelve-foot sculpture of a miner mounted on its roof. While Ronan was in near daily contact with Big Bill via telephone, with spies everywhere, some things were better left in person. Such as Leprechaun's treason and what to do about it.

After entering Haywood's office, he took one look at Big Bill and swore, "Jaysus! Looks like those bulls used you as their punching bag."

Since Haywood was on the phone, he just grinned, shrugged his shoulders and continued his conversation, apparently with Vincent St. John, president of Telluride's union and leader of their strike. While Haywood was no stranger to brawls, this one had been a fight against local bulls with brass knuckles doing a dance on both his and the WFM's president's face and body. In response, Haywood had plugged one of the coppers three times. The fact that he was here in his office rather than a prison cell showed the man had survived.

To give Haywood and St. John a measure of privacy, Ronan crossed to one of the floor-to-ceiling windows. Six stories below, horse-drawn carriages, delivery wagons, bicycles, the occasional automobile, streetcar and pedestrian went about their day. While Ronan wasn't a fan of cities, compared to the District, Denver was a pretty lady indeed. No blast-and-pray prospect holes, belching smokestacks, headframes rising like grotesque insects above slap-dash buildings surrounded by mountains of waste dumps and mill tailings. The scene reminded him of *A Trip to the Moon* which he and Maeve had seen at the Topic Theatre. He'd been captivated by the film short—scientists who built a cannon-propelled capsule that shot them to the moon—which actually possessed a human face. He'd laughed as the characters had jumped and run and rolled about. The best part was that the action had all been silent. Explosions were mere puffs of smoke; mouths pursed or smiled or otherwise moved minus voices. He wished he could turn off the volume in his own life so easily. Respite from the endless nattering: "Ronan, do this," "Mr. Doyle, can you help with that?" "Bossman, we've a situation..." "Ronan Doyle, you're under arrest..."

"I've some ideas about how we can shake up things in Telluride," Big Bill was saying to St. John.

Ah, Telluride. With mountains that guarded the town like malevolent beasts and twelve-thousand-foot-high mines with no safety measures and winters so brutal they could freeze a man's lungs just stepping out his door.

Maybe it was the Arctic temperatures that completely shattered the hearts of Telluride's owners. Their universal attitude was that corporations could dictate every aspect of the workers' lives without feck all from the workers themselves. Far worse than the District, at least until this current mess. There had been that fire in the Smuggler-Union Mine killing twenty-five miners while the superintendent worried more about saving its Winchesters and munitions than men. The Liberty Bell snowslide that killed seventeen and was explained away as the wrath of God being visited upon unions, thug deputies beating up strikers and burning property, running gun battles with deaths on both sides.

"Okay, Adonis," said Big Bill, after hanging up. "Now we've no spies skulking about, tell me all you've got on that midget piece-of-shite traitor."

Ronan blinked himself back to the present.

"Timmy Fein's been carrying messages since before I was arrested the first time, back in September. Though Timmy didn't know anything about them other than that he handed them to—I have the list—" Ronan placed a paper among the chaos on Big Bill's desk. "He was paid two bits for delivering each message, some directly connected to the mine owners. Others were go-betweens, we figure, to be passed through until they reached their target. We're thinking even to Sherman Bell himself."

Haywood leaned back in his chair and stretched his arms above his head, like a boxer declaring victory. "Wonder how much McParland and the Citizens' Alliance are paying our own Benedict Arnold?"

Voices from the hallway and other WFM offices drifted through the open transom window.

"He's clever though. He quit passing his schoolboy notes and graduated to the telephone. Reporting to McParland himself, I'm thinking, which is the way most of those on Pinkerton's payroll do." Ronan himself had been one of those following Leprechaun, tracking him to the public phone outside Pioneer Mercantile where he made his calls, regular as clockwork, right at dusk, thinking the uncertain light would protect him, when it just as well protected anyone watching and listening in.

"The time'll come when we take care of him," said Big Bill, skimming the paper with Ronan's list of names. "A traitor to his class. If I believed in hell, I'd send him there myself."

Ronan sighed. Leprechaun's betrayal had cut deep. And he was far from the only one. "That bastard banker Gould was right when he said he could hire one-half of the working class to kill the other half."

Big Bill stood. Full height he matched Ronan, though he bested him by a good fifty pounds. "I've been thinking about our next move. A way to help our Telluride brothers and sisters, all those fightin' the good fight across the state." He threw a beefy arm across Ronan's shoulder. "Come along, Adonis. You and me're gonna put those sons a bitches on the back foot one more time. Just wait till I tell you how."

Anyone familiar with labor history has seen the iconic poster of the American flag sketched out by Big Bill Haywood and Ronan Doyle that December afternoon, soon printed and distributed to strikers across Colorado.

The WFM's Declaration of War:

A barely rippling flag on a flagpole against a buff background reminiscent of the parchment upon which the Declaration of Independence had been written. Forty-five stars in blue on the top left corner, like the mailing address on an envelope; stripes of red and the same buff color as the poster background.

Above an American flag against the parchment-colored background: IS COLORADO IN AMERICA?

In each of the stripes a statement is printed:

Martial law declared in Colorado!

Habeas corpus suspended in Colorado!

Free press throttled in Colorado!

Union men exiled from homes and families in Colorado!

Constitutional right to bear arms questioned in Colorado!

Corporations corrupt and control administration in Colorado!

Right to fair, impartial and speedy trial abolished in Colorado!

Citizens' Alliance resorts to mob law and violence in Colorado!

Militia hired by corporations to break the strike in Colorado!

Followed by the declaration of unions' right to organize, asking for donations and signed by Charles Moyer, president, and Bill Haywood, treasurer.

President Moyer and Haywood were later arrested in Telluride for "desecrating the flag" and for having signed the poster. Haywood was beaten again, this time so badly his right ear was nearly severed. When the civilian courts ordered the National Guard to release them, they refused. Later he and Moyers were found not guilty of desecration and freed.

Upon seeing the posters, Sherman Bell's response:

"Habeas corpus be damned! We'll give them postmortems!"

PART EIGHT

Today

❧

Lost causes are the only ones worth fighting for.

— CLARENCE DARROW

Nineteen

P adrick Mooney was looking for answers. Now that he'd read his sister's journals, now that he knew the District's doomsday clock was rapidly approaching midnight, he lay awake, his wife sleeping peacefully beside him, trying to fit pieces together that didn't fit, no matter how he tried to force them.

He'd been with Nana Grace in UC Health's emergency room when she'd died. Remembered one moment in particular: His grandmother turning her head to him, wearing that sly expression he, all the Mooneys had been conditioned to dread. "We O'Connors can make time dance," she'd smirked. "Too bad your blood can't."

Rearranging the pieces yet again. Might his grandmother's "walkabouts" have been trips down the White Rabbit? Could she somehow fine-tune the exact date she would return to? Unlike Maeve, whose time on the other side seemed to correlate directly with here in the 21st century. Because Maeve was a Mooney rather than an O'Connor?

This is what had brought Padrick to the Mooney library on this dreary November morning. Seeking answers to questions he couldn't even properly articulate—here among thousands of books, properly collated thanks to Mooneys' past and present; old newspapers and magazines, shelves of local histories, family photo albums and decades of personal farm journals, along with a century of legal documents tucked away in a battered filing cabinet.

He didn't find anything that even vaguely "clicked" until he returned a folder containing Shamrock Ranch's original deed of trust to its place in the filing cabinet. And spotted the corner of what looked to be a notebook, mostly hidden beneath a jumble of other files. After pulling it out, he recognized "Padrick Sean Mooney" in his great-great-grandfather's careful handwriting on the cover.

And wondered whether this might be what he'd been seeking.

Here's the truth of it. Ronan Doyle was a pretty face and nothing more. With leaders like Doyle, the WFM was bound to lose anyway. No sense of strategy. No guts. He was weak and shortsighted, not willing to do what it takes. Which is why he failed at everything in the end.

While I...well, I had the luck of the Irish, didn't I? Started out a bit rough with my little Byrdie pregnant and none too pleasant about it, and always complaining about my gambling and drinking, which were of no consequence. Besides, Byrdie ought not to have been flapping her gums about an occasional tipple, since there was a time she could outdrink most any man. But with Byrdie, she was afflicted with a preponderance of the seven deadly sins—greed, wrath, lust and envy, I'd say. With greed being uppermost. She was the one who'd suggested high-grading, which earned Harry Orchard and me a tidy extra. She was the one who nagged and nagged about the Pinkertons until I had no choice but to toss them a bit of extra information for cash. And I sure as hell would've never made that devil's bargain with Big Bill, if she hadn't been on me like flies on shite.

Padrick put down the notebook and ran a hand over his face. Why would a man confess to such baseness? As if it was something to brag about? Had Nana Grace stumbled across this notebook and because she had appointed herself both guardian and destroyer of reputations, decided to meddle in the past? Had her O'Connor "blood" somehow allowed her to do that?

For the next hour, Padric read his great-great-grandfather's version of his life, which unfolded like a novel—or a case jacket. How Saint Paddy and his brother Tommy had come to Colorado Springs as young men; how they'd robbed a motorman because they wanted to attend a circus but were broke. How Tommy had accidentally shot and killed the motorman. How Paddy had fled to the silver mines in Aspen, only reading about his younger brother's death in the newspaper.

And because it was always about the man himself: *Best of luck for me was that Tommy gave his last name to Johnny Law as "Lawton," and no one investigated different. Looney was our proper surname, and after changing the "L" to an "M," I was a man reborn. Like probably three-quarters of those who found their way to the District.*

"So, we aren't even Mooneys?"

If any of this were even true. He suspected Nana Grace had believed it to be so. But why would that so alarm her? Every family had their share of rakes and outlaws...and flat-out narcissists like Saint Paddy.

Now I'm here to tell the truth about something—the WFM and the strike. The WFM had a reputation for violence, but their supporters claim to this day there was little of that in 1903-04. The truth is Big Bill was one tough son of a bitch and paid us good money to carry out his mischief and that stupid Ronan Doyle never knew what was going on under his nose.

Long and short, after the First National Bank of Victor went bankrupt and me losing every cent I'd deposited, I had to do something different. So, I became a paid assassin for the WFM.

Paid assassin? Really? "With all due respect, you're a bullshitter slinging bullshit," Padrick said to the empty room.

Don't get me wrong, I played all sides, but the WFM paid the best. They were also behind most of the violence in the District. There was the Vindi-

cator Mine Explosion in November of 1903. Me and Harry Orchard'd been high-grading again, but when prices fell and we could only get fifty cents to a dollar a pound for the ore, it wasn't worth the danger. During one of our forays into the Vindicator, we discovered a stored car-load of dynamite in a crosscut on the eighth level of the mine. One of the union bosses offered us two hundred dollars to blow it up, saying the union needed to do something to scare off the scabs and keep our men in line.

So, we did. Blew the Vindicator all to hell, though we made a mistake our two along the way. But we were never caught and we were paid.

Padrick's stomach roiled. He'd experienced a range of human behavior, but had he ever encountered such casual evil? What if Maeve somehow crossed him or even Byrdie? Was that even a possibility when you inserted yourself back in time? All the tropes said you couldn't actually change events, at least major ones. Still...

Maybe I have more to worry about than an explosion.

Padrick skimmed the rest of Padrick Sean Mooney's "memoir," not believing the half of it, yet worrying it could be true.

Big Bill and the WFM paying him and Orchard to toss "hell-fire" bombs down mine shafts and into railcar windows carrying scabs. Fill beer kegs with dynamite, attach a time fuse to each, roll them down the mountainside into the town of Telluride. Poison Telluride's reservoir with cyanide and potassium.

"Nothing came of anything but I was paid well for doing nothing."

Apparently, the *coup de grâce* was the WFM's plan to blow up Governor Peabody himself.

"So's, I agree to kill him. First, I scope out the governor's residence and monitor his movements, figuring I can shoot him full of buckshot on his way home. When his schedule proves too erratic, me and Big Bill decide I should just blow the governor up, kind of the way we later did the Independence Depot. Big Bill called that off too, but it was a good practice run for the Independence, and once again I got paid."

Saint Paddy's tale ended with:

"By the time the strike was crushed, me and Byrdie and the baby had a good nest egg. Add the money Horace Strank gave me after I set fire to

Strank's Manse—and he made a pretty penny off of insurance, saving his fortune—and that's how I bought Shamrock Ranch."

Was this the true Mooney legacy? Selfishness ratcheted to such a degree that it swallowed any vestige of what made a man human?

Padrick shook his head. "That might've been your legacy, *Grandfather*, but the rest of this family ain't claiming it."

Padrick returned the notebook to its original hiding place.

And turned his attention to a far more pressing matter.

THE DISTRICT ~ DECEMBER 1903–MAY 1904

Shadows crawled across Bennett Avenue with the waning afternoon light. Maeve hurried the three blocks to her rooms at the Gold Nugget carrying two bags of presents. IS COLORADO IN AMERICA? posters were everywhere, ripped down nearly as soon as they'd been put up. And put right back up again.

A week before Christmas, and you could taste the dread. Tension inhaled with the knife-sharp air; faces, young to old, tight with stress; newsboys half-heartedly waving newspapers and parroting headlines from pro-miner, anti-union newspapers...

Total lawlessness: the Bill of Rights suspended, assemblies forbidden; weapons and ammunition must be surrendered! (Most everyone simply hid theirs.) Military courts handled all but the most minor criminal and civil cases. More union officers arrested—some on a catch and release. Others permanently banned from the District. Still others murdered in their beds.

Lower officers, drunk on their power as well as actual spirits, harassed whomever they pleased. Teachers on their way to school were stopped and run off. Sentries stationed near Cripple Creek's high school tried to flirt with female students through the windows, threw notes into the building, and harassed them after classes. Should a woman cross from one side of the main streets to the other, she risked being ridden down. If one man harbored a grudge against another—and tensions between those who supported the strike and those against it ever simmered beneath the surface—he need only label his enemy as an "agitator" and military authorities arrested him. Overheard disparaging the militia? You were promptly hustled off to the bull pen, which held nearly as many women and children as men.

Like everyone who'd ventured out, Maeve walked with her head down, so intent on her destination that she wasn't sure when she realized she was being followed. There were the usual city noises along with the rustle of her bags, the slap of her boots on the boardwalk. Nothing out of the ordinary—at least *après* martial law ordinary. But there it was: that feeling you get when the hair on the back of your neck prickles and you know you're being watched. Maeve glanced over her shoulder. Only one person behind her, walking fast, quickly closing the distance. The man was as big as Ronan and even bulkier. Straightening her shoulders—*don't look like a victim*—Maeve increased her pace, though not too much. Just as if she were eager to get home and out of the cold.

Nothing is going to happen in the light of day, she reminded herself, as though people weren't being kidnapped or harassed at all hours. And unable to turn to the ever-lurking soldiers for help because they were the ones breaking the law.

Another backward glance. Wearing Carhartt overalls and jacket, a wide-brimmed hat slung low over his face. Maeve crossed the street, then back again. She was sure she could hear his feet, the quickening of his pace. One last glimpse. Closer. Face in shadow. Huge, the biggest man she'd ever seen. One of the criminals up from Canon City's state prison, hired by the MOA, thinking to snatch her bags? A Pinkerton goon, singling her out? "She's just as guilty as her union boyfriend, filling his head with nonsense," they'd say. Or "We'll kidnap her and hold her for ransom. Call off the strike and we'll free her!"

Maeve imagined giant hands grabbing her shoulders, dragging

her off into an alleyway, snapping her neck. Intent on sprinting the last yards to the Gold Nugget, she placed her bags in one hand and picked up her skirts with the other.

"Stop!"

Maeve began to run.

"Goddamnit, Moonface, stop! Right the fuck now!"

A millisecond to register that oh, so familiar voice. She stopped as abruptly as if she'd smacked into a glass wall.

Whipping around, Maeve watched the figure approach. She couldn't yet see his facial features but his build, the way he walked were so familiar. As was his voice. She'd know her brother's voice anywhere.

"Padrick?" She stared at him, disbelieving.

He held out his arms and Maeve ran into them. "Padrick, Padrick, what are you doing here?" She found herself crying and laughing simultaneously.

"I've come to take you home."

On Christmas Eve, Padrick dressed up as Santa to hand out presents Maeve had purchased for all the children on Golden Avenue. Toys that contemporary children would dismiss as boring were oohed and aahed over. Little Folks Painting Books, original coloring books which possessed drawings intricate enough to frame; newly invented crayons, dime novels, jacks, tops, cracker jacks, marbles, Old Maid and baseball cards.

Maeve was positively glowing. (At least most of the time.) She felt safe with her big brother here, like a Zoom call with her family, who Padrick informed her, had received all her journals, and while they agreed they were more exciting than even *The Lord of the Rings* series, it was time for Maeve to return home.

That part she ignored.

"Yes, Moonface, Cripple Creek is plenty fascinating, I'll give you that. But I know how this ends, and it's not safe to stay."

That part Maeve ignored, as well.

Yes, Padrick was impressed with Ronan Doyle. "Too bad you couldn't have met your handsome union man in your own century, the way everybody else does."

For God sakes. Couldn't Padrick pretend like he was on an extended LARP? He'd made financial arrangements for Celia and Lily before leaving, so quit nagging!

She knew she was on a timetable, but like Scarlett O'Hara, she'd think about it tomorrow.

On the eve of New Year's Eve: National Guard thugs came for the Pick-Axe's hidden cache of weapons. All firearms in the District were supposed to have already been confiscated, though compliance remained a joke. Tired of the continued resistance that met them at every turn, the militia grew increasingly agitated. The strike had been going on for more than four months now, with no signs of a settlement. The mine owners and their alliances were slow paying, which further angered troops. If something didn't change soon, military leaders threatened to pull out of the District altogether.

When the guard arrived, Uncle Liam, Ronan and Padrick were playing Faro, Timmy and Danny Fein were sprawled near a glowing coal stove reading their Christmas novels, *The Time Machine* and *Journey to the Center of the Earth*, while Annie and her daughters were in the backroom making sugar cookies. Maeve, who'd been playing Christmas carols on the piano, watched in horror as soldiers went directly to the back room, to the hidden trapdoor that held the cache of weapons she'd seen months ago. *Leprechaun*, she thought, heart pounding. He'd betrayed them yet again. But when the soldiers pulled back the rag rug and opened the trap door, it was empty.

The furious lieutenant in charge arrested Ronan anyway and marched him away at bayonet point.

Afterward, regarding the missing cache, Uncle Liam said, "God is good but never dance in a small boat." Translation: Knowing the traitor in their midst, he and Ronan had removed the rifles and dynamite.

Ronan was released in time to enjoy the sugar cookies, still warm from the oven and in the shape of stars, Christmas trees, and Santa Claus.

Twenty

*J*anuary 7, 1904: The military implemented a "vag" law, meaning anyone who chose to "idle" rather than return to work would be imprisoned—and some of them forced to work in chain gangs—or escorted to Teller County's boundary with orders never to return.

The WFM responded by issuing circulars reminding union members that courts had ruled in the union's favor.

"Keep your union cards and refuse to be driven from home. If compelled to leave by force of arms, union men are advised to return immediately to the Cripple Creek district. The Western Federation of Miners will provide for all striking miners' families."

In Victor, Danny and Timmy Fein, who their mother swore would lead her to an early grave, tacked the circulars on billboards and telegraphs. Soldiers followed behind tearing them down before invading the *Victor Daily Record*, which had printed the circulars, and ordering employees to cease and desist. Military leaders branded the *Daily Record* the District's lone "outlaw." Declaring they must "protect" citizens from the "contaminating influence" of its editorials, officials placed the paper under military censorship.

No more statements emanating from WFM headquarters would be printed in the *Record*. No more editorials lamenting the loss of a free America.

Timmy and Danny Fein were arrested and imprisoned for several hours. Both later swore they enjoyed the experience.

When the *Daily Record* reopened, the paper championed the side of mine owners.

On January 26, a cage of non-union miners broke from the hoist at the Independence Mine. Fifteen men fell to their deaths. The coroner blamed management because their greenhorn hires had improperly installed safety equipment. Management countered that the WFM had tampered with the lift. The union had no access to the property, which was under military protection. One hundred sixty-eight men quit the mine.

While mine owners swore their properties were operating just fine, actual numbers told a different tale. Of the original thirty-five hundred strikers, three hundred had returned to work. Those were largely unskilled employees, costing management more because of lost time and downtime.

From mid-January to late March, street fights between Victor strikers and the National Guard became commonplace. Each altercation was carefully planned and carried out by leaders of the guard, who ordered their troops to literally "knock strikers down, knock their teeth down their throats, bend in their faces, kick in their ribs and do everything except kill them."

The Mine Owners Association fell further behind in funding payroll. Sherman Bell complained to Governor Peabody that he didn't have the funds to procure coal, hay, food, or any of the necessities needed to properly supply his troops. Peabody countered that the MOA wasn't paying its bills and threatened to pull out all remaining militia. Disgruntled higher-ups decided to nudge the MOA into loosening their purse strings. They hired two thugs with orders to shoot employees coming off their early morning shift at the Vindicator Mine. Since the departing men generally boarded an electric car that stopped directly in front of the shaft house, thus making them poor targets, the thugs pumped sixty shots inside the shaft house itself.

The MOA quickly made payroll.

Governor Peabody and General Bell, who knew in advance of the plan, didn't even pretend to investigate.

"You need to tell Ronan the truth, Moonface."

"I will, I promise."

"Tell him"

"He won't believe me."

"If you don't tell him and you suddenly disappear, that'll be even worse."

"I will! I'm just trying to figure out how to say it so he won't think I'm crazy."

"Maeve, you're making this harder on all of us."

"Maybe after I tell him, I can convince him to return with us."

"That doesn't strike me as the man Ronan Doyle is."

"We need to go home before the District blows. You need to tell him *now*!

"If you don't tell him, I will."

In mid-March, when patches of grass appeared through lingering snow, Padrick and Ronan rode to the rock formation near the entrance of what would become Shamrock Ranch. After they'd settled onto one of the ledges, with a clear view of Strank's Manse, the carriage house and the original headframe, Padrick told Ronan the truth—about how he and Maeve had found themselves in 1900s' Cripple Creek. Maeve might continue to procrastinate, but decisions had to be made. In less than ninety days, the strike would be smashed. He and Maeve needed to return to the future, not only for their own safety but because witnessing the annihilation of all those dreams would be too painful for them both.

From an inner pocket of his Carhartt jacket Padrick produced colored photos, unlike any Ronan had ever seen—the before and after of Shamrock Ranch, of Cripple Creek, Victor and the District, of Colorado Springs and Denver. He shared photos of jet airplanes, automobiles, rocket ships, television, computers, all sorts of mad inventions. Ronan accepted each photo, listened to each explanation with a mixture of curiosity, skepticism, and excitement. As he did when reading scientific romances like *Journey to the Center of the Earth* or *Twenty Thousand Leagues Under the Sea* and *The Time Machine*. Fantastical yarns that might contain a nugget of truth at their core that he was happy to entertain.

"And what will happen to mankind in this, our twentieth century?" Ronan asked after Padrick returned the photos to his pocket.

The answer was like something plucked out of the Book of Revelation with the Four Horsemen of the Apocalypse unleashing war, famine, plague, destruction and annihilation. Not a future for the faint of heart. Still, the way Padrick spun it, life would ultimately improve for many ordinary folks. Implying that the moral arc of the universe might be fractionally bending toward...if not justice, the hunger for it. Or maybe the moral arc of the universe simply ebbed and flowed.

While Padrick's revelations were undeniably fantastical, Ronan had grown up with faeries, bantees and banshees, phookas and leprechauns and the rest. That was just part of being Irish. Furthermore, his Catholic faith was filled with impossibilities—Jesus's resurrection and ascension into heaven. His many miracles. Saints who bore the stigmata, or could appear in two places simultaneously; who levitated; whose corpses never rotted and smelled of roses; who could survive solely by ingesting the eucharist. Ronan's patron saint had raised the dead; his relics cured dumbness and demonic possession. Francis of Assisi had tamed wild animals and brought them to God. The French saint, Denis, carried his own severed head six miles to the spot where his basilica—the future resting place of France's kings—would someday be built, and with his head preaching the entire journey.

Nor were impossibilities limited to the sacred.

Hadn't a tommyknocker warned of his Da's impending death? His uncle's handprint remained on his jail cell when he'd proclaimed his innocence and no amount of washing or repainting could erase it. While Ronan sat at his mother's bedside, she'd conversed with Da and Ronan had felt his presence as surely as if he could actually see him. Here in the District, when children sickened from typhoid or other diseases, some mothers swore faeries had exchanged their healthy babes with changelings.

"I do believe you," he said finally. The late afternoon sun had set the windows of Strank's empty mansion ablaze. Ronan imagined a party of ghosts inside suddenly shaking themselves awake, imagined them stuffing their gobs in a room the size of a great hall, waltzing past the wee hours in a ballroom glutted with mirrors and chandeliers and *nouveau riche* excess. He thought of bloated, duplicitous, eager-to-please-his-handlers Horace Strank, destroying all that was right and good and holy via the MOA and Citizens' Alliance. He had not asked Padrick about the outcome of the strike and noted he had not volunteered it.

Easing himself off the ledge, his backside and thighs numb from hours of sitting, Padrick said, "What happens next is up to you. You and Maeve."

Twenty-One

I t's cold in here. Cold and dead. Peculiar noises. Could make a man believe in ghosts, though it was most likely mice or even something larger. Hell, a herd of Bighorn Sheep could be hiding in more damn rooms than he could count.

As Horace Strank sat in front of a struggling fire, he surreptitiously rubbed his stomach through his brocade waistcoat. Digestive problems. Losing weight. All that stress. Damnable strike.

After it's won...has to be won...I'll be needing to pour money, money, money into this dry hole.

Once Horace had been so proud of Strank's Manse. He looked back with nostalgia on the summer before the strike—like so many, he divided his life into "before" and "after"—imbuing it with the brilliance of a midsummer afternoon. Picnicking in meadows blanketed in blues and whites, pinks, reds and purples, bearing names like harebells, beardtongues, columbines and chiming bells. Autumn when the aspen quivered, their leaves crackling beneath his feet, and he imagined himself as King Midas trodding upon a pathway of gold. Or as a second William Jackson Palmer, one of Colorado

Springs' founders, who'd built Glen Eyrie Castle for his wife Queenie with the Garden of the Gods smack-dab in his backyard.

But instead of gold coins or an actual Tudor-style castle, Horace Strank was saddled with leaking roofs, shutters hanging askew, peeling wallpaper, cracked glass in the bay windows and he could swear his front porch steps were beginning to rival the Leaning Tower of Pisa in their slant.

Hemorrhaging money. Bleeding out like a slaughtered calf.

The wail of a baby from an upstairs bedroom reminded Strank he was very much not alone. No doubt Baby Sean would holler his lungs out before being properly tended to. Mrs. Mooney wasn't much of a mother. But was that a surprise? Bridget Kehoe-Mooney might have dressed herself in a more staid fashion and pretended to be all that, but she was still Sundown from Pearl de Vere's first brothel. A whore and a thief. Also, a drunk, at least he suspected so. Good thing she was pouring formula into the wee thing rather than her breast milk which must be hundred-proof alcohol. Baby Sean looked healthy enough, though he was an unusually crabby creature.

I'd be crabby too if I had to look at that wrinkled mug all day.

The fire in the parlor fireplace flickered and smoked and sizzled. Probably green wood. Leprechaun was proving himself an indifferent caretaker. Hardly surprising, considering his many distractions. Chief among them was probably his fear of getting unmasked as a Pinkerton agent. Ending up with a bullet to the back of his head courtesy of Ronan Doyle or one of Doyle's goons. Better to lie low and shun dark alleyways. Besides, allowing Mooney and his wife to stay here was cheaper than maintaining staff and Strank so seldom visited...

"Whiskey!" Horace bellowed. He shifted his gaze in the direction of the parlor doorway, through which Leprechaun eventually appeared.

"On it, Cap'n." Leprechaun offered an exaggerated salute before crossing to the sideboard where the liquor was kept. For some ridiculous reason, Leprechaun called him "Captain," when Strank had never been in the military, had never wanted to be in the military and after the strike's ending, hoped never to see another soldier.

Leprechaun cranked up the gramophone near the sideboard from which emanated a tinny *My Wild Irish Rose.*

> *...the sweetest flower that grows*
> *You may search everywhere,*
> *but none can compare with my wild Irish Rose.*

Strank rubbed his stomach again. Maeve Mooney had sung and played *Rose* so prettily, looking like an Irish rose herself. Such a shame she'd thrown in her lot with that anarchist when she could have done so much better. *Him* for example. Not to marry, but for *adventure*. Currently, he had his eye on a Denver socialite, but *that* depended on the outcome of this debacle.

Leprechaun handed Horace a drink and placed a bottle of Jack Daniel's on the side table between them before easing himself down in an adjacent chair.

After pouring himself a shot, Leprechaun raised his arm in a toast. "Here's to us, Cap'n!" He tossed his drink back in one gulp. They sat in silence, not companionable—their stations were too different for that—but comfortable enough. As the liquid warmed Strank, he wished he could risk a cigar, but not with his unpredictable stomach. Maybe another trip to the Spa of the Rockies over in Glenwood Springs was in order. He'd enjoyed the amenities at its Hotel Colorado, which rivalled Europe's grandest accommodations. It even possessed an indoor waterfall, which reminded Strank of his empty trout pond in the manse's entranceway, further darkening his mood.

Gah, better to just burn this folly down and collect the insurance.

"Did you hear the story about Mick and Finian after they were sent to prison?"

Strank grunted. The way this worked, Leprechaun had to tell a joke or two before shutting up or getting down to a serious conversation.

"Now Mick and Finian want to stay in touch inside so they invent a code where they can tap out messages to each other. Which works as good as good can be till the boyos are transferred to separate prison cells!"

...my one wish has been that someday I may win
The heart of my wild Irish Rose.

"Shut up that blasted song," Strank growled, ignoring Leprechaun's stupid joke. "Not in the mood for any of your Mick lachrymosity."

"Aye, Cap'n." Leprechaun scurried over to the gramophone, replacing *Rose* with a disc of *Bill Bailey*.

Leaning his head against the upholstered back of his chair, Strank closed his eyes, his brain pulsating with images of yesterday's Decoration Day, which, according to Leprechaun, had seen the miners out in full force, honoring real war veterans rather than the tin soldiers who currently occupied the District.

"And everyone as cheerful as could be," Leprechaun had crowed when recounting the parade. "Waving flags and the band playing 'Stars and Stripes Forever' and marchers with a spring in their step as if they hadn't a care in the world." Often Strank wondered what side Leprechaun was really on. He suspected Leprechaun wondered as well.

"No violence either," Leprechaun had added, as if to further sour Strank's mood. Okay, though the truth was that, while the WFM was peopled with socialist ruffians who delighted in beating up non-union replacements and running Bohunks and their like out of the District, Horace could admit—in the privacy of back rooms, no, late at night when sleep eluded him—that they, the good guys, burned down union homes and assay offices that were in the business of high-grading. Gunmen had been given the green light by their MOA employers to kill as many strikers as possible and to destroy union stores. But no matter what was thrown their way, the strikers and their families didn't break. Sure, the strike had split families, but most kept to their opposite corners and survived as best they could.

Overhead, Baby Sean had started up his crying again. *Thump.* Hope Mother Bridget hadn't dropped him. For the good of humanity, some women should never be allowed to breed.

Blast it all, thought Stank, returning to his obsession. The way it was looking, the strike could last longer than the Thirty Years' War, which he didn't know much about other than it had lasted thirty years.

What progress are we really making? Production was down. Profits had collapsed while strikers continued receiving their strike benefits, their collective stores remained running and leaders even managed the occasional community entertainment to keep spirits up. Who was really being hurt here?

Beside him, Leprechaun warbled *"Won't you come home, Bill Bailey? Won't you come home?"*

I'm in hell, thought Strank. If he believed in hell, which he didn't, though you had to pretend among all those Protestants. Well-educated, sophisticated, most having impeccable pedigrees so why couldn't they outsmart half-illiterates like Charles Moyer, Bill Haywood and Ronan Doyle? Maybe that's why that particular trio didn't realize they were dead men walking. Why didn't they concede defeat so that he and his compatriots could go about the business of America, which was money? The making of it. The spending of it. The amassing of more of it via proper stewardship rather than being forced to negotiate with anti-capitalist hooligans. Governor Peabody, all the members of the various Alliances, strong-armed senators and congressmen in Capitol hallways and industry heads in private boardrooms with their message. From Peabody to McParland to the politicians to the press they repeated some form of the following: "We, the righteous...battle between good and evil... violent, anarchistic labor leaders who advocate the fallacies and realities of the socialistic doctrine... rebellion!... revolution!..."

"*Mo ghrá geal*, my darling!" Leprechaun cried, leaping to his feet. Strank hadn't noticed Bridget Mooney standing at the bottom of the stairs in the adjoining entryway. Leprechaun scurried across the parlor to his wife, who stood gripping a newel post. Bridget wore a rumpled wrapper and a scowl. In the light filtering through the sidelights flanking the great front door, her hair, which had once been so beautiful—not red exactly, more the color of a pumpkin— but soft and shiny and so long she could sit on it when she left it unbound, appeared as frazzled as she obviously felt.

Strank returned his gaze to the flickering flames. By unspoken agreement, he and Bridget pretended they'd never previously known each other, though he had no idea how much Leprechaun might be aware. Maybe they all three were pretending.

While Leprechaun and his wife engaged in murmured conversation, Strank's thoughts continued their endless circling. The bills for the militia continued piling up and Sherman Bell and militia heads always yammering about being paid. "*Not enough! We need more!*" Do your damn job then! Crush the strike! And once this is over, you, Governor James Peabody, had damn sure reimburse us like you promised you would.

Exhausted by his conversation, Horace Strank slumped back in his upholstered chair.

Something has to be done.

He just had no idea what.

After downing his third bourbon and slamming the shot glass on the tabletop, Leprechaun grinned. "Now if that ain't a miracle cureall for anything that ails a man." Shadows hung like cobwebs in the corners of the parlor, even with the lanterns he'd lit in order to save electricity. Turning serious, he said, "We're at a stalemate. After nearly a year."

Strank grunted.

"We need something more. We need to blow everything up."

"Any grand ideas?" Strank absently rubbed his uneasy stomach. "I'd say we've tried them all."

"Not this one."

It was Leprechaun's job to please his meal ticket, whether that be the WFM, the Pinkertons, the MOA, Horace Strank or a combination of them all. He couldn't realize his ambitions on the Pinkerton's $18 a week plus a few bucks from the strike fund. Besides, Ronan Doyle had been freezing him out, though that could be because Doyle wanted to hide the fact he'd gone arseways on the strike and had no idea what he was doing. A man had to weigh all the odds and look out for his own interests since no one else would. And then there was the other thing, that he knew was true but didn't want to think about. His wife was intent on destroying Liam and Ronan Doyle. Leprechaun wasn't so stupid as to think Bridget loved him, or that she was driven by anything other than revenge. In fact, if she'd left him alone through every phase of the strike, he'd probably not have been at this juncture, never have turned double agent, but Jesus, Mary and Joseph a man had to have peace in his home. And he had his next generation to build a legacy for.

"I've been rolling this particular plan round my noggin a while now," Leprechaun smirked at his morose companion. "Watch, Cap'n, listen and learn!"

Twenty-Two

Maeve refused to talk to Ronan about the time travel business. "I don't care about it. I didn't exist before you. I've no interest in the future."

If Ronan expressed curiosity, and he did, he spoke with Padrick. Maeve pretended and pretended and the days passed until they'd bumped up against Dedication Day, the future Memorial Day, which had been Padrick's hard limit.

"If I have to knock you out and carry you to the White Rabbit, I'll do it. And Ronan agrees."

Which made Maeve want to throw and break things. How could Ronan so easily let her go? She was sure Padrick had told him the fate of the strike and yet he insisted on walking into that burning building, knowing it would collapse around him.

～

Maeve rested her cheek upon Ronan's bare chest, his chest hair prickly against her skin. Her fingers idly played with the medals on his necklaces, which she knew by feel—St. Christopher, St. Barbara,

THE GOLDEN PROMISE OF CRIPPLE CREEK

patron saint of miners; St. Patrick, and the Celtic cross nestled above a regular crucifix. Over the months, it had become a habit, fingering them as if they were her own personal worry beads. *Never again.* A lifetime without tracing their surfaces, his body heat warming their metal.

Everything ends. At least I know so I can savor each moment.

Stoical, she would be. Chin jutted out, eyes narrowed, face to the wind, a Celtic warrior woman dispassionately surveying the remains of a battlefield. Accepting your destiny. Better yet, embracing it. A Celtic warrior woman who never cried, no matter what. But all Maeve did was cry. She likened her tears to a reservoir that surely should have drained long ago. Yet, in the next moment the tears overflowed the dam and she'd be off again. And again, no matter how she ordered her tears to stop.

From the moment Padrick had warned her, "We have to be gone before the District erupts. Two days, Moonface, no longer."

She cried alone in her rooms, in public, whenever she even looked at Ronan. She would turn away pretending she wasn't crying; Ronan would pretend he didn't notice. While her lover was the main focus of Maeve's pain, she mourned the Feins and Uncle Liam and all those she'd met, some she'd come to love and others who'd shaped this period of history for good or ill. A history she'd been lucky enough to experience in real time, aware of its importance even as it unfolded. Such things had become important to someone who'd been the worst of the smartphone age, not caring about— and ignorant of—anything beyond herself.

I'm blessed for that. And I'll not forget it. I'll not go back to my selfishness. Cripple Creek will not be a mere way-stop in my life.

Their last night together, holding each other, speaking in low voices or simply lost in private thought, Maeve tried to come to grips with these past two and a half years, to put them in perspective.

I knew you for less than a thousand days. Loved you half that time. But that wasn't true. She'd been obsessed with him since she was a teen, staring at the tintype of a WFM man named Ronan Doyle. In all the ways that counted, he'd been in her life forever.

The boarding house had settled into a silence broken only by occasional muffled voices in the hallway or in the streets beyond, the blast of mine whistles, as ubiquitous as they'd always been; the rumble and shake of a related explosion, the mournful wail of a late-running train.

"You can come with me," she said aloud. *Please come with me.*

Ronan shifted so his chin rested atop her head. "Tell me, Maeve Mooney, how my life would be if I followed you." He stroked her unbound hair, now cascading down to the middle of her back. Would she cut it upon her return? Dye it? New hair extensions?

Who had that Maeve Mooney even been?

"We'll build a house," Maeve said, sketching her vision as if it were real. As if she believed. "On top of the ridge overlooking the red rocks and the Rockies. Where I've hiked a thousand times. The air is so pure and crisp because the mines have been gone for decades and it's so quiet the only sound you hear is the soughing of a breeze through the pines. And maybe Lily's donkey because Padrick and his family will live within walking distance."

Ronan's fingers continued their exploration. "What sort of house will we build?"

Images popped into her mind: a thatched roof cottage. A stone hut. Log cabin. Glass and steel cube. "What would you like?"

Ronan stayed silent, as if considering, as if any of this could possibly be real and they weren't playacting to keep the truth at bay. "It needs to be white so I can see it when I come home late at night. Otherwise, I might miss it and stumble over the ridge to my doom."

Maeve laughed. "But what if it snows? If it's a blizzard and everything's white? And there's such a thing as porch lights, you know. I'll be able to turn on so many lights that the house will glow like a Christmas tree. And I'll wait up for you. Because I can't sleep until you're beside me."

She could imagine it, tucked snugly beneath a pile of comforters with the furnace registers tick-ticking, and the winter wind howling outside. She'd hear the front door open, Ronan stomping the snow off his boots, shedding his clothes after he reaches their bedroom. And when he slips in beside her, she'd say, "Your skin is so cold. Let me warm you..."

"I don't want a big house. But I think I'd like a tower maybe, where I can get away from you and our wee ones. A library. With a grand telescope. To watch the stars. And the man in the moon."

"So, we'll have...children...will we?" Something they'd never discussed. Something she'd never even contemplated, and he'd said he'd never live long enough to sire. Her voice didn't sound so casual, did it? As if she were choking on the words. *Children.* Already she felt the loss of that dream.

"We'll have at least four—two and two. But what sort of work would I be doing in your world?"

A social media influencer? A waiter at Olive Garden? A union electrician or lineman?

"You wouldn't work. You've already worked enough for ten lifetimes." She paused. She could picture it so clearly, and she hated it because it was a fantasy she wanted to be real and it never would be so what was the point in constructing imaginary castles? "Our house has a porch that covers the entire front and you'll sit there every day on your wooden bench playing with our children until they're grown, and then until you're an old man drowsing in the sun." She swallowed hard, trying to ease the lump in her throat. "You deserve at least that."

"I wish it could be so."

I can do this. Weaving fantasies, not even pretending this can't become real. And yet she couldn't stop herself. "It could be." Impossible to hide the desperation in her voice. "It will be peaceful and happy and we can make a new life for ourselves—"

Ronan sighed. They'd had some version of this conversation ever since Maeve announced her and Padrick's leaving. It wasn't like taking the Short Line to Colorado Springs. Stepping into the future? In a way it would be exciting. But the die of his life had already been cast.

"I can't leave my uncle. He's all the family I've left. And I have to see this through to the end. You know I do."

"I know Padrick's told you the outcome." In a week, the miners would be run out of the District in their own version of the Trail of Tears. And Ronan would vanish. Would he emulate Big Bill Haywood, becoming one of the founding members of the International Workers of the World? Would he end up alongside Haywood in Bolshevik Russia where both would die of alcoholism and smashed hopes? Would he fall in love here and create the four children they would never have together? Would he be shot dead when the National Guard opened fire?

"Just because I know isn't enough. This is my life. It's not like reading a book where you see it on the printed page, but it's not *real*."

Real? What did that even mean? What was real about falling down a shaft into the past, about shopping at stores that didn't exist, eating food that was dust, about resting in the arms of a dead man?

"You don't love me enough," Maeve cried. She shifted away from him, giving him her back. She would never forgive him for not leaving with her. He could. She loved him, hated him, had no idea what she was feeling, and simultaneously couldn't blame him, or deride him for believing as he did. There was no right or wrong here, just two people groping their way through life, doing the best they could with the way they'd entered the world and how that world had shaped them. But how could she bear it when all she'd soon have would be the photographs Padrick had taken of them with his newly purchased box camera?

"It's not about love, *a stóra*/my treasure," Ronan wanted to say. He loved Maeve more than he'd thought it possible to love a woman, far more than Byrdie, and he was grateful he'd had the experience. Losing her would be painful, but his life, all lives were chock full of pain and loss. It was a lovely dream Maeve dreamed, but dreams can't live past the dawn.

"*In the gardens of memory, in the palace of dreams, that is where you and I shall meet,*" he whispered, quoting the Mad Hatter. He pulled Maeve back to him; she allowed herself to be fitted against him a final time.

Ronan knew it wasn't enough. But it was all he was willing to give.

Maeve lay with the moonlight from the lone window slanting across their quilt and onto the opposite wall, a blank screen upon which she projected her future and her fears. How pointless to contemplate any future. And her fears? It was impossible to sort through any of her emotions. They were too overwhelming, too contradictory, too un-Maeve like. From the first moment she'd laid eyes on Ronan Doyle, it was as if she'd struck out for a walk along Bennett Avenue only to end up on Mars.

At least I had this experience. Most people never will. At least I met you, loved you. That could never have happened if not for the White Rabbit. If not for magic.

Ronan's limbs twitched. Sometimes he muttered or made gasping noises that slid into soft snores. Still, his arms remained firmly encircled around her. Rather than counting sheep, Maeve counted her lover's breathing. She thought of other moments, too numerous to count—seconds that would bleed to minutes that would bleed to hours, days, weeks and months until it would all collapse like a demolition building.

With the dawn, Maeve slipped out of bed and slipped on the jeans, sweater, shacket and boots in which she'd arrived.

Standing beside Ronan, she gazed down at him, glad that his

beautiful face was peaceful, his breathing even. It was fitting she would slip away without him even knowing.

She bent over and mouthed, "I love you," against his lips. Surprised when he looped an arm around her and pulled her tight against him. She inhaled the scent of his Florida water, felt the softness and warmth of his skin.

"We'll meet in the palace of dreams," she whispered before breaking free and hurrying to meet Padrick.

PART NINE

June–September 1904

Whether or not individual members of the Western Federation of Miners committed violent acts during the strike, violence was not union policy. It was, however, the policy of the (Cripple Creek) Mine Owners' Association, the Citizens' Alliance, and the militia.

— ELIZABETH JAMESON, ALL THAT GLITTERS—
CLASS, CONFLICT, AND COMMUNITY IN CRIPPLE
CREEK

Twenty-Three

It should have been easy to avert the crime. Most everyone knew "something" was in the air. In the preceding days, an unusual number of gun fighters, parolees and ex-convicts showed up in the District where they were hired by the MOA to act as detectives, spies and mercenaries.

The militia, MOA and Citizens' Alliance, who had happily hired similar men throughout the strike, warned that "something" was going to happen soon. "Be ready," they ordered.

Large cases of ammunition were brought to the Victor Armory, while the Victor militia performed an unusual number of drills. A final inspection was ordered of the arms and supplies, ensuring they'd be ready for immediate use. One of the generals offered five hundred dollars to any of the men there gathered who agreed to commit the act. The night of June 5—in the hours before the horror—several of the men who would later be fingered as carrying the "infernal machine" to its destination, ate and drank and hung out in Goldfield and Independence saloons. Witnesses later commented that the men acted differently—as if "preparing for some extraordinary piece of work."

Most of the militia and prominent members of the Citizens' Alliance stayed at Victor's glamorous Baltimore Hotel, though few took advantage of its spacious rooms. Rather they congregated in the bar and lobby, all with an air of "anticipation."

In the minutes before, A.E. Carlton, president of the MOA and principal owner of the Findley and Shurtloff mines, telephoned the Findley Mine with the intention of delaying workers from leaving after they finished their graveyard shift. After failing to make the connection, Carlton called the manager of the Shurtloff and told him to order the miners to "stay back" past quitting time.

In the immediate aftermath, the WFM offered a five-thousand-dollar reward for the capture of the assassins; the various Alliances declined to do the same. A prominent mine owner announced the perpetrators would never be discovered. General Sherman Bell soon contradicted him.

"I have undisputed evidence in my possession which will lead to the conviction of between thirty-five and forty union men," Bell publicly announced. "We are only waiting to capture two or three more men before telling what our evidence is."

No evidence was ever brought forth; no such men were ever brought to trial.

Locals whispered the identities of the actual perpetrators, though they never dared speak openly. Some of the conspirators were rewarded for their perfidy—one, after being pardoned by Governor Peabody, gained work as a guard at the El Paso Mine; another, hired as a deputy for an MOA-appointed sheriff, raped a fourteen-year-old girl and was sentenced to fourteen years in prison —after which he was paroled and relocated to Denver where he ran a saloon. One of their murderers was "punished" with a job as a saloon keeper in Goldfield where he bragged he could make the MOA pay him eighty thousand dollars any time he wanted. Others who knew too much did not fare as gently. Two locals, after hinting at "dark truths," were gunned down. A woman who cohabited (simultaneously!) with two MOA detectives and gunslingers implicated in the explosion, fled to Pueblo where she was murdered. One of several mysterious "disappearances" was rumored to be lying at the bottom of a deserted mine shaft. Several died under "peculiar" circumstances. At least one was sentenced to life in prison.

Harry Orchard was the only man who ever publicly confessed to the crime—years later, when facing the death penalty for blowing up a former Idaho governor. Then the ever-odious James McParland helped Orchard pen a confession in which Orchard admitted to the deed, along with at least sixteen other murders.

Orchard's reward?

He was spared the rope.

The town of Independence lay in a deep valley, a half mile from Victor and just below Altman. Many of the richest mines in the District were located in this area, which accounted for the particularly unsightly terrain—mountains of tailings with the occasional tree poking out of the rubble like a troublesome weed, and gullies deeper than a man was tall. Poorly lighted, lending an air of menace to the darkness. The perfect place to commit crimes without fear of being caught out, many said. Or maybe they only said that in hindsight, following the disaster.

Independence Depot, one of several railroad depots in the District, sat high upon a hillside. It was built in the typical manner: a rectangular design topped by a gable roof with wide eaves to protect waiting passengers from the elements and a wooden platform extending along the track side for easy boarding and disembarkation. Over time the Independence had become more of an afterthought, in need of maintenance and minus a station agent to service customers.

June 6: early morning. Half-moon and a dusting of stars. Unusually cold. Frost crunched beneath the boots of the twenty-five or so non-union miners who'd just exited the Findley mine, heading for the depot where the F.& C.C. railroad would provide special cars to carry them home. The Findley's regular shift change had occurred at two a.m. Now it was closer to 2:30, with tonight's train chugging along, approximately two hundred feet from the depot. Late arrivals from the Shurtloff and Last Dollar Mines scrambled to climb on board or scurried alongside, tin dinner pails clanking against their legs.

Fifteen or so Findley men already huddled on the Independence's platform, faces turned toward their approaching ride. Oblivious to the infernal machine half buried beneath their feet. One hundred pounds of explosives attached to a slender feed wire, the kind used to fasten stove pipes, that ran some fifty yards before being wrapped around a discarded chair leg. When the murderer jerked the leg, it would pull the trigger of a revolver aimed at the hidden explosives, causing the bullet to discharge.

Boom!

An infernal machine indeed.

The locomotive slowed as it neared the depot. The shriek of its whistle pierced the quiet landscape. As if that were the murderer's signal, he jerked the chair leg. The revolver discharged. The dynamite exploded. The blast was so powerful it extinguished lights in Altman, a mile and a half away, shattered windows in Goldfield and Independence and destroyed nearby homes.

An afterthought to the real horror: not the great chunks of flying earth and wood and pieces of the Independence's platform that caused the building to resemble a grotesque game of Jenga. Not the shattered windows, the sprung foundation posts, the entire western front that had collapsed in upon itself. Not the broken timbers in the basement where the explosives had been hidden, or the gaping holes in its roof.

Thirteen men killed outright. In all, twenty-seven killed or wounded.

That was the real horror.

Men were blown one hundred fifty feet straight up the hillside and mutilated beyond recognition. Screams, shouts, and confused voices of residents and miners racing to the scene. Some searched by lantern light for the wounded, others retrieved arms and legs and other body parts scattered across the terrain like leaves in autumn. Bits of flesh and bone were gathered into tin pails, the same way rag-and-bone men collected trash for resale.

With the dawn a special train left Cripple Creek for the depot. Inside was A. E. Carlton, who'd called the Findley and Shurtloff mines in order to detain their miners; Cripple Creek's Sheriff Henry Robertson; deputy sheriffs, and medical personnel. Law enforcement roped off the space around the depot to search for clues.

And set the cover-up in motion.

Within an hour following the explosion, the surrounding area was placed under guard and patrolled by those ex-parolees, thugs and hired guns who'd recently flooded Victor, those whom locals later whispered had planted the "infernal machine." In one voice, the Alliances' mouthpieces denounced the WFM, accused them of blowing up the Depot and called for every single member to be deported. Or hanged.

It was a marvel really, how such a vast number of company men could assemble so quickly—and carry out their superiors' orders with such efficiency.

While lanterns dotted the blackness and voices buzzed like angry insects, Ronan stood in a secluded enough area where he could view the entire area, including arriving and departing trains, without being seen. Ordinarily, he and members of his local would have been in the midst of the carnage, helping as best they could. Not now. This was something different. Now, Ronan was here as a watcher, keeping vigil over the corpse of the WFM. So that when the killer shuffled past, the corpse would reveal its identity to those who'd been appointed to observe. "You murdered me," the corpse would signal with a twitch or a sigh or an opening of its eyes.

No need for that.

Ronan already knew.

He might have been watching a version of *Swan Lake* at the Topic Theatre, the entire ballet choreographed down to the simplest *plié*. Pre-planned and flawlessly executed. If you put your emotions aside—and he had, though perhaps he was simply numb —he admired the members of the Alliances, the Pinkerton and Baldwin-Felts detectives along with their lackeys for so impeccably performing their parts. How long had the planning taken? Luck had certainly been with them, or perhaps God was on their side, the way Bishop Matz had declared it was early in the strike. Automatically, Ronan reached up to clutch his row of necklaces, the imprint of the Celtic cross that hanged low rough against his palm.

Despite the cold, Ronan felt too hot in his Carhartt jacket and Levi's. While he loved his church, Bishop Matz's betrayal was simply one in a long line. Obviously, when Jesus said, "Blessed are the poor in spirit...those who mourn...those who hunger and thirst for righteousness...those who are persecuted for righteousness' sake," his earthly spokesmen, with their fuschia-colored sashes and unctuous smiles, meant, *"Except for those who want to join a union. For those who seek a living wage and safer working conditions."* Ronan's uncles, all the twenty who'd been hanged following the Molly Maguire's sham trial, had been excommunicated and denied proper Christian burial.

To the east, purple limned the horizon. Ronan's mind continued to race. Not focusing on the explosion, but viewing every aspect of these past fifteen months—from the day the Colorado City strike had been called to the explosion, from a different vantage point. Like observing the Earth from a hot air balloon. How different things would look. Searching for what he might have missed, earth-bound as he was. Some larger meaning? Some connection? What? A different truth than what he'd always assumed?

Which hit him like a sudden punch to the gut.

How had he missed the obvious? The "before" and "today" and the link between the two. Always there—a spectre which had only materialized after Ronan's vision had cleared enough to see what was before his eyes. He'd been raised on explosions and plots hatched by politicians and coal owners who, using James McParland as their Angel of Death, had annihilated the Mollies so thoroughly that to this day, relatives dared not breathe their names.

And who is the mastermind behind this current horror?

James McParland?

I'd bet my life on it.

Ronan wished he could share his suspicions with Uncle Liam so his uncle could respond, "You're onto something, laddie," or scoff that he'd gone barmy. Or Maeve. But Uncle Liam was safely away in Palmer Lake with his new family, working in some fancy hotel, and Maeve...well, Maeve Mooney was lost to him forever.

About that connection...

Feckin' hell. He'd been like the Israelites wandering in the wilderness for forty years when all they'd had to do was keep walking in one direction until they'd eventually run smack dab into the Promised Land.

Pennsylvania's Long Strike of 1875. Lasting seven months. Bloody on both sides, though it was the coal authorities who'd formed the police force whose sole purpose was to kill violent strikers. And fancy that—the increase in violence had coincided with the arrival of Pinkerton agents, James McParland in particular, who'd been tasked with infiltrating the Mollies long enough to gather—and plant—the "evidence" that would destroy them. Simple enough since, from investigation through arrest and prosecution, everything had been orchestrated by the coal barons.

And now here we are three decades later. Only our strike is still going strong after nearly a year.

Had the explosion been McParland's way of ending the stalemate?

Sure, the government, the MOA and Citizens' Alliances and military were ostensibly in charge, but who had experience destroying a union?

James McParland.

Cunning and shrewd, like *Paradise Lost*'s Beelzebub, flattering and cajoling and acting as Satan's most trusted confidant so Satan could more easily orchestrate his demonic army's revenge.

McParland had been hired early on in the Colorado City strike. All those reports you send to your overlords. All those men, good union men or sympathetic strangers just wandering into the refining mills the way McParland had wandered into Pennsylvania's coal patches, sabotaging union actions or instigating violence. When the current strike had spread to the District, McParland had entrenched himself ever more quietly and methodically. Whispering in the ears of idiots like Horace Strank and James Peabody, manipulating events in order to...what?

Take out the last of the Doyles?

Nonsense! Ronan thought, though goosebumps rose on his forearms. The Molly Maguires had all been Irish—Irish Catholic, to be precise—but the WFM was comprised of different nationalities and faiths. And the District's membership numbered in the thousands, not the dozens who'd belonged to the Mollies.

This isn't about me. Certainly not McParland's twisted plot to finish off the remainder of one insignificant family. McParland was too calculating to be ruled by hatred or jealousy or something so petty as a personal desire for revenge. He'd been best friends with Black Jack Kehoe, King of the Mollies, yet had perjured himself and later watched Kehoe hang without a twinge of remorse.

You have to possess a soul in order to feel emotion.

When the sun peeked above the horizon, Ronan knew it was time to go. Victor was where the armory was located, where the bodies would be taken, where the rest of this charade would unfold. He'd head there. He inhaled the brisk morning air and glanced one final time in the direction that, had he been able to see through mountains and into the future, Maeve's home would reside. Was she just awakening in her childhood bedroom with its pink bedspread and butterflies? Or had she, so recently alive in this time and place, been startled awake, if only by the echo of the Independence Depot explosion, calling his name?

It felt surreal...

All that we see or seem
Is but a dream within a dream

She would be thinking of him, he knew that for certain. Often, he could feel her thoughts mingling with his, even carry on silent conversations—fancying they could engage in a back and forth, just as they had after lovemaking, while holding hands, or simply sitting side by side, not needing to speak at all. She would be thinking of him now, knowing this was the day. Worrying for him, mourning the death of his dreams and the dreams of all those who'd remained loyal from the beginning. She'd been the smart one, to grieve a century into the future rather than in real time when it was more likely one could literally die from a broken heart.

He remembered Padrick Mooney's warning about the strike, "You'll be annihilated." Maeve's face whiter than the snow blanketing the Sangre de Cristos, when she'd cried, "You don't love me enough." He hadn't. Perhaps. He wished he could claw his way back to the before time, where he might have made a different choice. No, he wouldn't have. But Ronan would give nearly anything to be able to dip back into their happiest moments together, freeze them, at least until he could relinquish them without regret. Knowing that he and his Maeve could create new, even happier memories together.

He wished he'd had the courage to follow Maeve to the White Rabbit, to take her hand in his and fall into the future. Or to death, perhaps, if her and Padrick's stories had been nonsense.

But how could he give all his love to a woman when he'd given it first to a belief?

~

By eight a.m., all the mines in the area, save for Jimmy Burns' Portland, were shut down. Workers, armed by their employers and under their instruction, began gathering in Victor, three miles from the town of Independence.

Bloodhounds were sent for in order to track the killer or killers, but... odd. The most experienced bloodhounds were housed right in the area, yet new dogs were ordered shipped from Palmer Lake and Trinidad. By the time the hounds arrived, the trail had grown cold. Still, the dogs quickly picked up a scent that led them to a house occupied by a professional gunman for the MOA and after that, to the powder house at the Vindicator Mine. Since the powder house had been off limits to union miners since the beginning of the strike, it was a mystery how they could have removed one hundred pounds of closely guarded explosives without being seen.

The hounds were immediately called off.

After the remains of the dead and the bodies of the wounded were placed in railroad cars and transported to Victor, the wounded were removed to the Victor and Red Cross hospitals. The dead were loaded into horse-drawn hearses, and with grim-faced locals flanking either side of North Fourth Street, driven to the Dunn undertaking parlors, where the coroner's office was located. When Coroner Doran made the mistake of referring to the explosion as an "accident," the leader of the militia, a fanatical union hater, ordered the bodies transferred to the undertaking parlors of a more sympathetic-to-the-owners' J. H. Hunt.

An increasingly agitated crowd gathered along Diamond Avenue, between Fourth and Fifth Street, where the Red Cross Hospital, formerly the Gold Coin Club the Woods family had built for their employees, was located and where the wounded were being treated.

Relatives, friends, loved ones could be inside, their identities yet unpublished, which increased the bystanders' rage, their threats to lynch members of the WFM, even to burn them at the stake.

Prudently, all of Victor's saloons were closed, though the narrative was already in place, the scapegoats identified. Which made it easier for the various Alliances to perform their deeds without opprobrium.

Under pain of lynching, members of the "inner circle" of the MOA forced Henry Robertson, Cripple Creek's sheriff and a union member, to resign. Robertson was persuaded by the mob outside Alliance headquarters, where he'd been brought, and who had torn down nearby billboards in preparation for constructing makeshift gallows. The *crack!crack!* of gunfire finally convinced Robertson he'd best resign and depart the county, as demanded. Robertson was immediately replaced by another member of the Citizens' Alliance, Edward Bell—no relation to the hated-by-the-strikers General Sherman Bell. After that, all of Teller County's regularly elected undersheriffs, judges, commissioners, and other civil officers were forced to resign, to be replaced by mine owners, mine superintendents and other members of the Mine Owners' Association. Even Coroner Doran, who'd referred to the explosion as an accident, was given the choice of resigning or being hanged.

In the space of a few minutes, every law enforcement position in the District was occupied by someone employed by or in the pocket of the mine owners.

Ronan had ridden the streetcar to Goldfield, after which he decided to walk the rest of the way to Victor. Craving his own musings rather than the opinions of yet more people who knew less than he did. He was certain of one thing: this day would be the denouement, not of a book or a play, but of the strike and perhaps his life.

Was this what Padrick Mooney had hinted at, refusing to give him details other than that one pronouncement, like Moses coming down off the mountain? Still, Ronan didn't need Padrick Mooney to confirm what must be obvious to even the most obtuse. Or the most delusional.

Other than the sound of Ronan's boots on the graveled path and a trio of camp robbers that took flight upon his approach, the area had a stillness to it, as if the world was wrung out and needed to rest. He halted to look back at Goldfield with its bull pen tents dotting the plain, and Independence on the hill above. Far enough away to look peaceful, rather than the hellscape it had become.

When God had given man dominion over all the earth, had He envisioned this trash heap would be the result? All for the sake of gold bars and baubles? What had this land been like when the Utes had roamed the hills and plains before being corralled into reservations? Even twenty years ago?

Is humankind meant to be a scourge on the planet, a scourge to each other, or are there a multitude of alternatives we're too straitjacketed to even imagine?

Ronan stretched, a weariness setting over him. Judging from the position of the sun, it must be close to noon. What...adventures... awaited him upon reaching Victor? What more carefully planned "surprises" did the MOA and Citizens' Alliance have in store?

When Ronan turned to continue his journey, he spotted a figure, one leg bent as he leaned against a tree stump, alongside the trail, perhaps thirty feet ahead. Familiar. Little taller than a boy, western hat tipped back, cigarette dangling from his lips, looking calm as calm could be.

Ronan's heartbeat exploded, thundering in his ears. What was *he* doing here? Ronan hadn't seen him in more than a week, so why would he turn up now? Coincidence? Not with Leprechaun's record. Had he been part of this heinous plot, the way he'd been part of the plot to derail the F.& C.C. back in November? At the heart of most every evil, Paddy Mooney was bound to be somewhere nearby.

Ronan broke into a run. Just as the smaller man became aware of his presence, Ronan tackled him.

"You did this, didn't you?" Hands around Leprechaun's throat, pressing, pressing into his windpipe. "You and McParland and the Alliance."

Leprechaun's eyes bugged. He tried to speak, but Ronan tightened his chokehold. Leprechaun clawed at his hands.

"I know about you; I've known for months. You betrayed us, betrayed the cause. I should kill you on the spot."

Leprechaun's face was the color of puce. He bucked beneath Ronan, attempting to shake free, but Ronan easily held him down.

Gazing into that contorted face, Ronan considered. Choke him to death? Pummel him until that smirking mug was the texture of hamburger? Too bad he hadn't carried his pistol. A bullet to the gut and his death would have been long, drawn out and agonizing.

Instead, Ronan removed his grip and eased off the flailing body. He stood over Leprechaun, watching him roll over, gasp for air. He struggled to rise, failed, curled into a fetal position.

"I know who you are, Paddy Mooney. I hope you rot in hell."

Ronan drew his leg back. As if kicking a football, he caught Leprechaun with his hobnailed boot, right in the stomach. Leprechaun screamed as he was lifted into the air. Slammed back to the ground. Lay still.

Ronan didn't bother to check to see if his former friend still breathed. Rather, he stepped around Paddy Mooney and continued on his way.

Twenty-Four

W ord spread that a mass meeting was to be held at 3 p.m. The place: a vacant lot located on the corner of Fourth and Victor, near the spot where Sheriff Robertson had been threatened with the erection of a makeshift gallows.

Nearby, the Victor Armory, formerly a hardware building and sometimes a dance hall, had been designated headquarters for the State Militia. Soldiers now clustered on its colonnaded porch and in the surrounding area to monitor the rapidly swelling crowd.

Michael O'Connell, Victor's forty-three-year-old marshal, was alarmed by the size of the gathering, now approaching a thousand. He could imagine the incendiary speeches soon to be given by mine owner mouthpieces and how that rhetoric would inflame already unstable tempers.

There'd been enough blood shed for one day.

Since most of the leaders who'd instigated this morning's firings, including newly-appointed Sheriff Edward Bell, were ensconced inside Victor's Armory, Marshal O'Connell determined to meet with them. If this afternoon's gathering could not be cancelled, he intended to plead for enough soldiers to maintain control. Unfortunately, he was barred from even entering the Armory. Why? Because he'd maintained from the very beginning of the strike that he could keep the peace without calling in the militia. And because he remained a card-carrying member of the WFM.

Once O'Connell was refused help, he quickly assembled one hundred union men and appointed them deputy policemen. After passing out white ribbon badges inscribed with "Special Police," along with rifles, shotguns and revolvers, O'Connell positioned his men on three sides of the yet vacant lot.

A member of the WFM taking charge? Not on June 6, 1904. Not within a four-minute walk of the Red Cross Hospital where doctors were frantically working to stitch back together mangled remains and previously hale miners. Where corpses laid out at Hunt's undertaking parlors were being readied for their coffins while devastated families wept over their losses.

Sheriff Bell and his cohorts dismissed O'Connell and his deputies at gunpoint.

Clarence C. Hamlin was a small man with big ambitions. Secretary of the Mine Owners Association and an attorney with a gift for oratory, Hamlin knew how he would frame today's closing argument: Good v. Evil. "It is our duty to protect life, liberty and property by annihilating the WFM, in particular," he would declare. "For they are the chief union seeking to overthrow Colorado's laws and replace them with their own."

And organized labor's defense as embodied by troglodytes like Big Bill Haywood? *Something for nothing, lads, and to hell with those who risk their capital in business endeavors that pay your wages and allow you to prosper.*

As an American, Clarence Hamlin might not believe in the divine right of kings, but he certainly believed in the divine right of capitalism. And this morning's published ruling from the Colorado

Supreme Court provided further confirmation. In short, the justices had held that Governor Peabody enjoyed the exclusive prerogative of determining where and when a state of war exists. Translation: When James Peabody declared the present action in the District to be a war, it was a war. Therefore, any citizen could be lawfully arrested and held, regardless of the writ of habeas corpus.

Which means we are unrestrained in our actions. We can do what's necessary without fear of reprisal.

Hamlin had nearly laughed aloud—while maintaining a decorous facade because of the uncollected body parts still dotting various hillsides—after purchasing a newspaper from one of the few newsboys braving the chaos, and scanning it to read an alarmed reporter's interpretation of the ruling, *"Strikers resisting with arms, may be stood up against a wall, after a drum-head court martial, and shot to death."*

Hamlin would not deny that this morning's carnage had been horrific. Should those who'd planned it speak honestly among themselves—which they would not—they'd lament the number of unexpected deaths. Like bowling a strike when you expected a split. However, being a top-shelf lawyer, he would take advantage of changing circumstances. It was he who'd been instrumental in forcing Sheriff Robertson and the other union stooges to resign.

He had already loaded one final bullet into the chamber of his revenge, after which... Blam!

At 3 p.m., Clarence Hamlin strode to the lone transfer wagon that had been placed on the lot and which would act as a speaker's box. The militia, rifles at the ready, were positioned on the bluff behind him in front of the Gold Coin Mine's shaft house. After taking his place on the bed of the wagon, he straightened to his full diminutive height and adjusted his suit coat. Deep breaths, centering himself as he would before launching into a closing argument.

And then, like an Old Testament prophet, he called down the wrath of God upon the Western Federation of Miners.

This is all a set piece, like Nativity scenes at St. Peter's, Ronan thought, standing amidst a sea of bowlers, fedoras, western hats and the occasional Gainsborough, adorned with feathers and flowers. *Only there is nothing holy about this.*

As detailed as the timetable for arrivals and departures on the Short Line.

2:30 a.m.: Blow up twenty-seven men.

12 p.m.: Oust Sheriff Robertson; force every official connected with the county's civil government to resign; Replace all with MOA loyalists.

1 p.m.: Call for a public meeting across from the Armory where the militia is gathered.

2 p.m.: Oust Marshal O'Connell and deputies.

2:15 p.m.: Move militia into place behind vacant lot.

3 p.m.: Light the fuse.

Ronan was tall enough to enjoy an unobstructed view of Clarence Hamlin. With his high starched collar, precisely parted hair and calculating eyes, Hamlin looked more like some fussbudget bank teller than what he was—an alpha wolf about to signal his pack that their prey was at its weakest; time to take it down.

Ronan scanned the surrounding faces, half expecting to see James McParland grinning at him like Ammit, Devourer of the Dead, come to feast on his heart. Women, some with children, were sprinkled among members of the Citizens' Alliance and Mine Owners' Association; strikebreakers who, judging from their pale, hungry look, were newly arrived from big city slums; and hard cases from Canon City's Colorado State Prison where they'd been incarcerated for crimes mine owners now paid them to commit. Since most of the District's mine guards also had prison records, Ronan reckoned the strike had provided employment for half the state's parolees.

"You will be annihilated." Padrick had warned. Yet, fool that he was, Ronan still could not quite believe the lifeblood of the WFM was about to bleed out as swiftly, as effortlessly as a pig in a slaughterhouse. Somehow, because his cause was just, some part of Ronan must naïvely cling to the fantasy that the God of Creation would mercifully alter fate's trajectory.

When Ronan shifted position, he felt the unyielding outline of the revolver tucked between his belt and Levi's. Marshal O'Connell had provided the Peacemaker along with the white ribbon badge proclaiming Ronan and one hundred other union brothers his deputies. As if a lone weapon and a handful of bullets would make a difference among a thousand similarly armed men.

When Clarence Hamlin howled his howl and his pack rushed in for the kill, would Ronan even care? *How many more breaths am I meant to draw? Will I die quickly as Da—one moment here, the next blown into so many pieces not even God could have reassembled the parts—or waste away like Mam until she drowned in her own blood?*

Ronan ignored the glares directed at him, even from some who'd once proudly carried a WFM card. The next few minutes would once again prove Jay Gould's truism that he could hire one half of the working class to kill the other half.

My fault. No excuses. I was warned. Ronan could have moved in with Uncle Liam and his new family. He could have flung himself down Maeve's White Rabbit in hopes of reuniting. He could have ridden a train to some Massachusetts's sea town, joined a whaling crew and prowled the Atlantic for his own white whale; he could have disappeared into the Rockies.

Out of an infinity of choices, I continued playing this part, as if I had no agency.

How stupid. How predictable.

"United States citizens must arm themselves and drive these

Western Federation men to the hills!" Hamlin was bellowing from his platform.

Anger crackled like lightning; the air thickened with menace.

"They—the WFM—are responsible for the Independence explosions and the deaths thereof."

Regret flooded Ronan—regret he allowed himself to indulge in even at this inflammatory moment. He regretted he'd sacrificed so much fighting for a cause sacred to him but shunned by so many. That he hadn't followed Maeve into the future. He could have turned his back on that seven-year-old breaker boy, on the child clutching his mother and his Da's hands as they witnessed the sudden drop of his uncles' bodies, their necks snapped as easily as you'd wring the neck of a chicken.

You could have created a life in a world far more forgiving than this one.

"...Gang of cutthroats," Hamlin boomed from his platform, jolting Ronan back to the present. Oh, this mouse could roar. "Their membership in the WFM is a badge of murder and arson."

"Lynch them," yelled a man Ronan identified as a Pinkerton spy. Because of course, McParland would salt this crowd in a twisted homage to the way WFM organizers salted non-union jobs.

"You must drive them out, drive them over the hills!"

The storm was upon them, exploding in fury. Several union men pushed against the tide, heading for the safety of the nearby WFM hall.

Hamlin lifted his arms to the sky in imprecation. "Run 'em all out, all their lice and nits too!"

Ronan found himself consumed by such rage that he could have smashed everyone within reach, whipped out his revolver and put a bullet through Hamlin's brain. Blaspheming Annie Fein and her children, all those women who toiled from dawn to death, who brought babies into the world because that's what the Church commanded them to do in order to please God, but it's really so you and your offspring can provide more bodies to be broken on the rack of capitalism.

Because me and Big Bill and the WFM ultimately failed you all.

Ronan slipped his right hand up and back to curl his fingers around the grip of his Peacemaker; eased it out of his belt.

"Kill them!" shouted a woman holding a boy in a sailor suit.

Aye, thought Ronan, pistol at his side.

"Lynch them!"

"For the blowing up of those brave boys, fifty union men should be shot down like dogs and as many more swung to telegraph poles. Every Federation man is a criminal, and it is up to you men to drive them over the hills with your guns."

"Whadda ya mean by 'them?'" roared a miner Ronan recognized as Alf Miller, six feet some and two hundred pounds, full of liquor and indignation.

Someone struck Miller over the head with a revolver. A fistfight broke out.

The storm broke wild.

Shots rang out. A woman screamed. More yelling. "Kill them all!"

Stay? Risk a shot at Hamlin or retreat? Split-second decision.

Ronan forced his way in the opposite direction of the fistfight, away from the center of that particular chaos, back toward Fourth Street and the shelter of Victor's WFM hall. People falling, slamming into each other, pushing and shoving, intent on breaking free of the chaos and seeking sanctuary alongside streets or inside buildings. Ronan pushing against jostling bodies. Someone grabbed him from behind. Hard. A half turn and an uppercut to the side of the head with his free hand and Ronan continued moving, maneuvering around a prone body. Dead or alive he didn't stop to look.

Victor's union hall was located on the second floor of a large building constructed from red brick in the Italianate style so common in contemporary Victor. On either side of the hall, huge awnings sheltered Palmer's Billiard Hall and the Simonton Grocer

Co. Ronan's destination—the double doors between that would lead to safety.

More screams. A volley of gunfire. Most likely the militia from their position on the ridge. Soaring above the cacophony, Clarence Hamlin, his screed reduced to "Kill! Kill! Kill!"

Ronan and a handful of others reached the doors between the awnings. Overhead in elaborate grillwork, "WFMA" and above that "Victor Miner Union No. 32."

Sanctuary. For now.

Ronan raced up the staircase. Small landing at the top. Narrow hallways leading to four offices. Huge meeting hall where dozens of miners had congregated and were leaning out of four tall windows, monitoring events on the square below.

Ronan recognized most of them, who greeted him with a wave or a short nod. Men whose houses he'd visited; who'd patronized the Pick-Axe and sung along with Maeve during her piano sets, baseball games, picnics at Pinnacle Park, marched beside at parades, part of a brotherhood that had remained stoically loyal during the strike...

Crossing to the first window, he studied the scene below.

"Two dead, we're hearing."

Ronan positioned himself on the other side, so he had a clear view. Soldiers everywhere. He counted five bodies. Low voices around him, those at the windows describing events for those behind.

Ronan hadn't been at the hall since he'd attended the funeral service of the local's president, William Dodsworth, back in November, after Dodsworth had plunged to his death in the Delmonico mine shaft while mending a steam pipe. During Dodsworth's ceremony, Ronan had been marched out of the ceremony by a file of officers, one of whom now stood next to Clarence Hamlin from his perch atop the transport wagon while Hamlin vomited his hate to an increasingly empty square.

Maybe Dodsworth had the best of it, Ronan thought, his gaze

sweeping the scene below. Not living to see this. But it was important to remember, if he lived so long as to pass along the memory.

Across the street was an advertisement painted on the entire
side of a building: The word "Cremo," the "o" touching an enormous cigar shaped like a submarine, and below, "5¢." A deserted
trolley car, tangles of telegraph and electricity wires atop wooden
poles.

Padrick's a lineman; annihilated, annihilated, annihilated...

A handful of figures were hurrying along a nearly deserted
Fourth Street in one direction while right below the hall, a man
emptied his revolver at someone running in the opposite direction.
Behind the ridge where soldiers had been standing guard
throughout this dustup, the Gold Coin Mine, with its stained-glass
windows and state-of-the-art equipment, rose like a benevolent
landlord over the entire city.

Never again. All that had died with the Independence explosion. No, with the strike.

More men clustered at the windows; one who'd leaned out
farther than prudent on the wide window sills in order to obtain a
better view, suddenly breathed, "Jesus, Mary and Joseph!"

Ronan, they all saw it then; militia marching from the direction
of the Armory, positioning themselves around the hall's exterior
and beneath the awnings covering the billiard hall and grocery
store. More on the rooflines of the buildings across the street—
buildings taller than the hall so soldiers could easily shoot into its
windows. Extending to the bank building next door, which over-
looked the hall's skylight, was another easy target.

Ronan felt a thrill of something, even a fierce joy? If it came to
this, that they would all be mown down in a hail of bullets, wasn't
that better than the long, slow slide toward death from black lung
or being asphyxiated in a tunnel no wider than your body, or being
shot in the back running away rather than making a last stand,
returning fire for fire because "This is what I believe. This is what I
am willing to die for."

There were approximately fifty miners in the room; fifty against hundreds. Pistols against Winchester and Springfield rifles? Or would mine owners and their goons save their ammunition and rig a second explosion?

Will they say we blew up ourselves or something equally as outrageous? Everyone will know it's a lie and no one will care.

Unless someone like Emma Langdon, the courageous savior of the *Victor Daily Record*, decided to immortalize them. Ronan rather liked that idea. Would Maeve stumble across Emma's articles in some long-forgotten newspaper series stashed away in Shamrock Ranch's library? "How did I miss this?" she'd say. "So that's how Ronan Doyle met his end." Perhaps she'd shed a tear or two before going about her life... though Ronan knew better.

The rifle barrels of the soldiers positioned on the rooftop gleamed in the afternoon sun. A pleasant June day. Colorado's summers consisted of such days, each more exquisite than the last. Not like Pennsylvania's, so grey and muggy and depressing. He hoped Uncle Liam wouldn't decide to relocate his family back east because of this. But if he did leave, perhaps he and Annie could buy a farm somewhere on Colorado's eastern plains. Ronan had worked with a miner who'd come from a tiny town, Snyder, it was called, which ran along the South Platte and where you could raise cattle and grow cantaloupes the size of a man's head and where you never again had to schedule your life by the shriek of a whistle or worry whether the price of gold would suddenly collapse the way silver had following the repeal of the Sherman Silver Purchase Act and your skill would be as worthless as a three-headed dog. Had he and Uncle Liam ever talked about Snyder? About farming and cattle ranching? Probably not because Ronan, fool that he was, had given his heart to the mountains and the union.

The door to the outside landing was locked and bolted, so the miners didn't at first hear Sheriff Ed Bell, accompanied by a troop of soldiers, arriving at the bottom of the staircase.

Bell climbed the stairs. "Surrender your arms and go home," he shouted outside the door.

"The hall is our home," yelled one.

"We own the building," yelled a second. "And if we think to leave the hall, we'll be murdered single-handed by either you or the mob."

"We have no intention of harming anyone, but there's an insane mob out there."

Not a mob so much now, but the militia, only awaiting the command to let loose their vengeance. Ronan had removed his pistol again, as had many others. That peculiar detachment remained, as if he were standing beside himself, with his doppelganger taking note of it all. No doubt Bell was playing for time, making certain his militia and sharpshooters were in place before he took them out like metal ducks at a carnival game.

Losing patience—or perhaps all his troops were properly positioned—Ed Bell shouted. "All right then. We'll take you by force."

Almost immediately, a fusillade of shots was fired into the hall windows and through the skylight. Ronan hit the floor near the edge of one wall, away from the exploding windows. Glass from the shattered skylight rained down like deadly icicles. Bullets everywhere. Caught between a crossfire, with shots from the militia above angled down, while those from below shooting upward. Men yelling and diving and crawling away or crouching with their hands over their heads to protect themselves from falling debris.

Volley after volley, slamming into plaster, brick and wood; ping, ping like insects beating against a porch light. Someone crying, "I'm hit," others cursing. The walls and windows were totally demolished. Yet, despite the weapons, none of the miners shot back. Before they could reach a window to return fire, they knew they'd be taken out. And as if by silent accord, they'd adhered to the WFM's pledge of no violence. Despite what the rest of the world would say.

The length between volleys lessened. Then scattered shots like a rainstorm as it eases off.

Silence.

"We're done," said one miner into the surrounding ruins, the scattered bodies.

Aye, thought Ronan. *We can go out in a hail of bullets, believing we'll be remembered in glory. Or we can surrender and tell ourselves we'll live to fight another day. Which we will not.*

Someone risked a move toward one of the shattered windows, keeping to the wall, pulled out a white handkerchief and waved it toward the militia. "Stop, stop shooting. We surrender."

The handkerchief was immediately riddled with bullets.

So, this is how we'll go, Ronan thought. Despite the shards of glass that could slice his chest to ribbons, he could crawl to one of the windows. How many could he kill before his turn? One of the mob below? A nameless soldier on a rooftop? Or should he unbolt the door and take down Ed Bell, that scab, that tool of all that was evil, as his last out?

Ronan edged toward the door.

"Cease fire!" Ed Bell yelled.

A patter of shots; then a final raindrop. Silence. The storm had passed.

Ronan looked around. He was surprised no one had been killed, though he counted four who appeared to have been wounded.

"We need to get them help," he said. Others had risen to their feet; some tending as best they could to their fallen comrades.

"It's over then?"

Ronan nodded. "Unless they shoot us on the way out."

In twos and threes, they exited the hall, with Ronan near the end.

"Hands above your heads," bellowed Sheriff Bell. "And keep 'em there."

While Bell lined up the strikers, the crowd flanking both sides of North 4th Street screamed for vengeance. After Bell's soldiers divested the arrestees of their weapons, the bystanders swarmed—shoving, kicking, beating. One miner was nearly scalped with a bayonet; Ronan had a pistol jammed down his throat, with the thug screaming, "Why shouldn't I blow your brains out?"

If Ronan had been capable of replying, he would have taunted, "Go ahead!" As if anyone yet believed life was worth clinging to.

After the mob's fury had largely dissipated, one of the sergeants called a halt to the abuse. While the prisoners were being marched to the Armory Hall, some bystanders tried to take photos, only to have their cameras knocked to the ground and stomped on. Single file, hands above his head, Ronan scanned the faces in passing, recognizing so many, from grocers to assayers to patrons of the Pick-Axe, well enough to call them by their god given names.

What was this? Genuine hatred? Pandering to the moment? Fearful that their own previous sympathies, their own secrets might be uncovered if they didn't show proper loyalty to the mine owners and their thugs?

At this moment, Ronan realized what he perhaps should have understood far earlier: *I have no understanding of human nature.*

The Armory hall was reconfigured as a temporary bullpen. While armed guards kept watch, more arrestees arrived, hour after hour until three hundred were jammed into a room meant for half that.

Little sleep. Less food. To keep the ever-lurking fear of claustrophobia at bay, Ronan distracted himself imagining a future he might never possess. Why not a horseback ride to Breckenridge? Another mining town he'd never visited. Pack his horse's saddlebags and wander across endless hills and forests and meadows thick with herds of elk, antelope, and deer—without another human to be seen. By his lonesome, except for maybe a dog. He liked that idea. Not those irritating Chihuahuas gentlewomen carried around like some sort of parasol. Why not an Airedale Terrier that could hunt birds and game and was small enough that, if it tired, Ronan could lift it up and cradle it before him while riding?

I might call him—it should be a him—Puck.

Hadn't that been the name of his Uncle Mikey's mutt? Michael Doyle, the last of his uncles to be hanged.

Puck and I will ride the high country.

On the second day, Ronan and his fellow prisoners were removed from the Armory Hall and marched to Victor's rail yard. Once again, their route was lined with shouting, fist-waving bystanders. Interesting that locals seemed to have a sixth sense as to their whereabouts. Courtesy of the MOA, for certain. Once at the tracks, the prisoners were herded to a narrow-gauge boxcar topped by armed guards monitoring their movements. Several more were already boarding the passenger car behind.

"Hurry it up!"

Poking, prodding, shoving them into the space, soon packed in so tight a man could drop dead and remain upright.

Breathe! Think about...nothing...

After the door was slid shut and locked from the outside, Ronan feared his heart would explode.

He closed his eyes. *You survived the cage. You survived the tunnels.*

Knowing there would be worse to come.

Throughout the six-mile ride, Ronan distracted himself with deciphering the shouts from the guards, outside on the rooftop, counting the endless crack of rifle shots. As if they were engaged in some grand celebration.

Which they were. Sprawled before them, the carcass of the WFM, already riddled with bullet holes and betrayal.

Upon reaching Cripple Creek, the prisoners were marched to an empty building that had formerly served as a gymnasium. Jammed together once again, while guards bearing sawed-off shotguns and six-shooters monitored them from a balcony. Citizens had surrounded the building, howling and pounding on the front door, seeking entrance. It reminded Ronan of that book he'd recently read, about Count Dracula, tucked away in his castle in Transylvania, with wolves outside baying at the moon and poor Jonathan Harker locked inside with those intent on sucking out his life. It was unnerving, the rise and fall of such hatred, the craving for retribution the way those female vampires had craved Harker's blood. Stirring the mob would be Pinkerton spies, MOA plants, and turncoats fearful that, if they did not denounce former friends and a cause they'd recently championed, they'd end up among the condemned. Judging from the tense faces of the guards overhead, they were protecting Ronan and the others as much as guarding them.

"Sweet Mother Mary," cursed one of the miners. "They're making more noise than my wife when she snores."

Which caused Ronan to smile. A hardy bunch, as Uncle Liam would say. And tough enough to survive anything thrown at them.

Days passed. No beds or bedding; Ronan slept seated, his legs stretched in front of him, his back against a wall. Always hungry: a ham sandwich at night, an egg sandwich for breakfast and a coffee, if you could dip your tin cup quick enough in the five-gallon can provided.

Still, Ronan was no worse off than his union brothers and that gave him comfort. He often thought of his uncle, hoped he'd married Annie as he'd promised and was working in that grand Palmer Lake hotel. Thought even more often of his Maeve. Dreamed of her.

Ronan couldn't regret not following her.

Yet he wished he had.

Immediately after Ronan and the miners had been marched to the Armory on June 6, locals had rushed Victor's union hall, smashing furnishings, defacing walls, tearing down curtains, destroying books and union papers. Any uncovered charters and membership ledgers were carted off to the Citizens' Alliance.

Across the District, WFM halls were ransacked, including Cripple Creek's No. 40 where doors were broken down, furnishings demolished and the windows of the reading room and secretary's office smashed. Once again, the locals' records were swept away, ostensibly to be used as incriminating evidence in future trials that would never be held. Which provided an added benefit for the mine owners and their stooges because history would record their voices rather than those of the vanquished.

Engineer's hall No. 80, WFM, an especially finely appointed building, had its new piano flipped over and smashed, its Brussels carpet and various rugs torn and bayoneted, banners shredded, portieres ripped from windows and torn into rags. Hundreds of its library books were hurled from windows to the sidewalk below. All official records and books from the various organizations that met there were hauled off to military headquarters.

Written in blood, the following message was left on a blackboard: "For being a union man, deportation or death will be your fate. 'Citizens' Alliance.'"

The *Victor Daily Record*, Emma Langdon's newspaper, was raided, its printing presses and linotype machines destroyed.

Every union store was burgled. Stock was tossed into the street; coal oil poured over provisions like flour and sugar, rendering them inedible. Looters and members of the Citizens' Alliance carried off the rest of the groceries so that the remaining strikers' families risked starvation.

Whitecappers reappeared, harassing, sometimes kidnapping and torturing anyone union affiliated. One mine superintendent tore off a woman's clothes and kicked her to near death for being a union sympathizer. The Citizens' Alliance set up a seven-man commission—dismissed by locals who yet dared to speak out as a kangaroo court. Ultimately, General Sherman Bell "tried" nearly sixteen hundred union men. Almost immediately after the explosion, the first batch was deported to Kansas.

"They need harvest hands," said Bell, referring to Kansas farmers. "They can get eight weeks' work there and they can't come back here." Except prisoners were dumped in the middle of scrub brush and dirt and a landscape as alien as the moon with not a wheat or corn or hay field for days.

Ronan was tried soon after. The president of Local 40 was an important enough fellow to receive press interest. Particularly if he would repudiate the WFM and turn over his union card. Unfortunately for reporters, Ronan Doyle turned out to be a disappointment. Other than a "Never," when the commission demanded he renounce the WFM, he refused to speak. What sort of a headline can you make of that?

Hardly surprising, Ronan was on the next train bound for New Mexico. A long and wearying journey, nearly seven hundred miles. Lined faces, dirty, with cramped muscles and for most, stomachs that nearly touched their spines. Endless darkness. Stifling heat. Stench of bodies, piss and shit.

When the door to the box car finally slid open, Ronan and his companions gazed out at a desolate plain, white from alkali, and with not so much to be seen as a bony cow nudging sagebrush.

Ah, but the sun was bright and the air was pure. Once Ronan stumbled down the ramp, he gratefully filled his lungs, luxuriated in the endless sky, and spread out his arms to embrace the limitless space. He grinned at the miner next to him, Charles Anderson, one of the Victor miners who'd endured the hail of bullets along with him. Anderson grinned back.

"Move it!" A soldier shoved him from behind, though without enthusiasm, for they were as weary of the journey as their captives.

The miners walked nearly a mile before being halted by a stone that officially marked the line between the state of Colorado and the territory of New Mexico.

So, here we are.

The soldiers and deputies began walking back to their train, nearly a mile away. Charles Anderson raised a hunk of bread and shouted, "Give me liberty or give me death." Beside Ronan, a second miner began singing, "Sweet Land of Liberty, of Thee I sing." Ronan and the others repeated the words, though just the two lines, a chant rather than a song. Ronan thought of the flag he and Bill Haywood had created: IS COLORADO IN AMERICA? and he felt a sudden swelling of pride, so vast it brought tears to his eyes. The WFM might not have won this battle, but they'd done their best and this would be a war of a long season, with his kind nowhere defeated.

The train pulled away, its smoke low as a hovering spirit, but Ronan raised his arms, as he used to do after winning a bout at the Topic Theatre, and shouted to the sky.

This is what freedom feels like!

PART TEN

July – September 1904

❧

Life moves on, whether we act as cowards or heroes.

— HENRY MILLER

Twenty-Five

On July 26, Governor Peabody officially ended martial law and deactivated the National Guard, though whitecappers continued their vendetta. More breadwinners were driven from the District, leaving behind families with no means and no money. Members of the Women's Auxiliary, bankrolled by the WFM, secretly distributed food, after which they were rounded up and put in pens. Used to the harassment, upon release they resumed feeding families as best as they could.

A total of two hundred twenty-five men were deported. That did not include all those who disappeared into the mountains or simply walked out of the District and then the state.

C.C. Hamlin, who had instigated the June 6 violence with his speechifying, was soon elected District Attorney. When court cases were brought against anyone—whether mine owners or managers or members of law enforcement—for deporting strikers or for any related violence and property destruction, Hamlin refused to prosecute.

The mines reopened without union labor.

In November, James Peabody lost his re-election.

~

Ronan arrived in the town of Palmer Lake when leaves were just beginning to turn. Mostly he'd ridden the rails north—sometimes alone, sometimes with others—sleeping and eating with hoboes who'd pass along information about sympathetic locals, what town had a union hall or lodges and friendly law enforcement, which places to avoid. He found work on farms and ranches, in smaller towns as a dishwasher, stable hand or janitor and once as a handyman for a widow in exchange for room and board. Early on, he'd shaved off his beard and cut his hair, though he still kept his WFM card inside his boot. It wasn't until he neared Pueblo, with Colorado Springs the next city, that he grew more cautious, staying to the shadows on the off chance he might be recognized. While Sherman Bell and the rest had banished strikers as punishment, Ronan largely counted it a gift. Three months free of responsibility for anyone other than himself and with time enough to dig deep into his thirty-four years, reassess his past and plot his future.

In Palmer Lake, he rented a room from a WFM brother, Aidan McCartney, who'd once worked Leadville's silver mines. The WFM had its own underground, if you knew how to look for it. Not much needed to be said, and wasn't. It was just understood.

"Welcome, Colm Murphy!" Aidan said, opening the door to Ronan's room and gesturing for him to enter. Ronan had adopted his father's first name and his mother's maiden name. Most likely Aidan knew that wasn't his actual name. Most likely he knew exactly who Ronan was, but that was the way it was with the underground. Telling lies in order to protect a larger truth.

Right away Ronan liked the feel of Palmer Lake. Mountains close on two sides and air smelling so pure and sweet, surpassing even the times when he'd passed through parts of Colorado that had never known a mine or a factory or most likely, more than a sodbuster or two. Palmer Lake was located along the Denver & Rio Grande Railroad, which was how Ronan, now adept at train hopping, had arrived. Because it was both a resort town and a sanitarium for consumptive patients, Ronan imagined himself and Uncle Liam packing up his mam and bringing her here to recover in this fresh air and tender climate, though they'd never even heard of Palmer Lake and he didn't have the emotional energy to add one more regret to his ever-expanding list.

That first night, Ronan slept well, knowing his uncle was nearby and that the initial phase of his plan would soon be completed.

The next morning, Ronan pulled his cap low and set out to explore the town. Hotel Rockland, where Uncle Liam should still be employed, was his first destination and such an impressive sight, Ronan's breath caught. Situated near the base of a mountain, the hotel was the biggest sprawl of buildings he'd ever seen, all pitched roofs, angles and porches. Made completely of wood, without a hint of brick, so its builders obviously weren't concerned about fire. A huge porch for tubercular patients who spent most of their days outside, even in winter.

Guests, most of them wealthy from the look of it, strolled the lawns, which, because of the nearby mountain, would be cast all in shadow by mid-afternoon. Children clustered around a petting zoo, while other guests headed for carriages that would take them to the Chautauqua, which was Palmer Lake's claim to fame. Every summer, tent universities were set up. Besides plays, concerts and family-friendly versions of Vaudeville, the lectures were the main draw. Some of the lecturers were famous, all of them eager to share their knowledge concerning the secrets to better health, prison reform, women's rights, literature, and the latest scientific theories. Ronan wondered whether the labor wars had already been a featured topic. Some pompous ass blathering, "The unions sowed class consciousness, after which it sprang up to destroy them." Though Ronan couldn't imagine these delicately dressed women with their smooth, thin, graceful, fluttering gloved hands and the birds' nests perched atop their heads ever concerning themselves with such an uncivilized subject.

Uncle Liam had chosen an ideal place to raise his new family, Ronan would give him that. How different his own life could have been if he'd realized a man's opportunities could extend beyond mining.

But I'd never have met my Maeve then.

Cripple Creek must possess some peculiar magic. Maybe all those holes punched into the earth or driving down deep had stirred other worldly forces. The Irish already lived half their lives in unseen worlds or writing tales about unseen worlds or living in fear of them. So, a White Rabbit wasn't so far-fetched, if you thought about it.

Still, Ronan didn't regret the arc of his life.

The only thing I regret is that we didn't win.

Ronan purchased a bottle of Jim Beam, which he presented to Aidan McCartney upon his return. After grabbing shot glasses from the parlor, Aidan settled them both in rocking chairs on the front porch, which provided a picturesque view of the lake itself. Train idling on the tracks, row boats skimming the water, fishermen casting lines from the banks, picnickers lounging on blankets or wandering nearby trails to pick wildflowers.

"Do you know a Liam Doyle?" Ronan asked without preamble.

If Aidan was surprised by the question, he didn't show it. "We attend the same church in Monument, the next town over."

"Tell me."

Aidan turned to study him. There would be no mistaking the family resemblance, though Ronan wouldn't elaborate.

Aidan stretched his legs and sipped his drink. "In the winter, Palmer Lake pulls itself back in with all the tourists returning to their fancy Denver homes. Then the biggest thing is harvesting ice blocks," he waved his hand holding the shot glass at the lake, "and storing them for summer use. The trains still stop cuz they need to take on water here on their return from the Palmer-Divide summit. We're the only natural water supply year-round." He paused. "Otherwise, I might go days not hearing anything other than the occasional whistle. That's the grace of Palmer Lake, its peace."

Figuring this was Aidan's way of getting around to answering his question, Ronan waited.

"I see Liam Doyle at Sunday Mass, him and his pretty wife. A fine family they make with two handsome boys and girls always so well-mannered."

Ronan smiled at the image. His uncle deserved a ready-made family. "Does he work at Hotel Rockland?"

"He and his missus both. He's a bartender. I see him when I'm in the mood for a drink and something more than my own company."

Ronan nodded. That made sense. Unlike Ronan, his uncle wouldn't have to hide himself. He'd always been known more as a saloon owner than union-affiliated, and he'd left the District before it had blown.

"His wife is a housekeeper, which'll keep her plenty busy with sixty-one rooms and guests that are here to recreate and not concern themselves much with the welfare of the help."

Wasn't that ever thus, though Annie would be used to that. Aidan said he saw the boys hanging about the lectures. Danny would set up tents, put up and remove chairs and "flirt with the lassies." Timmy sold lemonade and popcorn outside the tents, "but he's ever poking his head inside to listen to the speakers."

"Aye, that's Timmy. He has a brain on him."

Palmer Lake sounded ideal, and he was happy for them all. As he was suddenly impatient for their reunion. Now that they were so near, Ronan could allow himself to miss them. Otherwise, he couldn't lose emotional control enough to mourn something or someone forever lost to him.

"Do you know where they live?"

Aidan poured them both a second shot. "That I do," he said.

~

Ronan approached the cottage, larger than the Fein house on Golden Avenue. Honeyed light spilling onto the patch of lawn. Watching Uncle Liam through the window, rising from the dinner table, Annie supervising the girls cleaning up.

A sight that gladdened his heart; a sweep of his uncle's face confirming his sober state.

"This is the land of lost content, I see it shining plain..."

Comforting to know that out of them all, Uncle Liam need not look with regret on a happier past, for he was living contentedly.

Ronan knocked on the front door.

Uncle Liam embraced him in a breath-stealing hug, Annie cried into her apron, the girls hopped around excitedly, though he doubted they even remembered him. Timmy stood back shyly, while Danny, when it came his turn, extended his hand for a manly shake.

Everyone speaking at once.

"I can't believe you're here!"

"Let me fix you something to eat."

"You've cut your hair."

"I'd not have recognized you without your beard, Mr. Doyle," that from Timmy, clutching a copy of *The Sea Wolf* to his chest.

For this moment, Ronan himself felt content and was grateful that this was a daily condition for Uncle Liam.

It was only later when Annie was putting her girls to bed and the boys had disappeared, that Ronan addressed his uncle. "Let's walk."

Outside, the Hotel Rockland sprawled behind them, blazing like a giant sword across the dark of Chataqua Mountain behind it. This part of Palmer Lake consisted of a handful of cabins and tents for the poorer or more adventuresome tourists. Overhead, a velvet night, a riot of stars, a sliver of moon. Ronan felt the peace of the area, just as Aidan McCartney had said. They walked in silence along a deserted dirt road with only the soft thud of their boots, the swish of their clothing disturbing the quiet. Whereas Cripple Creek was ever a jangle of noise and chaos. Would it be so, even now that the WFM was broken and the mines running open? Ronan's cope was that he felt in his bones the District would never recover from the government and mine owners' desecration. They might have destroyed the strikers, but they'd killed the goose that laid the golden egg along with it.

Beside him, Uncle Liam finally spoke. "Wasn't sure I'd ever see you again, lad. All of it's a feckin' heartbreak, yet here it seems a lifetime away, as far removed as Schuylkill County."

Ronan nodded into the darkness. "Good has come from it. Did you make an honest woman of Annie?"

"Soon after we arrived. Church service and all."

Ronan didn't offer that he'd not stepped into a church since Bishop Matz's betrayal. It would take longer than this lifetime for him to forgive the Catholic Church's betrayal of his union.

"What about you and your Maeve?" His uncle had no way of knowing what had actually happened, certainly not the truth of her time travel or her leaving.

"I'm planning on reuniting soon," he said. They continued their walk. Inside the occasional tent, silhouettes outlined in the light from kerosene lanterns reminded him of shadow puppets thrown upon a wall.

He summoned the resolve to ask what had niggled at him since Leprechaun and Bridget Kehoe's wedding. While no one save him and his uncle and Bridget herself might end up knowing the truth, he would appreciate the confirmation. Particularly if the answer altered the storyline of the Mooney family tree.

"Tell me. Bridget Kehoe's babe. A boy named Sean, I'm told. Is it yours?"

He heard his uncle's sharp intake of breath, imagined the stiffening of shoulders, the guarded expression. His silence confirmed Ronan's suspicion, though he still wanted an explanation.

"Truth is, I don't know. You know how I tried to stay away from her. Jaysus, I couldn't stand the sight of her."

Ronan didn't say that he understood the allure of Byrdie Kehoe because he was so far removed from any feelings for her that they might have happened to another man. But the things a man would get up to when drunk...

"If Bridget Kehoe didn't want a baby, she wouldn't have had one," he said instead. "She'd spent enough time on her back to know how to take care of inconvenient consequences. And you and I know, she'd not be wanting Paddy Mooney's brat."

"One night. It's all so hazy. I wish I were certain."

Afraid that if he further pressed, he might trigger another of Uncle Liam's drinking bouts, Ronan dropped the subject with the warning, "You've got a good woman. Don't be feckin' that up."

Uncle Liam paused to face his nephew. Two shadows in the darkness of an empty road. "Aye, *nia,* I'm well aware that not all of us are granted the chances I've been. I'd say we've got more than a handful of Doyles acting as our guardian angels." He flung an arm around Ronan's shoulder. "Now it's time for you to be findin' your own pot of gold, even without the rainbow."

When they returned, Timmy was peering out the window. While Ronan and his uncle were saying their goodbyes, Timmy slipped outside to stand awkwardly nearby.

"Might we speak, Mr. Doyle?" he asked, after Uncle Liam finally released Ronan from a final bone-crushing embrace.

To Timmy, Uncle Liam said, "Now you're knowing you didn't see anyone here tonight, don't you, lad?"

Timmy nodded solemnly. After his stepfather disappeared inside, he stood in front of Ronan, head bowed and shuffling his feet.

"Timmy?" Ronan prodded.

"How is Miss Mooney?"

Ronan smiled. "I'll be seeing her soon, and you know she thinks of you often." Two things he could not know but hoped were the truth.

"A terrible thing happened." Timmy's gaze remained on the ground. Ronan couldn't think of anything much worse than what had already happened, but he wasn't a twelve-year-old boy.

"What might that be?"

"The last time Mr. Leprechaun had my *Alice in Wonderland*, he never returned it. If you see him, would you get it back for me? It always reminds me of Miss Mooney, and I miss those memories. They seem to slip further into the past by the day."

"I will," Ronan lied, for with any luck Paddy Mooney was dead, and when he returned to Cripple Creek, he intended to be just another ghost no one would even sense.

"Until that time." Ronan reached into his pocket and withdrew a pair of silver dollars. "I spotted a bookshop along your main street." He placed the coins in Timmy's hand and closed his own over it. "Buy yourself another copy while you wait. When I tell Miss Mooney, she'll agree it's the right thing to do."

Timmy gave him a quick hug. Gazing into those huge brown eyes, Ryan hoped he'd grow up to the life, he, they all deserved. He'd not be thinking of the apocalyptic future Padrick Mooney had painted that afternoon in March when he'd revealed the secret of the White Rabbit.

"You know, lad, you could set your sights on something grander. Perhaps even Colorado College. Colorado Springs isn't so very far away, and with a proper education, you'll achieve far greater dreams than the rest of us. I wish that for you."

As if he were a magician who could conjure such a thing. Ronan watched Timmy retreat, closing the cottage door behind him.

After which, he stepped into the dark.

Part Eleven

⌒∿⌒

TODAY

I can't go back to yesterday because I was a different person then.

— LEWIS CARROLL, *ALICE'S ADVENTURES IN
WONDERLAND*

Twenty-Six

My first month back, I slept more than I was awake. My parents fretted, particularly since Padrick had seamlessly settled back in, though we sometimes hiked long-familiar trails and talked. Or he listened to me natter on about Ronan.

"I know it's painful," he said more than once. "But what an experience for both of us."

As if Ronan could be dismissed as an "experience." Sensing my displeasure, he threw a huge arm across my shoulder. "Helluva man, Moonface. No matter what the century."

Sometimes I visited our library. Padrick had shown me Leprechaun's memoir, but I didn't even want to touch it and ordered him to put it away. I was done with Leprechaun and Bridget, though I enjoyed perusing local histories, more the photos than the text. Touching base with familiar landmarks, always seeking a glimpse of *him*.

I did find something interesting. Pulling down the ancient copy of *Alice in Wonderland/Through the Looking Glass* so many of us had carried around as kidlings. The cover had faded to a weathered grey, not the emerald green I'd purchased for Timmy Fein, and the corners were badly frayed. Yet when I opened it to Chapter One, "Down the Rabbit-Hole," and skimmed the first page, *"Alice was beginning to get very tired of sitting by her sister on the bank..."* I wasn't really surprised when I saw penciled circles throughout the text, as they'd been in Timmy's copy. Nor that when I rearranged the eleven circled letters, they spelled T-I-M-O-T-H-Y F-E-I-N.

How did Timmy's copy of *Alice* come into our possession? However, I felt warm and happy simply having it.

While I missed Ronan every moment of every day, what I never shared was that we met nightly, in the palace of dreams, just as he'd promised. At first they were more disjointed memories—picking wild flowers, strolling through Cheyenne Park, a duet of "Danny Boy." But the more I slept, the more easily I opened myself to the experience, the more realistic the incidents became. Sometimes more than my memories. Swaying box cars; hour after hour of bleak landscape. Images flitting like moths: slapdash towns in the middle of nowhere; darkened hovels, curious faces; switch yards; freight hopping, Pikes Peak rising beyond the plains. I dreamed of Ronan, whispering close to my ear. *"This is what had happened." "This is what's happening now."* So long as I remained in our dream palace, I experienced his world alongside him.

The one thing I knew for certain was that Ronan Doyle wasn't dead, as had been the fate of so many other strikers. Which was kind of an oxymoron. Because the Independence Depot explosion had occurred well over a hundred years ago.

Do the existential math.

It would have been so easy to sleep my life away, to perpetually hover between the past and present, an astronaut floating in space. But I'd made my choice and I accepted the consequences, determined to grope my way forward, inch by inch.

Maeve Mooney, Survivor.

Sort of.

After I'd properly settled in, my family sometimes brought up incidents from my journals, eager for a discussion. Impossible. My throat would immediately close and my pulse ratchet until I felt as if my head would explode and I'd simply shake my head, "No."

"You need time to heal," Mama soothed, thinking she understood.

What I needed was to learn to live my life without Ronan.

And be grateful.

I knew I'd never marry, but I wouldn't be sad either. How many could have experienced such an adventure? Been blessed to meet and fall in love with their own Ronan Doyle?

Time. It was all I had. All any of us have. I'd been lucky it had once made a detour on my behalf.

I purchased an electric bike and rode from Shamrock Ranch through Cripple Creek to Victor, six miles one way. That was difficult. Nature's landscapes—Mount Pisgah, the Sangre de Cristos, and Battle Mountain would never change, but detritus was all that remained of the Portland, the Independence and the other mines that had earned Battle Mountain the epithet, "richest hill on earth." So many towns like Independence, where the explosion had occurred, might contain a crumbled shack, a fallen length of fence, a rusted automobile. Wilderness had largely reclaimed the Woods family's Skaguay Dam, Reservoir and Hydroelectric Power Plant which had brought electricity to the District.

And Pinnacle Park. That was the toughest to revisit, for that's the day I realized I just might be in love with Ronan Doyle. I would settle beside one of the stone arches that had once housed wolves and other animals, close my eyes and remember. The dancing pavilion so vast four hundred couples could waltz without touching; its zoo and baseball stadium seating a thousand. Shooting galleries, trapeze artists and high wire acts, swings, slides and an electric carousel, though the biggest draw had been the moving picture machines.

What I remembered most was Ronan, standing in the pavilion, long hair catching the sun, pouring out his heart on behalf of a doomed cause.

Once the District had hummed with energy, manically embracing the siren song of capitalism. You noticed it, now that the hum had been replaced by bird calls, small animals scurrying across CO-67 and the occasional passing car. The open pit Cripple Creek & Victor Mine did create its own sort of noise, a low-grade tinnitus, with its monstrous machines scraping away the earth and its explosions, though puny echoes of the past, still causing the air to tremble.

Cripple Creek had devolved into an unfinished sketch of itself. The Pick-Axe was gone, along with Ronan's union hall and the National Hotel. Not even a foundation remained of Annie Fein's house high on Golden Avenue, though I sometimes visited nearby St. Peter's Catholic Church, which largely looked the same. Where we'd sat together, Ronan's thigh against mine, shoulders touching. Everything reminded me of him. Whether it was, "Oh, this wasn't here," or "That building hasn't changed hardly at all."

I couldn't shake free that other, far more exuberant Paris of the West. With department stores rivalling those on Denver's Market Street, where one of its two opera houses had feted Sarah Bernhardt, who'd performed "La Tosca," and according to legend, invited Ronan to her suite afterward for a private dinner.

I remembered the Black preacher, Parson Holmes, who'd park himself in front of Cohen's Thirst Parlor regular as clockwork, hop up the back of his wagon and exhort sinners to repent. I remembered boardwalks teeming with women grocery shopping at Smith's Market, miners at the Miner's Emporium, crib girls slipping into W.L. Shockey's Cripple Creek Pharmacy in order to buy health products containing laudanum and cocaine, while their more refined sisters purchased custom-fitted gowns from the Elegant Boutique.

How puny, how inadequate this contemporary version.

I spent more time in Victor, retracing what I'd researched about June 6, 1904. Often, I felt as if I were looking at events through Ronan's eyes. That he was beside me, whispering, "This is where we ran to the hall." "There is where the bodies lay sprawled in the lot." "Up on the roofline we spotted the soldiers, their barrels flashing like signal mirrors." Was that part of his nightly re-tellings, the story of the death of his cause?

It was hard to reconcile this sleepy little patch with that larger-than-life city, eager as a race horse trembling to be cut free. *Fortunes to be made! Adventures to be experienced! Life to be embraced!* Miners spent a dollar a night to sleep on a billiard table in the back room of a saloon or to bathe in a makeshift tub courtesy of a local barbershop. Its red-light district far out-sinned Cripple Creek's.

But Victor also had the Woods family, who'd founded Victor after discovering a twenty-inch-wide gold vein that became the Gold Coin Mine and created Victor out of its rock and hardscrabble. I was one of those with a soft spot for Victor, which at the time I knew teemed with a population of thirteen thousand. Now its entire population could probably fit into the Gold Coin Club, still standing over on Diamond Avenue.

Ronan and I had dined at fancy restaurants advertising seventy-five-cent steaks and ninety-cent plates of ham and eggs. We'd attended Shakespeare's *Julius Caesar* at the Victor Opera house, all twelve hundred of us seated in plush velvet seats, attired in morning suits and satin evening gowns. That was the thing. Particularly now that the preferred fashion of so many Americans seems to be rolling-out-of-bed-and-grabbing-anything-at-hand. When our ancestors had performed excruciating physical labor. When bathing generally couldn't be accomplished by turning a faucet and yet they'd cherished culture enough to dress for it.

Sometimes I'd spend the night at the Victor Hotel, formerly the First National Bank, which had gone bankrupt during the strike. The Victor Hotel was a lovingly renovated Victorian that housed the ghost of a miner named Eddy, who'd fallen down an elevator shaft when his elevator car hadn't arrived on time and he'd stepped into empty air.

I didn't need Eddy to see ghosts; they were everywhere.

Whenever I stayed at the Victor Hotel, I'd stroll the streets after the town had tucked itself away. Beneath my feet was a labyrinth of abandoned tunnels where miners had once shoveled ore for the Gold Coin Mine in the heart of Victor. At a cost of two hundred fifty thousand dollars, the mine had been a marvel of engineering and elegance, housing the latest compressors, boilers, and a great hoist that could drop a double-deck miner's cage fifteen hundred feet in a minute. By 1920, its great sprawl of buildings, all of it, had been dismantled and hauled away.

A lightning strike had pretty much finished off Victor's WFM building, though its brick façade remains where you can place your fingers in its bullet holes. On the vacant lot where C.C. Hamlin had demanded fifty union men be slaughtered, J-E-T Repair and Service Station is located. The Victor Armory, which had housed Ronan and his fellow strikers following their arrests, is now Elks Lodge 367.

On each visit, I would stand outside The Gold Coin Club, that wondrous establishment the Woods brothers had gifted their employees and which had served as a hospital the day of the explosion. How many times had I taken a five-cent trolley from Cripple Creek to entertain there or to accompany school children giving performances?

I imagined the Gold Coin Club's doors flying open and the school children—laughing girls in starched dresses and long stockings, exuberant boys in Russian blouses and knickers—spilling into the warm afternoon.

All of it lost.

All of it like trying to capture sunlight.

Still, I had my palace.

∾

My dreams changed. No longer in technicolor, but in chilly blues, as if viewing figures trapped in ice. I didn't like it. One night, Ronan and I danced all alone in a decaying ballroom I'd never seen before, wearing clothes we'd never worn. And then, the way it is in dreams, he's standing in the doorway, bathed in those icy shadows. He tips his hat, as if in greeting, as if mocking me. I reach for him and he shatters into a thousand shards that fly away like tiny birds.

I carried around an uneasy feeling. Dreading now what the night might bring. Here we are again, embracing beneath a harvest moon so swollen it consumes the sky. Around us, vague shapes like those artificial ruins once built to mimic ancient Rome and medieval castles. I feel your breath on my cheek, the warmth of your hands while in the background the suppurating moon drip, drips and I awake with a scream lodged in my throat.

Something's happened. Something's wrong. These certainly didn't belong in our garden of memories.

Once I woke to the scent of Florida water. Another time, I swore I heard music, *"It was fascination, I know,"* drifting to me in my sleep. Clawing myself awake. The unease deepening. The axis in our world had shifted. What did that mean?

"There's no record of him after the explosion," Padrick had once said.

What if we'd not met in a palace, but Ronan was calling out to me from purgatory or beyond?

In the last dream, he waited in front of a darkened mine entrance, lantern in hand, again as I'd never actually seen him. Twilight shades of blue. "Time, Maeve," he'd said before turning his back and disappearing into the blackness.

Time for what? Had Ronan found his way to the White Rabbit? A man who was forbidden to set foot in Colorado, let alone the District lest he be shot on sight?

Was it time for me to let him go?

Was the mine a symbol for something? Couldn't be death, could it? Wasn't that too obvious?

Then again, why *had* he turned his back on me? Why had he walked into the darkness?

That night I woke to find my bedroom bathed in the eerie light of my dreams. I lay still, listening for what might have awakened me. I'd fallen asleep with the photographs Padrick had taken of us clutched in my hand. Now they were spilled across my comforter. Quiet from my parents' bedroom at the far end of the hall. No warning bark from Mutt, curled in his usual spot on the first floor near the front door. Distant hoot of my Great Horned Owl, most likely prowling the ruins of Strank's Manse, eyes glowing, talons curled.

My thoughts spun to the night I'd fallen down the White Rabbit. Black upon black upon black. This had the same feel. As if magic had once again taken up residence. Slowly, I eased out of bed. Paused. Listened. Bare feet cool on the hardwood floor, I crossed to my window, open to the fall air, and leaned my elbows on the sill. Like the ghost girl I'd glimpsed peering out the window at the Turf Club.

Searching the lawn, cast in indigo.

To the figure there.

As I'd known he would be.

Gazing up at my window.

As I'd known he would.

Or at least that's how I felt tonight. That this was inevitable, that all these months I'd simply been marking time, awaiting his return.

Could this be another one of my dreams?

No. The chill air on my face was real. My elbows were sharp on the windowsill. My chest pressed against the wood beneath. The inhale and exhale of my breathing.

Ronan, not moving. Waiting.

I recognized him immediately, of course. He was hatless, so I could more easily see that he was beardless and his hair shorter, but

I would never mistake him. Odd that I wasn't excited, that my heart wasn't tripping. My major feeling was one of relief.

"What took you so long, Ronan Doyle?" I called out.

"Came as quick as I could, Maeve Mooney," he replied.

"Are you going to leave again?"

There I saw it, Ronan's mouth kicking up on one side in a half-smile. "Not in this century," he said.

After which I raced down the stairs and out the door, arms outstretched, running to my beloved in the moonlight.

END

Notes and Acknowledgments

Having lived much of my life in Colorado and decades within forty minutes of Cripple Creek and Victor, I knew a bit about the District's history. I'd vaguely heard of strikes and bullet holes in a WFM building, which, given my blue-collar background, I marked for further exploration. "Someday." Marshall Sprague, a popular author and chronicler of early Colorado Springs and the District, wrote one chapter on the strike which, given our state's tumultuous labor history, is puzzling. Rereading Sprague's recounting, I sensed his disapproval of the strike, certainly of Big Bill Haywood.

My research led me to a different conclusion.

As I investigated the events surrounding Colorado's Labor War, I was reminded that wealthy places like Aspen, Vail, Breckenridge and Telluride (where Butch Cassidy robbed his first bank), were once hardscrabble mining towns where miners fought and died seeking a wage of three dollars for an eight-hour day and for the right to form a union.

While the Cripple Creek District is known as the "World's Greatest Gold Camp," it enjoys little of the cachet of those other mining meccas. Open pit mining, gambling and tourism are its major sources of revenue. It does remain rightfully proud of its past. You can spend hours in the Cripple Creek Heritage Center which overlooks the town itself, as well as tour several museums. The Cripple Creek and Victor Narrow Gauge Railroad recreates the route (partially) to Victor via an old-fashioned steam engine. Townsfolk celebrate their history with parades, art shows, cemetery tours and events such as Donkey Derby Days and Victor Gold Rush Days.

While researching the District's past, I sometimes became frustrated with the many conflicting accounts of various events. Perhaps scholars and historians have sophisticated ways of arriving at definitive conclusions, but I am neither. I found myself weighing the sources of information—pro or anti or somewhere in the middle—and defaulting to "this makes sense." Was the WFM winning the strike before the Independence Depot explosion? Some sources say yes. Others say that the mines were running at near full capacity from early on. Was the WFM as violent as its critics maintained? Only one newspaper, the *Victor Daily Record*, was explicitly pro-union, while others such as *The Gazette*—still going strong after nearly one hundred fifty years—has always been unashamedly pro-business.

WFM leaders, particularly Big Bill Haywood, certainly had a reputation. Union members sometimes used violence to run non-union workers or businesses out of the District. But during the strike, the entire power of the state plus the mine owners was directed against the miners. After martial law was imposed, citizens had virtually no rights. When acts of sabotage occurred in the mines, newspapers generally blamed the strikers. Maybe so, but in addition to having their mouthpiece papers, the mines employed non-union labor and non-union guards patrolled the premises, making it difficult for "socialist agitators" to carry out said crimes.

Finally, who blew up the Independence Depot, which abruptly ended the strike? For me, it always came down to one question: Who benefited? Following the explosion, mine interests swept in so quickly, shut down any investigation pointing away from the WFM, and immediately replaced all law enforcement and legal authorities with those properly loyal to "capitalism."

Later, the conman/assassin Harry Orchard, after being arrested and thrown in jail for the 1905 bombing of Idaho Governor Harry Steunenberg, signed a sixty-four-page confession detailing crimes committed at the behest of the WFM, including the Independence Depot explosion. However, Orchard spent a year honing that confession with the help of Pinkerton James McParland and the jury didn't buy it.

One final rant: James McParland, the Pinkerton detective who destroyed the Molly Maguires and whose agency—he headed the Denver branch—played a large part in destroying District miners and their families. I despise the man. If you're unfamiliar with McParland and prefer movies to books, spend a couple of hours with the 1974 movie *The Molly Maguires*. McParland committed crimes and sent men to the gallows via perjured testimony simply because he was carrying out "God's will." He hated unions and he successfully broke them.

I wholeheartedly agree with the curse Jack Kehoe (Sean Connery) hurled at McParland (Richard Harris) before Kehoe was sent to the gallows.

"There's no punishment this side of hell that can free you from what you did."

Some notes on the story itself. All my main characters are fictional. Many of the sentiments expressed by men like Ronan Doyle, Governor Peabody or James McParland are taken, often verbatim, from speeches of the day.

Strank's Manse is based on "Finn's Folly", built by Cripple Creek attorney and mine operator J. Maurice Finn. The garish twenty-six-room nightmare was built and demolished within a span of twenty years.

The ghostly handprint on the wall of Pennsylvania's Carbon County Jail is a real thing. On the Day of the Rope, one of the

Mollies, Alexander Campbell, swore he was innocent of the murder of a mine boss. Before being hauled off to his execution, Campbell slapped his hand on the cell wall, swearing the print would ever remain as a reminder of his innocence. And it has.

Before ending, I owe many, many thanks to Victor historian La Jean Greeson, whose help and expertise were invaluable in my research. She generously shared old photos, articles, and maps, patiently answered my questions and guided me to websites containing source documents. La Jean also hunted down the District map that graces the front page of *The Golden Promise of Cripple Creek* (Linda Irene Tingvik collection/ CrippleCreekRailroadsDotCom).

I am forever grateful to the Victor Heritage Society for their invaluable website, https://www.victorheritagesociety.com/. Not only is it easy to navigate, but it also possesses a cornucopia of information on Victor's remarkable past. The saying, "Cripple Creek gets the glory, but Victor has the gold," is quite true. Its sister site, https://www.rebelgraphics.org/wfmhall/history.html, has downloaded several contemporaneous books on the strike. Emma Langdon's *The Cripple Creek Strike,* which provides a day-by-day recounting, is particularly helpful.

Of all the books I read during my research, a shout out to my favorite: *All That Glitters: Class, Conflict and Community in Cripple Creek* by Elizabeth Jameson.

Finally, a special thanks to my forever friend, Sheryl Harrell, for providing invaluable suggestions after reading a draft of *The Golden Promise of Cripple Creek*. I hope the changes were successful!

About the Author

I've lived in Colorado much of my life and never tire of its heart-stopping scenery. What I, enamored as I am of medieval England, never paid much attention to was Colorado's history. Second state to give women the right to vote, etc., etc. But all around me and across the state, you can spot weathered headframes, entrances to long-abandoned mine shafts, beautiful orange-colored—and totally polluted—mountain streams in the vicinity of wealthy resort towns such as Breckenridge, Aspen, and Telluride. All of which were once hardscrabble mining camps where newly minted millionaires existed right alongside men and women who worked too hard and earned too little. (**Fun fact:** Telluride is the first bank Butch Cassidy robbed, riding away with half a million dollars in today's currency.) Living forty minutes from Cripple Creek and Victor, I was vaguely aware that these quaint towns with their red-brick, frontier-style buildings had once been part of the richest gold camp on earth. I'd heard about a long-ago violent strike, which, being from a union household, snared my attention. *Someday I'll explore that further*, I used to think. *And I'll put my fingers in the bullet holes gouged into the brick of that old Western Federation of Miners building after the National Guard decided they'd had enough of those miners who just didn't get the fact that they really **must** work for longer hours and lower wages.*

I did put my fingers into those bullet holes, and I've explored many of the places I write about in THE GOLDEN PROMISE OF CRIPPLE CREEK, my third time travel historical romance.

I've done my best to recount the exciting, courageous, and ultimately tragic story of the WFM miners, their families, and the union that fought valiantly against the power of the state. And, of course, I tell it all via the love affair between my (initially) self-absorbed social media influencer and my idealistic (and devastatingly handsome) labor leader.

I hope you enjoy THE GOLDEN PROMISE OF CRIPPLE CREEK: Love During the Boom Times. I am also the author of the six-book KNIGHTS OF ENGLAND historical romance series and two other time travel romances, ETERNAL BELOVED and BEFORE I WAKE.

When not writing, I enjoy travel, my children and grandchildren, and Karma, my German shepherd, whose main talent appears to be shedding!

www.maryellenjohnsonnauthor.com

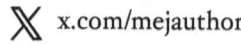 x.com/mejauthor